HAiRDO

HAiRDO

SARAH GILBERT

WARNER BOOKS

A Warner Communications Company

The author wishes to thank the South Carolina Arts Commission for Fellowship in Literature.

Warner Books, Inc., 666 Fifth Avenue, New York, NY 10103

W A Warner Communications Company

Printed in the United States of America
First printing: February 1990
10 9 8 7 6 5 4 3 2 1

Library of Congress Cataloging-in-Publication Data

Gilbert, Sarah.
  Hairdo / Sarah Gilbert.
     p.   cm.
  ISBN 0-446-51526-4
  I. Title.
PS3557.I34228H35   1990
813'.54—dc20   89-40045
                                                         CIP

Designed by Giorgetta Bell McRee

With Love for my Mother.
*And for Aunt Sally's tree
out on the road to Edisto.*

HAiRDO

1

The phones had been ringing at The Celebrity Styling Shop all morning and Ruby McSwain didn't know what to do. She pushed at her stomach, pressed at her updo and said, "Well now, isn't that something. Going off and having a nervous breakdown just like that."

She was talking about her cousin, Gladys Bessinger, who had hung up her CLOSED sign across the square, leaving most of the blue rinse set in the town of Stuckey, South Carolina, without a hairdresser. The only thing left for them to do was telephone and see if Miss Ruby could take them.

"Well you won't find that happening in this shop. Whoever heard of such a thing?" she asked as Yvonne put the finishing touches on her hair. "A nervous breakdown." She said it again as she shook her head and looked at Gladys' dark TRES CHIC sign.

The phone was still ringing and the cars were beginning to line up outside but Miss Ruby was not about to open the front door until her hair was ready.

Yvonne put one last finishing touch on her updo, stepped away, and with the comb still in her hand, she rubbed the

1

small of her back. "Hon, you look like a queen. A real queen."

This pleased Miss Ruby so much that she swiveled around in her chair and lit a cigarette. Then she raised her arm, and like the conductor to an orchestra, she waved for everyone to be let in. "Where's Thurston?" she asked.

"Honey," said Yvonne still rubbing her back, "don't get me wrong. It's not that I dislike gays. But it's like I've always said. I wouldn't want one working in my shop. For one thing he is always late. And for another thing," she said picking up the appointment book, "he is always overbooking. Look at this. Just look." She tapped the book with her comb. "Three people for the same nine-thirty. Three! And you know who's going to end up doing most of the work, don't you? Me." Yvonne poked the comb at her chest, and carrying the book to the front door, she unlocked it and let in all the frantic women.

Some went and immediately picked out all the newest magazines, hugging them to their breasts for the duration. Some came in and asked for the coffee that had yet to be made. Some went straight to the shampoo bowls expecting to be shampooed even though it wasn't their turn yet. And some went straight up to Ruby and said, "Never. *Never* again. I will never trust that woman for as long as I live."

And, "I knew something was wrong with her. Last week she acted like she was on some kind of drugs and just ruined my hair. Just look at it. Five minutes. She cut it in five minutes flat and now *look*!"

And, "I *know*! Here my sister's getting married next week, and you know, Gladys has just been acting so funny lately. She won't even come to the phone. Just puts on that damned answering machine." This last voice belonged to Louise Stokes, who had a shock of white hair running across the top of her head. Louise had left Ruby for Gladys over a year ago and now here she was, back. Louise was still complaining, "And she never returns your calls either. I just knew something was up. Oh, I forgot how *small* it was in here.

2

Why Gladys' shop just goes on and on, doesn't it. I guess it's all those mirrors."

Miss Ruby, who was trying hard not to look delighted with Gladys' breakdown, Poor Deared, Poor Deared the new clients up to the front desk. And as she put them down for Thurston and Yvonne, she couldn't help smiling as once again she looked at the dark windows of the Tres Chic.

Ruby said, "Yvonne, be a dear and make sure everyone is comfortable and gets a doughnut and some coffee."

Yvonne Tisdale, who was from the old school of Cosmetology where the idea was to keep all the patrons happy, loved making the morning coffee. She loved setting up Miss Ruby's china tea set and counting out the spoonfuls of Maxwell House that went into the percolator. But even more than that, Yvonne loved serving the little cups on her very own silver platter. The one she brought from home every day. It was the same platter that she had won at her very first hair show, years back, when hair was still hair.

"Honey," said one of Thurston's three nine-thirty appointments, "I'd like three sugars, please." The woman held her hand out without even looking at Yvonne. "Is he here yet?"

"Who?" asked Yvonne. "Thurston? Stars are never on time."

And as if on cue, Thurston pranced in pushing at his chest as if he wore a D cup. "Oh my God oh my God oh my God! Did you see what Joan Collins was wearing last night? Gold lamé cut to here." He pointed down to his big turquoise belt buckle. "Oh, that woman, she is so meaaaaan. Move over honey," he said to Miss Ruby, sitting down on her stool, spreading out his floor length labcoat as if he were the Sun King.

"Thurston," said Miss Ruby, "I'm so glad you're here. Would you just look at that." She pointed across the square. "Look at whose lights aren't on this morning."

"Oh my Lord, I can't believe it." He clasped his hands together. "What happened to the Dragon Lady?"

3

"She's suffering a nervous breakdown as we speak," said Miss Ruby, spreading her hands out before her. Then she whispered, "And all her women are going to be mine now. And what I'm going to do is make them so gorgeous and so happy they'll never want to go back to that old Gladys Bessinger again."

"Well Ruby old girl," said Thurston, "if you're nothing else, you are a sympathetic woman." He stood up, crossed his arms, put one hand under his chin and surveyed the room. His eyes stopped on a woman who had hair at least half a foot high. "Oh look, problem hair," he said. He walked right up to the woman and touched her face. He pushed it this way and that way. "Darling, who did this to you? No, don't answer that. Yvonne, sweetie, drop what you are doing and shampoo this woman right away. This cannot wait." He was snapping his fingers. "We need to make her look young again."

Thurston gave the woman a once-over one more time, then came back to her hair. "Darling, this style went out with *Gunsmoke*."

The woman touched all around her hair and it was obvious that she felt like there was another whole head up there.

"Big, isn't it?" asked Thurston.

She was absolutely hypnotized by him. And not for the first time Yvonne saw that he had won yet another woman over for life.

Yvonne disapproved of just about everything Thurston did. Months back, when he had first come into the shop and used whatever it was that gay hairdressers seemed to have that attracted the women clientele, he had practically stolen all of her shampoo-and-sets away. He had shown them blowdryers, curling irons and their younger years. And the women had left Yvonne with little left to do except sweep up the hair she used to cut, and shampoo the women who used to tell her their problems. Now, while they still talked to her, it was about the weather and new shoes and other such trivial matters. They talked to her and treated her as if she had just finished, was about to start, or was going through a nervous breakdown herself. And Thurston would make it all the worse by coming around in his little Mumsy-Wumsy voice, saying, "Oh doesn't she give the most devine little shampoos. Why, yes, yes she does."

Yvonne had seen it a hundred times. Beauticians who overnight went from being the very best to assisting a man who didn't know the difference between hairspray and setting lotion, or men and women. And although it was happening to her now, she wasn't planning on letting it continue much longer. She was going to do something about it. It was just a matter of when. But now there was something else, something far, far more serious. Bebe Pointer had died, leaving her with a terrible problem. Yvonne decided she would deal with it later, when her head was clear and she had more time.

She swept her hand across the room and said, "Thurston, would you take a look around you? If you think I'm going to shampoo all of your clients, guess again. I've got my own nine-thirtys to do. Come on, Agnes."

Agnes Collins got up from the couch and Thurston went into his famous curtsy and dip, driving Yvonne up the wall and Agnes mad with desire. Then he whipped out his comb and fixed his bangs on the way to get some help from Miss Ruby.

One pout was all it took.

"Oh, all right, Thurston," said Miss Ruby. "I'll do your shampoos. Yvonne, sweetie, you've got another shampoo and set waiting on you." Miss Ruby hooked her head at a woman who was sitting on the couch wearing sweatpants with a matching teddy bear sweatshirt. She was trying to tear recipes out of a magazine without anyone noticing.

Miss Ruby knew that the woman had to be one of Gladys' clients, starved for the services of a real beauty shop. Gladys would no more let a client rip a recipe from a magazine than she would call a hairdo a hairdo. For Gladys it was

5

always everything in its place and everything had to sound French.

The woman with the magazine kept looking around, looking around all the time to make sure no one was watching. Miss Ruby reached over and nudged Thurston. "See her, Thurston? See that poor woman?"

"How can I miss?"

Ruby shook her head. "She's been going to Gladys' shop for so long with nothing to look at except herself in all those mirrors, and it's worn the poor dear out. It's just got to be real nice for her to come over here and let her hair down, so to speak."

She thought of Gladys and knew that if she were here now and seeing this woman, she'd put her hand to her heart like she was suffering a heart attack, only she'd laugh and say, "Can you imagine, Ruby, tearing out a lousy recipe for a meringue. It makes you wonder what their home lives are like."

But Ruby McSwain never wondered. She enjoyed walking around her shop with a certain air of supremacy, letting all the clients know that she was not wanting for anything and neither should they be. She so enjoyed her Celebrity Status. And thinking about her cousin Gladys suffering that nervous breakdown pleased Ruby so much she could barely stand it.

At Gladys' Tres Chic, less than a hundred yards away through the live oaks across the square, there were separate booths with lattice doors for each and every client. And every time one of the doors opened or closed a shot of perfume sprayed the air. Gladys had a makeup room stocked with little colored bottles of makeup and big colored bottles of skin cleansers, toners and moisturizers, all of which had her very own TRES CHIC logo on the sides. And there were mirrors everywhere. They were designed in such a way that when the clients walked in, the mirrors they were looking at had a draining yellow track light flushing down on them, making them appear fat and sallow. But when they left, after what Gladys called a "treatment" with Alexander or Rudolpho, the mirrors that led to the cash register were track lighted with a soft pink hue, taking ten years off their lives. And as if all that weren't enough, Gladys had a throne. A velvet throne, designed after one she had seen in Europe. But now the throne was empty, the TRES CHIC was dark, the morning mail was in the box and the morning paper was lying out there on the sidewalk.

For the first time in years Ruby McSwain's Celebrity Styling was swamped and the phone was ringing with new clients. And for the first time in years Ruby could feel the clients' needs so strong it was as if the air was being sucked right out of her. For a minute she thought she would need to breathe into a paper bag, like she used to when she was young and still married to her good for nothing husband.

But then the phone rang and Thurston leaned over the desk and answered it. "Ronder who?" he asked.

Miss Ruby's heart stopped.

"Ronder Jeffcoat?" He repeated it out loud, covering the phone. "Darling, she sounds like a bleached blonde."

Miss Ruby pushed the phone away and said loud enough for the entire shop to hear, "Tell her I'm going out. Ask her to call back some other time."

"Darling," said Thurston, tucking a lock of his long hair behind his ear, "in case you didn't notice, I am not an answering service." Then he pressed the receiver to his lips because someone had once told him that when he did this he sounded like Cary Grant. "Miss Ruby has asked me to take a message. She had to go to the jewelry store to look at some stones."

Miss Ruby was delighted. Here was Thurston talking about her jewels over the phone as if they were her second nature. It surprised her to hear someone talking about her that way. It thrilled her.

Ruby wore so many rings and necklaces and brooches it was hard to tell where the jewelry ended and the skin began. And while she may not have had a red velvet throne, she

7

did have her very own silhouette that had been made into a gold necklace, sewn on to her hankies, and painted on to THE CELEBRITY STYLING SHOP sign. As far as she was concerned, it was worth all the TRES CHIC HAIR logos in the state of South Carolina. Ruby knew for a fact that it was the one and only thing that Gladys Bessinger envied her for.

Ruby McSwain only set one woman's hair in town, and her name was Miss Harriet Rideout. She was a widow who painted little miniature silhouettes and sold them for $12.95 at the weekend flea market. It was a very profitable business and when news had reached Gladys as to where Ruby had gotten her silhouette done, it was reported that she had rushed right down and gotten herself one too.

But unlike Ruby, whose little nose turned up just so, Gladys had inherited a nose which tended to hook. When Gladys saw the end result she paid Miss Harriet the money she owed her and then doubled it to keep her mouth shut. Miss Harriet promptly spent the money on a new frosting at Ruby's shop and by mid-afternoon the news was all over town.

Thurston snapped his fingers in front of Miss Ruby's face. "Hey lady, are you going to shampoo my girl or not?" He didn't even wait for her answer. He just did two dips and turns instead of his usual one, and turned to walk away, saying, "Who would keep The Great Thurston waiting?"

Miss Ruby pushed at the back of her hair, "Okay, Thurston, but when Ronder calls back you keep telling her I'm busy."

"Darling, she said you're to call her back. She'll be waiting right by the phone. Persistent little thing, isn't she?"

"Like I said, Thurston, when she calls back you just keep telling her I'm busy."

Miss Ruby knew exactly what it was that Ronder wanted. She wanted her job back. She'd told Ronder this would happen the first time she'd laid eyes on that Buck Jeffcoat, and Ronder had asked to borrow money for the wedding.

"Sugar," Miss Ruby had told her almost a year ago, "I've

seen this kind before. They're trash. He's going to be money out of your pocket."

But Ronder had said, "Oh no Miss Ruby, he's got a job painting houses and you know something else, he's got the prettiest TransAm."

She had told Ronder, "I don't care what he's got, sugar. You'll be begging to get back to work after a couple of weeks with that redneck."

It was "that redneck" that had gotten the hairs up on the back of Ronder's neck and made her so mad that she had just marched right out of the shop and eloped with Buck anyway. And when she left, she had left two ladies under the dryer reading their *Redbooks*, and she had left Miss Ruby with not a soul to fix their hair except Yvonne.

"Well," said Thurston, who had taken a carnation from the front desk arrangement and was now putting it in his labcoat buttonhole, "whatever you say, but if I were you, I'd call back."

"Well since you aren't me . . ." said Miss Ruby trailing off and into the other room.

"Women," huffed Thurston, shaking his head.

Miss Ruby had no intention of calling Ronder Jeffcoat back. Ever. She was not about to give her the satisfaction. Secretly she was ecstatic that Ronder had called and knew she'd call back, again and again and again. Because Miss Ruby knew it was Ronder's nature to use the phone whenever she possibly could.

It took Miss Ruby less than ten minutes to shampoo two of Thurston's regulars, and in less than ten minutes more he was back up front with one of them, already moussed and blowdried, ready to face a new day. Miss Ruby herself hated for anybody to spend less than thirty minutes on her hair, and preferred forty-five, which is what she got, since the main reason she had bought the shop in the first place was so that she could have her hair styled any time she wanted for as long as she wanted as often as she wanted.

She looked at the finished woman's fingernails and then at her rings and knew within seconds that those rings came from a wholesale store, not only because they looked it, but because her orange frosted nail polish was chipped so badly that half of the free edges were showing. Ruby, a diamond wearer herself, knew that a woman who wore real diamonds would never let that happen.

"That's a beautiful setting you have, dear. Twelve fifty, please," and Miss Ruby, who only gave full attention where full attention was due—to the women with real jewelry—

worked the cash register and eased the woman out in record time.

Thurston was now touching the teased hair of the woman who had torn the recipes from the magazine. "Darling," he said, circling her and studying her, "your hair does not fit the way you sit in that chair." Then he turned to Miss Ruby. "Hon, is she on my books? Put her on my books."

Then he turned back to the woman and asked, "What did your last hairdresser have on his mind when he let you walk out of the door like this? What I'm going to do is cut this immediately," he said pulling out a strand of the woman's hair. "We've got to do something to these ends. Oh dear." He examined them. "Have they been this way for long?" He was so disgusted. "Darling, didn't you know that you can't wear that kind of hairstyle with a square face? It makes you look what I'd call rather long in the tooth. I don't know. It does something to your mouth, enlarges it or something."

The woman's eyes grew bigger and bigger as Thurston talked and she covered her mouth.

"Thurston, she's Yvonne's," warned Ruby.

"Oh," he said staring at the woman. "Well, darling, better luck next time." He cracked himself up and Miss Ruby shot him a hard dark look.

"Just a joke, just a joke," he said. "You'll just love old Yvonne. I swear you will. She's got those Sixties do's down pat." Thurston circled his hands above his head and did a pirouette.

Miss Ruby knew that in most businesses anyone would gang up on somebody who tried to steal someone else's customers away, but she also knew that there was an unwritten law in the hair business that said it's everyone for themselves. But she was beginning to feel sorry for Yvonne, so she made an effort not to laugh. Still, she couldn't help it.

The woman who had succeeded in tearing out most of the newest recipes from the newest *McCall's* was horrified.

She went straight up to Miss Ruby to make sure she was changed over to Thurston's book right away. As she stood there, she tightened her lips, convinced now that her teeth were as big as a mule's.

"Thurston, Yvonne's not going to like this," said Miss Ruby shaking her head, "she's not going to like this at all."

"Well, I am not Yvonne's customer," said the woman, "whoever she is. And this man is right. Gladys Bessinger has been trying to talk me out of this old thing for years and I guess now is as good a time as any."

At the mere mention of Gladys, Miss Ruby began erasing the woman's name off of Yvonne's side of the book as fast as she could. Just the thought of being able to do for a woman what Gladys never could sent chills running up and down her spine.

Thurston came around the desk and sat down next to Ruby again. He crossed his legs tight and tucked his toe around his ankle like a model. "Ruby baby, don't worry about Yvonne, hon. It could be worse. Take, for instance, the news. Did you happen to hear about those two gays that abducted that old lady?"

Ruby's eyes got big. "Oh my God, Thurston. Abducted?!"

The recipe woman forgot about her teeth. "What happened?" she gasped.

Thurston looked at her and then at Miss Ruby and then he looked to the ceiling and sighed. "Well, one tied her down," he said, then looked at the woman and cocked his right eyebrow for effect, "while the other did her hair."

"What a hoot!" said Miss Ruby dropping back into her old redneck years, slapping her knee.

And the woman, who looked like she hadn't smiled in a year, just cracked up too.

"Ohh baby," said Thurston hugging himself, "when I see those teeth, I can't wait to do your hair."

She reached up to cover her mouth but he grabbed her hands away. "Beautiful teeth, love," said Thurston, "just beautiful," winning yet another client over for life.

"Thurston, you are such a fool," said Ruby, tousling his hair.

Thurston pulled back. He hated more than anything for someone to touch his hair.

"I don't see what's so funny about that," said Yvonne, who was a sleepy looking woman when she was mad. "I mean, that could be a true story and a real live person. It wouldn't be so funny then," she said. She stood there holding her gloves, which had been stained with the Tempting Taffy hair dye she had earlier applied to Agnes Collins' hair.

Agnes had been wearing the same hair color for years now, and no sooner than Yvonne began to apply it, Agnes had said, "Thurston tells me this color is all wrong for me. He said I should go with a bashful something or other. Hold on and I'll check. It's in here somewhere." She dug around in her pocketbook and pulled out a Kleenex which had been folded into a small tight square. An old Raisinet was stuck to it. Agnes knocked it off. Unfolding the Kleenex, she began reading it out loud. "Bashful Blonde, yes, that's what it was. Bashful Blonde. He said it would take the edge off my ruddy complexion."

"Is that so?" asked Yvonne.

"Not only that," said Agnes, who always got very excited and sort of jumped around in her seat whenever she talked about Thurston, "he said that I was just the type of woman who could carry off a sophisticated color like that."

"What else did he say?" Yvonne rubbed some color around the base of Agnes' hairline.

"Oh, just lots of things. He even fixed my bangs. You know, my husband wouldn't stop staring at me. Said I looked as young as I did the day he married me."

Yvonne was horrified. "Agnes, when did Thurston fix your hair?"

"Oh no, not my hair, just my bangs," she said proudly.

"Okay, when did he fix your bangs?"

13

"The other day." She folded the Kleenex back neatly into its square and stuck it carefully into a side pocket of her purse. "As a matter of fact it was right after you fixed it. He just walked right up to me and said, 'Darling . . .' you know, in that movie star voice of his? And he said, 'Darling, let me show you what's missing in your life, darling . . .' and you know something, Yvonne, he really is sort of cute, isn't he?"

"He's just a sight, Agnes, I swear he is. But what did he do exactly?" asked Yvonne as she rolled the heating lamp over and adjusted it above Agnes' head.

"Oh, he just went right to work. It's the strangest thing, Yvonne, but I could hardly feel he was touching my hair at all and at the same time it felt like there were about fifteen little hands flying all around me. Now he is a *real* professional if you ask me. Ouch! That's burning my head, hon," she said, jumping.

"Hold still, sugar." Yvonne adjusted the lamp higher while Agnes sat back again, zipping and unzipping her pocketbook, staring dreamily into space.

"Thurston called it the windswept look, but my husband, you know what my husband called it?"

"Do tell," said Yvonne, who was tapping her foot nervously. She couldn't wait to corner Thurston on this one.

"He called it sexy. And Yvonne," giggled Agnes, "Leonard hasn't touched me like that in years. And do you know what that rascal went and did? He got us reservations for a weekend at King's Mountain. Can you believe it? My Leonard? And all because of my hair. It was lovely."

Suddenly she twisted her head around and looked up at Yvonne, who had been standing behind Agnes the whole time clinching her teeth together tight.

"Of course," Agnes added, "I would never dream of leaving you, hon."

"Did Thurston say anything else?" asked Yvonne.

"No," said Agnes turning back around, "but he did say that I was using too much hairspray. Do you think he could

14

be right? Leonard always complains whenever it rains. He says it smells like it gets right up there in his nose and stays all night. Thurston says I can get just as good a set if I use some of that mousse. He even sold me a bottle. He said it was the best thing on the market. Do you think he could be right?"

"Whoever heard of such a thing?" asked Yvonne. "Agnes, you ought to know by now that you can't trust a male hairdresser, no matter what they say."

Some of the hair color began to stain Agnes' forehead so Yvonne took some ashes out of an ashtray and began to rub the color off the skin around her hairline.

"Ouch! That's too hard, hon!" yelled Agnes pulling away. "I swear it is. What's gotten into you anyway? Did somebody rain on your parade?"

Yvonne eased up. "Oh, I'm sorry, Agnes. But it just seems like everything is falling to pieces. First this Gladys Bessinger thing, and then . . ."

"What Gladys Bessinger thing?"

"Didn't you know? She's suffering a nervous breakdown. That's why the shop's so full. Her clients had nowhere else to go." Yvonne paused and looked at herself in the mirror. She was drawn and needed more sleep. "Agnes, I just have to talk to someone. It's about Bebe Pointer."

"Oh, Yvonne, that was so terrible and so sudden. We were in school together and I remember one time when . . ."

Yvonne interrupted, "Agnes, all these years Bebe was my client and now Thurston is going to do her hair. Agnes, I am just not going to let him do it."

"Oh, honey, a dead woman's hair? No, I could never do that, that's for sure. Have you ever done that?"

"Well," Yvonne crossed her arms and squeezed herself tight, "it looks like I'm going to have to. I'm not about to send her off to the Lord with what Thurston has in mind."

"Look at it this way," said Agnes, "it couldn't be any worse than that big old black thing she was always wearing."

"Agnes, that was Black Rage and it's one of the finest hair colors on the market," said Yvonne, taking a towel and checking Agnes' hair to see if it was ready. "Come to think of it, sweetie, it wouldn't hurt you to think about getting a little extra teasing. As we get older we can use all the lift we can get."

"Well, not according to Thurston. He says I shouldn't wear teasing at all. He says . . ."

"My, my, aren't we listening to Thurston a lot these days," Yvonne said, rigid as she set the timer for an extra five minutes.

"Well don't go getting all catty at me, hon. I'm just telling you what he told me. Is it ready yet?"

And Yvonne said almost and Agnes said she'd be glad to try more teasing just as long as she didn't turn out having big hair stacked up on top of her head like Bebe Pointer had.

"I don't want big hair, is all. Thurston says it is definitely out."

And this was the conversation that went on all the way through the rinsing, the rolling, and the comb-out, all the way up to the front desk where she wrote Agnes up a ticket and sent her on her way. But not before first checking to make sure Thurston didn't fiddle with Agnes' hair, and checking to make sure that her standing appointment was where it was supposed to be, under Yvonne's name.

"Well I'm serious," Yvonne said to Thurston after Agnes had gone. "I really don't see what's so funny about mugging a little old lady."

But Thurston just grinned, which infuriated her, because that was what he was always just doing. Then he motioned for one of his clients, one in a sequined paisley dress with designer hose, to follow him back to his station.

"Mildred darling," he said, putting his hands on the woman's shoulders, "as usual, you look simply gorgeous. I can't

16

see why you even bother coming in to have your hair done at all."

Thurston turned his head away and grimaced, letting Miss Ruby and Yvonne know he was lying. Then he smiled at the woman on the couch, the one who had just been transferred from Yvonne's side of the appointment book to his.

Yvonne noticed the change right off. She was furious. "Thurston, you get back here right this instant. Miss Ruby, did you see that? Do you see what he's gone and done?"

Miss Ruby was at a loss for words.

But Thurston said, "Mildred, darling, it looks like we have a possible scene on our hands. Go on back and I'll be right with you. But wait! Stop!" He was framing his hands in front of Mildred like a Hollywood director "Ooooh baby! You look so good! Where'd you get that devine ensemble?"

"This old thing?" crooned Mildred, pulling the dress away from her neck. "I've had this thing for ages." She giggled and smoothed down the front of her shimmering cocktail dress. Mildred had never dressed like that for Yvonne when Yvonne fixed her hair. Back then, she always just wore pant suits.

Thurston blew kisses at Mildred as she left, and Yvonne could have sworn she'd seen him goose her too. But she knew she must be seeing things if she thought she'd seen that.

"Now, Yvonne," said Thurston, walking up with his hips swinging, "I can't imagine what on earth you find so pressing that can't wait and be discussed over a beer. But since I'm here, let me show you a little something about hair that seems to have slid past you in the last decade. You got a comb, babe?"

She waved the comb she did have in his face and said, "I am furious with you. Why don't you just stop? And," she said, turning to Miss Ruby, "why don't you ever try and stop him? In case you didn't notice, he's taking all my clients."

"Not all of them," said Thurston, "just the ones who want to look good."

"See there, Miss Ruby! See!" said Yvonne, jamming her comb at Thurston again.

"Would yall quit fighting," said Miss Ruby. "I have something I want to show you two."

She smoothed a brochure out across the desk. "I have this wonderful plan. Now look at this. The Southeast Hair Show of the year. This is the Olympics of hair. It's where all the top notch European hair designers come to show off their latest. And Thurston, the way I see it, you're destined to win this thing for me. I can feel it in my soul."

Yvonne's heart sank. Right before her very eyes, not only did Thurston get out of his immediate trouble with her, but he was being rewarded as well.

"So?" asked Miss Ruby, "what do you think?"

"Well," said Thurston, and then he came in for the kill, "it will have to be first class all the way. And there will be no chintzing with the clothes. I'll get whoever I want to take as my model, and we'll spend as much money on clothes as it will take." Thurston dreamed his way right through Miss Ruby's checking account, her savings account, and was just about to start in on her CDs when she stopped him.

"Whoa! Whoa there, buddy," she said. "It looks like I'm going to have to go with Yvonne. I can't afford you. How about it, Yvonne, hon? Think you could win this thing for me?"

Yvonne began to dream of the old days when she had won her first perm contest and it all came swooping back to her. The pride, the glory, having everyone coming up to her afterward, asking her advice on hair. She couldn't wait. It was going to be her chance to show Thurston something for a change. Maybe she could even get the shop back to order, back to the way it used to be.

"Well then," said Miss Ruby beaming, knowing Yvonne could never win, hoping and praying Thurston would come begging his way back in, "it's all settled then. I can see great things in the future for you and me, Yvonne."

"Wait a minute," said Thurston holding up his hand. "Now wait just a slimy minute. This isn't fair. All right, all right. I'll get my own model and I'll take care of my own clothes."

"Splendid!" said Miss Ruby clapping her hands together. "You can both go. Oh, it's going to be so exciting!"

"No no, darling," he said, grabbing Yvonne by the collar, "surely you can't be serious. I mean, I couldn't possibly stand next to this THING. Look at her. Look at this uniform. It went out with the Sausage Curl."

Yvonne jerked away and started to laugh, but Thurston just kept on. "It's people like her that keep us listed under 'Chambermaids' in the Blue Book instead of 'Professionals'!"

"Chambermaids?" Yvonne was still laughing.

"The way I see it," said Miss Ruby, not paying a bit of attention to either one of them, "we'll get first class tickets on Delta and fly down. It does say it's in Atlanta?"

"That's what it says," said Yvonne, pointing to one of the brochures at a picture of Six Flags Over Georgia.

"I've got it." Ruby snapped her fingers. "We'll contact the papers and have them take pictures of us at the airport as we embark on our tour. Oh, that's good! That's what the headlines will say." Miss Ruby spread her hands high in the air. " 'Miss Ruby and Her Celebrity Stylers Embark on Their Tour.' And we'll get a penthouse suite at the Peachtree Plaza and ..." And Miss Ruby just went wild daydreaming. And a big part of the dream was the single fact that with Gladys in the loony bin, or wherever she was, she wouldn't be thinking about going to any hair show. Actually, it was Tom Jones who had started Ruby thinking about Atlanta in the first place. First prize for the hair show was a round trip ticket to Las Vegas to see a show, and afterward the winner would have dinner with him backstage. How Gladys would die with envy when she found out that Ruby had sat at the very same table with Tom! How she had eaten with him and drank champagne with him. How she had listened to his jokes, and how when they left, he had given Miss Ruby his unlisted telephone number in case she or any of her close friends wanted ringside seats to anything in Vegas.

Oh, and to have Tom's number and to be able to tell Gladys that she was a personal friend of his would make Gladys' hair curl. She could finally get Gladys back for all the mean things she had done to Ruby. Up to and including the time she had won a trip to Europe three summers back and invited Ruby's boyfriend instead of Ruby. Of course, he was a good for nothing nobody and Ruby wouldn't have been caught dead spending a summer in Europe with Gladys anyway, but that was beside the point.

Ruby was just going through the Europe trip one more time when the phone rang and Yvonne picked it up, but Thurston grabbed it right out of her hand and said, "Helloooo, Celebrity Styling. Ronder? Ronder who? Oh yes, Ronder Jeffcoat. Well, Ronder Jeffcoat, Miss Ruby's too busy to come to the phone right now. Is there something I can help you with? A color job, perhaps?"

Yvonne watched as Thurston wrote down Ronder's number and gave it to Miss Ruby, who promptly tore it up and threw it away. She understood Miss Ruby so well, and was glad that she wasn't on her bad side, but she felt sorry for Ronder, who was. Nobody loved Miss Ruby as much as Ronder did, and Yvonne knew she was desperate to get back with her.

Yvonne had heard all about Ronder's problem by way of Louise Stokes and Earline Maddox, who were sitting in the back; one freshly rolled and under the dryer, the other freshly shampooed, waiting her turn. They had been gossiping like high school girls at a basketball game, putting their minds in gear and letting them rip from A to Z. They stayed on G for a long time, talking about Gladys, and then they moved on down the line to R for Ronder, exhausting the topic. It didn't take a genius to see that Ronder Jeffcoat would be wanting to come back to work.

3

onder knew that it was going to take more than a phone call to break Miss Ruby. In fact, if anyone knew what Gladys was going through with Ruby, Ronder did. But it was worth it because Ronder wanted more than anything to go back to being a beautician.

When people asked Ronder why she had wanted to become a beautician, she'd look them square in the face and say, "I didn't. I always wanted to be married until I was. Then I wanted to become a beautician."

Buck was his name, and the first month after their honeymoon he was out of work and the second month he was in front of the TV for what looked like life. Ronder's next door neighbor had a Tupperware like party, only instead of Tupperware, she sold love gels and little lavender teddies, and edible panties for "him" and little marbles for "her" that the Chinese women had invented and are supposed to wear all day long while they vacuum their rugs or dust their tables. Ronder wasn't interested in that, so she bought a silky see-through pink thing with black gloves that went all the way up to her elbows. She'd never been one for that kind of stuff before, but Buck had started watching wrestling.

He'd even started the soaps and game shows to the point where Ronder could only talk to him during commercials. But then one day he started watching those, so she put on her little outfit and some high heels to match and walked into the living room full of amorous intentions and said, "Look, sweetie, here's baby," because that was what he used to call her, only this time he looked over and said, "Where'd you get the money for that?" and went right on back to watching *The Price Is Right*.

That's when Ronder decided it was time to leave her trailer and go back to work at The Celebrity Styling Shop. Even if it did mean acknowledging that Miss Ruby was right.

As far as Ronder was concerned, these last months without Ruby had been terrible. She picked up the phone and dialed again, not even counting if it was the third or fourth or fifth time she'd called. The same strange man she'd been getting all morning answered the phone delivering the same strange message. But it didn't matter.

Miss Ruby was right.

Ronder would be on that phone all day long. She had propped her feet up on the couch and stationed herself next to Buck, who was watching the same soap opera that was also on at the beauty shop. And with the phone still on her stomach, she began to dial a different number. She nudged Buck with the toe of her sock and he grumbled. "Turn that thing down, hon. I can't hear a thing ... Oh yes, hello? Gladys? Hello?" Ronder rolled her eyes and slammed down the phone. "Damned answering machines!"

After she had hung up, she laid back and tried to decide who she could call next to use up the thirty minutes before she could call Miss Ruby back.

After Yvonne had both Louise and Earline sitting snuggly under the dryers, she sat Miss Ruby down at her station for her mid-morning fluff and tease and watched Thurston as he got ready to give Mildred Shealy a cut and color.

Mildred bent this way and that. "I want it cut right here and not too short there and kind of long here," she said.

"Honey," said Thurston, "what you want is what you want. I'm going to give you what you need." He combed her hair out until a song came over the radio.

"Excuse me, baby," and he put his comb down, went to the middle of the shop and started dancing. He danced around all the women in the beauty shop, even the ones at the shampoo bowls, and then came back, picked up his comb and said, "Sorry, baby. I just love that easy listening. Now where was I? Oh yes, well, the way that Louise Stokes told it, was that Gladys Bessinger ran out the back of the A&P when she saw her and Earline. Said she left a full cart right there at the check out counter."

"That's what I heard too," said Mildred.

Thurston pointed to Louise and Earline, who were under the dryers and lifting their hoods and talking away. He shook his head. "If I saw those two magpies coming at me down an A&P aisle, I'd start doing my shopping at the Piggly Wiggly."

He picked up where he'd left off and began combing, then dancing, then combing some more.

Thurston kept dancing around Mildred as he sectioned off her hair. His pink labcoat, which he had designed himself, was silk, and when it ballooned and floated in the air, you could see the red and blue rhinestones on his high heeled boots.

"Look at that," said Yvonne pointing her comb at him. "Just you look at that."

"What is it, honey?" asked Miss Ruby, who always held her head high, as if she wore a crown that was too heavy for her to turn her head.

"God did not create man to set a woman's hair. Now, in the Bible it says a woman's hair is her crown and glory, but I haven't read a thing yet about a man fixing hair. I don't think it's right. It gets them all confused."

Miss Ruby tightened her thighs and hoped Yvonne wasn't about to go off into one of her big religious tirades. Whenever Yvonne got into what Miss Ruby called as "one of her moods," Ruby would square her shoulders and try to think about something else and not listen to a word of it. But once in a while when Yvonne rolled into a full sermon, there was nothing to do but listen.

Miss Ruby felt a great relief flush over her when Yvonne stopped talking. It was one thing, her going at it when the shop was half full, but now with the shampoo bowls and dryers busy with Gladys Bessinger's clients, Miss Ruby cringed at the thought of Yvonne marching back and forth quoting Scriptural support for anything that came down the pike.

Yvonne quietly sprayed the spit curls at Miss Ruby's forehead.

25

Yvonne, herself, was losing her hair and had already switched to a smaller roller in order to add some extra height to her bang area. Sometimes she would just stare at Thurston, who did have plenty of hair, even right on down to his chest, and then further, and it just made her shiver to think how much further. And she knew that given half a chance, Thurston wouldn't hesitate to let anyone see just how far that hair did go. It was ugly.

Yvonne knew that Jesus didn't have hair like that. He had soft light brown hair, with just a little wave—and no body hair.

She had never once thought about if the devil had hair or not, but having thought about it now, she decided it would be just like Thurston's—perfect, with a beautiful perm and a nice frosting.

Yvonne would never understand gays. And she certainly knew she'd never have one messing around with her hair. Most of them seemed too, well, too much like Thurston. Since the very first day he had come to the shop with his blowdryers and curling irons and pop music, her whole world began falling apart. And now, because of him, she was thinking about getting out of the business. There just wasn't any room for the shampoo-and-set crowd anymore. And on top of that, all her patrons were either getting too old to come to the beauty shop or they were dead.

Then she thought about Bebe Pointer.

Bebe had followed Yvonne from beauty school to shop to shop to shop—from the bubble to the pageboy to the beehive and finally to her Black Rage updo. Yvonne remembered when Bebe had come in and said, "I want to ask you something, but I don't want to upset you. Will you fix my hair when I die?"

Yvonne had said, "Honey, if it's the last thing I do for you, I'll do your hair."

The very next week Bebe had brought in her will, and in bold letters was her request that Yvonne style her hair at the funeral parlor.

Bebe was the one patron Yvonne thought she'd never lose.

That was until Thurston had come into the picture and told Bebe that her updo made her face look too long. That was all it took to transform what Yvonne considered a decent, respectable woman into a soap opera star look alike.

Every week after that Thurston tried out a new style on Bebe and each style looked as hideous to Yvonne as the one before. And now, today, Thurston was going to give it one last shot. Yvonne had heard him just this morning, laughing over the phone to the funeral parlor director, saying he thought Rachel's hair on *The Edge of Night* would be the perfect hairstyle for Bebe.

It pained Yvonne to think of sending Bebe to the Lord that way. Put a deep pain in her tired old beautician's back and made it hard for her to swallow. Sometimes when Yvonne got upset she would start to count her swallows, trying to get some control over her life, but then she'd get up to number five and not be able to get six to come from trying so hard and she'd feel like she was going to choke. That's how she felt now, staring in the mirror and looking at the set she had given herself just that morning. Yvonne stopped what she was saying in mid-sentence and kept spraying and spraying the right side of Miss Ruby's head.

Miss Ruby knew her hair must be soaked by now. She looked around, hoping no one had heard anything, hoping it was all finished. She knew something was bothering Yvonne. She had to remind herself that something was always bothering Yvonne, and she tried to bring her out of it. She tried to sound cheerful. "That Atlanta show is going to be so much fun, Yvonne. You know, I hear that the men outweigh the women there two to one. Why, two old bats like ourselves set free in a big town like that . . ." but it was no use. Yvonne wasn't having any of it.

She was in deep thought about herself, and about the shop and how it had changed, and about Gladys Bessinger and her nervous breakdown, and about how it seemed to be changing Miss Ruby. But then everything seemed to be changing. Then just as she was thinking about Bebe and Bebe's hair, and Rachel on *The Edge of Night*, Thurston went and changed the radio to a pop station and Yvonne couldn't even cry it made her so mad.

Miss Ruby got worried when Yvonne just left her sitting there with half of her hair sprayed wet, and the other half not sprayed at all, in order to go to Thurston's chair where Mildred Shealy was enjoying a cup of hot coffee and Thurston combing her hair.

"So now there I was, Thurston," said Mildred, crouched over her coffee cup as if someone was going to take it away, "all dressed to go to church, and my husband says to me, 'I can't go, I don't have a thing to wear.' And do you know what I told him?"

"Just what did you tell him, sugar?" asked Thurston as he swung the color cape around Mildred's neck like he was a bull fighter, shaking it out, saying, "Olé!"

"Oh, Thurston, you are such a ham. I told him, I said, 'If Jesus came down right now, what would you tell him then? That you had nothing to wear?' "

Thurston threw his hands up in the air, laughing with Mildred, who had tears streaming down her face. And when she looked back up, she noticed Yvonne staring down at her. "Oh, hellooo, Yvonne," she said. "We were just talking about Gladys Bessinger. Have you heard the news?" she asked, still laughing.

"When Jesus comes down," said Yvonne, "we're going to be on the toilet, in the bathtub, in the shower or even naked. Who cares what we have on?"

Mildred looked at Yvonne as if she were half out of her mind, then went right on back to talking to Thurston as if Yvonne hadn't spoken a word. "Anyway, Thurston, do you even imagine it did a bit of good?"

"Pray tell, honey," he said, putting cotton in her ears.

"Why, no, it did not. Not the slightest bit of good. He sat there and watched that VCR all morning while I went and prayed for his soul. Sometimes I think the Dear Lord is just going to have to turn His head and bless our husbands anyway or else there won't be any men in heaven when we get there."

"Ain't it the truth! And if there aren't, I'm not going," said Thurston, flipping his hand at her. "Now you just hold your pretty little horses because I've got to mix up that rare secret formula of yours. Oh darling," he said, framing her face once more, making her blush, "you are just gorgeous. Simply gorgeous!" Then he did his little twirl as he left. The kind he was famous for. The kind that got on Yvonne's nerves because first he snapped his fingers and she really hated that.

"Well, Mildred," said Yvonne after Thurston had disappeared into the dispensary, "I see you're getting your color done today." She stood on her toes and examined Mildred's scalp. "And not a moment too soon I might add."

"Now what's that supposed to mean?" asked Mildred, fingering the sides of her hair. "I'd like to know exactly what's that supposed to mean."

"Oh nothing, except, well, you never know when Thurston's going to bc well, Mildred. If you know what I mean."

Mildred sat up straighter. "No, I don't know what you mean."

"Oh well, it's nothing really," said Yvonne. "Forget I even said anything."

Although Mildred was now with Thurston, Yvonne had worked on her for more years than Thurston had owned his beauty license. She probably knew her better than anyone in town. For instance, she knew that Mildred was exactly like Gladys Bessinger when it came to gossip—both of them acted so disinterested when actually all they wanted was every juicy minute by minute detail and then more.

For a fleeting moment, just a fleeting moment, Yvonne considered walking away leaving old Mildred Shealy guessing.

"Okay," said Yvonne, "but just between you and me," she lowered her voice, "he's been known to take a pill or two and get a little bongo. You should have seen what he did to some poor woman's hair last week. She asked for a gentle trim, but she walked out of the shop with hair shorter than Gladys Bessinger's."

Yvonne walked away, leaving Mildred touching her hair, looking concerned. It was a fact that she was one woman Yvonne Tisdale had not minded losing.

"Miss Ruby," Yvonne asked, "have you ever seen these women that come in and just crouch over their old pocketbooks like we're going to steal them or something? Well, that is Mildred Shealy to the T." She picked up her wicker fan and began fanning Miss Ruby's hairspray dry. "Why, one time, and I'll never forget this as long as I live, she fell asleep under the dryer and when she woke up, she was screaming that I'd stolen the money out of her pocketbook. And the whole thing was just a bad dream. It took her the longest time to get it in her head that I hadn't done it."

"I remember that," laughed Miss Ruby, "but do you remember that woman who had that dream while she was under the dryer and woke up fighting? The woman who always wore those leopard pedal pushers?"

"Who could forget her?" Yvonne smiled. "She was always falling asleep under the dryer. Remember the time that it blew up on her and she woke up screaming, 'I've been electrocuted! I've been electrocuted!' "

Yvonne and Miss Ruby were laughing.

"And once, and this isn't even funny," Yvonne was bent over cracking up and hugging her stomach, "in beauty school this lady was under the dryer and her foot fell asleep. And when she woke up, she stood up and fell and broke her foot." Tears were streaming from Yvonne's eyes and she was holding on to Miss Ruby's chair.

Miss Ruby just loved her hairdressers. She could never tell what one was going to do next. They were all so unpredictable. Just minutes before, Yvonne looked as if she was on the brink of suicide, and now, here she was fanning Miss Ruby's hair, laughing and not even talking about religion.

"You know, Miss Ruby," said a calmer looking Yvonne, "Thurston can really work the women, I swear he can. But that doesn't mean he can do good hair. As far as I'm concerned, everything he sends out that front door looks like a chicken."

Miss Ruby was about to explain to Yvonne that things were changing from the old ways. She was just about to tell her how two old birds like themselves were going to have to get used to it, when the phone rang.

"How about you going and getting that, hon," said Yvonne. "I've still got to pull Louise and Earline out from under the dryer."

Miss Ruby picked up the phone knowing it was Ronder. She was eating something, Miss Ruby could tell, and she sounded as if she had been settled in the same comfortable spot for a long time.

"Hon, I've been calling all day. I swear I have, and I keep getting the strangest man. Is he funny or something? Miss Ruby, you didn't go and hire one of those gays, did you?"

While Miss Ruby negotiated the terms for Ronder to come back to work, Thurston came up front looking for her to do another shampoo. It was then that he noticed a woman wearing what he considered a beauty school nightmare. He tried everything he could to talk her off of Yvonne's book, but it was no use. She wasn't going for any of his square face, round frame routine, and when he tried it out on her, she made him feel like he had asked her for a pack of contraceptives.

"Yvonne," said Thurston, walking to the back, hitching his thumb over his shoulder, "you've got a live one up front. She's from Arkansas and she means business."

He paused long enough to do an imitation of what he thought every woman in town acted like, and in the high pitched voice that seemed to go with it, he said, "I want a shampoo. And I want it set. And I want heavy teasing. That's *heavy* teasing. And don't keep me waiting."

Yvonne ignored him and continued to comb Earline out, while Louise continued to work on yet another version of the Gladys Bessinger breakdown story. "Someone told me that not only did she have a breakdown, but she's putting her shop up for sale." She stepped in front of Yvonne's mirror and pushed her white streak down, then poofed it back up. "Can you believe that?"

"Well it serves her right," said the ever-flirting Earline, who was making eyes at Thurston. "I still can't believe she left me without a hairdresser. If you ask me, she's no better than that Ronder Jeffcoat."

"That's no lie," said Louise.

Yvonne turned Earline's collar out and said, "Now Earl, hon, you know Ronder was just falling in love."

"Love or no love, she still left me under that dryer. My hair was a mess."

Thurston reached over and touched Earline's hair and said, "Amazing! You must have used a stepladder to get to the top of this, Yvonne. Dolly Parton, eat your heart out."

Earline pushed down at her new style, and so did Louise, all the way to the front, where they paid their tickets and went out the front door.

"Thurston," hissed Yvonne cornering him at the shampoo bowl, "I thought we had an agreement."

Thurston put his hands in the air. "I meant it, I meant it. You really got her hair up there."

"That's not what I'm talking about and you know it. Now you know as well as I do that that radio is supposed to stay on my station until after lunch and it isn't lunch yet. So what I want to know is who gave you permission to change it?"

"Yvonne darling," said Thurston, kissing her on the cheek, "I had an early lunch."

"Ohhh you make me so mad!"

Thurston wagged his finger at her. "Uh-uh, that's not very Christian."

Yvonne tried to control herself and Thurston said, "Listen, sugar, I try. Honestly I do. But that stuff you listen to doesn't have any beat, and my clients are falling asleep listening to it. I prefer something a little more rhythmical, myself." Thurston began dancing to the music that was playing. It was a black station with rap music, and the only words Yvonne could even make out was some nonsense about how, without the man, the woman was just Cornflakes and water. She'd never heard anything so ridiculous in her life.

"It's good, isn't it?" he asked, still dancing. "I could dance to this all day, but I've got to go mix Mildred's color."

Yvonne followed him back into the color room, where he promptly forgot Mildred's color and sat down to have a cigarette. Yvonne didn't know one beautician who didn't smoke. But this time Thurston was going too far. He was leaving Mildred sitting there, not even processing, with clips sticking off of her head going in all directions, just so he could smoke. It would be like going to the doctor's and another doctor comes in and says to the doctor you're with, "Want to take a coffee break?" and he'd say yes and leave you there, all laid out for the world to see.

Yvonne was imagining herself lying on that cold

examining table with nothing on but a gown that tied in the back, wearing paper slippers, holding a worn out magazine that she'd never subscribe to in a million years, when Thurston sighed and said, "Lordy, Lordy, I'm tired."

The blasphemous remark raised the hair on the back of her neck. "You're calling someone that knows you, Thurston. And if He doesn't, you're in trouble."

Thurston kept smoking and Yvonne reached over and switched the radio back to the easy listening station. "Thurston, you are playing with evil and winking at sin."

"That's not what's really upsetting you, is it?" he asked, pulling a petal off his carnation. "You're upset because Bebe took you out of her will and put me in instead, aren't you?" Thurston blew smoke rings in the air and waited for Yvonne's answer.

She watched him with a tired face, with a pain stabbing her chest where Bebe's friendship used to be.

"Well since you're being so candid with me, Yvonne, let me ask you something else." He took a long pause before he went on. "Have you ever fixed a dead woman's hair before?"

"Thurston, this is a beauty shop, not a disco, and I, for one, would prefer it if you did your dancing at home."

"Just as I thought," said Thurston, this time blowing the smoke rings out the side of his mouth. "You've probably never even seen a dead woman before, have you?"

He smelled his carnation two or three times and now it was Yvonne who waited.

"Well Yvonne, let me tell you, being in a room with a dead woman is strange. Really strange. It always feels like they're going to sit up and start telling you something."

Yvonne was quiet for a moment, and then she said, "I would really hate to see her go to her grave wearing something that didn't look like her. Something too young. Thurston, you're not planning on that, are you?"

"You know, Yvonne," said Thurston, puffing at his cigarette with pursed lips, "if there is one thing I cannot stand, it's when a woman wears her dress at mid-calf. It's what I'd call an unfortunate length."

Yvonne didn't know what he was talking about. She looked down at her clothes.

"No no darling. It's Mildred," he said. "She always wears such awful clothes. Who'd have ever thought that one designer could ever come up with the idea of mixing brown paisley with sequins? It must have been a woman designer." Thurston put his hand to his forehead and threw his head back. "I can't breathe when I'm around paisley. It just makes my poor gay eyes grow old."

He stopped his clowning around and gave Yvonne the once-over. "Of course," he said, "I wouldn't go to town flashing that outfit around either. It could be hazardous to your sex life."

"At least I dress like I'm supposed to," said Yvonne.

Thurston crushed out his cigarette and poured Mildred Shealy's special rare formula, a basic Spun Sand, into a bottle and then added peroxide. "Yvonne," he said, "if I wore that uniform, they'd kick me out of the Drag Queen Hall of Fame. My sex life would be ruined."

Then he laughed because if Thurston knew anything, he knew that Yvonne didn't have a sex life.

Yvonne had always known that women her age didn't think about such things. In her book it was just a terrible sin thinking about sex at all unless you were married. Of course, it wasn't as bad as some sins.

The Bible said that one sin was as bad as another but she also knew, from the good raising she'd had, that this was just a way to keep people from sinning at all. Naturally a murder was a whole lot worse than, say, someone bearing false witness against their neighbor, which is exactly what Yvonne had done to Thurston when she had told Mildred he had a problem with pills. She'd never even seen Thurston take an aspirin.

Well, Thurston was not her neighbor and had he been, she surely would have moved out of the neighborhood.

She knew from reading the Bible that God hated homosexuals. It said so right in Romans 1:27. She knew it by heart. She said it out loud: "And likewise also the men, leaving the natural use of the woman, burned in their lust one toward another; men with men working that which is unseemly, and receiving in themselves that recompense of their error which was meet." She didn't exactly know what that last part meant, but she did know what the first part was all about and recited it right to Thurston's face. He didn't do anything but just sit there and smoke. So she said it again, this time closer and louder, and this time he laughed like a red devil with horns coming right out of his forehead, making the sign of the cross. "Yvonne, I think you missed your calling," he said, crossing his legs tight, hooking his toe around his ankle like he always did.

She was furious. "Thurston, it is not good to cross your legs like that. It cuts off your circulation and it's a good way to get a heart attack! Didn't your mama ever tell you that?"

"No," said Thurston, trying to get a good look at the back of Yvonne's legs. "She just said something about varicose veins."

Yvonne looked at her legs. She had worn support hose ever since her first day of beauty school because she had read once that doctors recommended it for beauticians and nurses who stood on their feet all day.

"I don't have any veins," she said proudly.

"That's not hard to believe."

"Thurston, let's just cut this out. What I want to know is what you're planning to do to Bebe Pointer's hair?"

"If you must know, which you always seem to think you must, I plan on giving her the deluxe treatment. I'm going to paint her fingernails and toenails with a pretty Park Avenue Pink and then I'm going to do her makeup and then I thought maybe I'd fix her hair to look like Linda Evans on *Dynasty*. Don't you think Peter at the Gates will just love that look?" Yvonne glared at him and he glared right back. "*If* you must know."

Neither one of them looked away. They just stared and stared. Then Mildred Shealy's timer dinged, and as Thurston moved to get up, Yvonne said, "You really must see your evil ways, Thurston. It's one thing for you to talk that way, but when you start inflicting it on others ... I mean, Bebe was never that vain and never once did she look like a movie star. It just isn't right sending her to heaven full of all that vanity."

Thurston nodded his head solemnly for a moment, as if she had finally gotten through to him. Then he crossed his eyes and lolled his tongue out like an idiot.

"Oh, there's just no talking to you," said Yvonne, exasperated. "You're sick, Thurston. Do you hear me? Sick, sick, sick! Give me those gloves. I'm going to check Mildred's color for you. She isn't safe with you around."

"For moi? You'd do that for me?" asked Thurston, sitting back down to light another cigarette. "Darling, you're utterly devine."

"Yoo hoo," said Miss Ruby, coming back, waving the appointment book at Yvonne. "That lady from Arkansas is up front having a fit. She wants to know what's taking so long."

Yvonne just stared at Miss Ruby, making her feel like she had food on her chin, and then Miss Ruby looked down at the appointment book and said, "I guess she'll be your last for the day. Your book's blank after that. Looks like Thurston's got a full day ahead of him, though."

Yvonne didn't even give Miss Ruby a chance to finish what she was saying. She just brushed past her in a fury.

"What on earth is wrong with her?" asked Miss Ruby when Yvonne was out of sight.

"She's crazy," said Thurston. "When I went to beauty school I did so many shampoo-and-sets I started to dream about them every night. Maybe they've gone to her head."

"Listen, do you know where the Nudeze is?" Miss Ruby asked as she began searching through the cabinets.

"I don't even know what it is."

"Of course you do. It's that wax that removes hair?"

"Oh, that. Well I used it on my legs just last night, sweetheart," said Thurston, pinching Miss Ruby's side.

"Stop that," she said, swatting his hand away. "This is serious, Thurston. I've made a decision."

"Oh, drum roll, drum roll," said Thurston, drumming everything in sight with his fingers.

Miss Ruby laughed. "We're going to start doing you-know-where hair in here," she said proudly. "I'm going to build a room off to the side for it, and for makeovers, too. And I'm going to add three more chairs, or maybe four. Gladys won't have a fighting chance after I'm through with this place."

Miss Ruby stared right through Thurston, trying to remember the last place she'd seen the Nudeze.

But Thurston got the wrong idea. "Don't you even *think* about it," he said, pulling back. "Don't you even *look* at me. You're going to have to get somebody else to do that. Somebody that really appreciates women. I am definitely not your man."

"Oh don't worry so. I've already got someone else in mind."

"Oh? Who's the poor unfortunate creature?"

"Hair removal is such a big business these days, Thurston," continued Miss Ruby. "And I'm not just talking about bikini lines. Have you ever noticed how many women have mustaches?"

"Noticed? Darling, I've never seen so many mustaches as I have since I came to work here. You ought to take a look at Mildred Shealy. When she purses her lips at me and says in that high squeaky voice of hers, 'Thurston Thurston Thurston make me beautiful,' and I see that hair around those lips, I thank God every day that he made men."

• • •

Mildred was ready because Thurston was so very good at doing color. But Yvonne was angry at him and even more so at Mildred, because when she walked up, Mildred had taken on a superior smirk. Ever since Mildred had switched over to Thurston, she had begun to act different. She walked lighter, kind of bouncy, and she always flipped her hair wherever she went, like she was back in high school chewing Juicy Fruit.

Yvonne decided it was time to put her plan to work. She put her hands on her hips and said, "Oh dear, Mildred, it looks like Thurston missed a spot."

Mildred stuck her head right up to the mirror to try and see, but Yvonne just pushed her calmly back down and said, "Well hold still and I'll just fix it right up."

Of course, there was no missed spot.

Actually Yvonne had no idea that she was going to do what she did next, until luck of luck, the phone rang and it was Thurston's lover, Duran. She could hear him all the way across the shop, "Oh Duran baby!" and it gave Yvonne exactly the time she needed to go in the back and mix more color. After she did this, she applied it all over Mildred's hair.

This would be a color job to remember.

When Thurston walked back ten minutes later, he was under the impression that Yvonne had already rinsed the color out of Mildred's hair. But the timer was set for twenty more minutes.

"Thurston?" asked Mildred. "I don't ever remember it taking this long to process. Shouldn't I be rinsed now?" And Thurston knew better than to say no, because a good beautician knows that covering up mistakes is half the secret of doing a good job. So he just held his breath, pressed his palms together and turned away to wait an extra minute or so, so that she wouldn't see the look of concern on his face. Then he began rinsing her off, cooing over the wonderful color, which of course had grabbed and now sat on top of Mildred Shealy's hair as a very drab lavender blonde shade that wouldn't come out for weeks. But maybe with a little help from a deep conditioner and a Sweet Cream temporary rinse, he could get her out of the shop without her noticing. The whole time he was just dying to get hold of Yvonne, but the shop kept getting busier, too busy for him to do anything about her just yet.

In the meantime Yvonne had just finished washing the woman from Arkansas' hair. It looked flat and oily, like it had been licked by a dog for a very long time.

"Oh my neck is hurting from that shampoo bowl," said the woman, rubbing the back of her neck. "And you got my collar all wet."

"I'll blowdry your collar." Yvonne took out a blowdryer and set it on normal speed.

"My girl back in Little Rock never gets me wet."

Yvonne held the dryer on the woman's collar.

"Ouch! That's too hot! You're burning me."

"I'm sorry," said Yvonne. "Excuse me for a moment please."

"My collar's still wet."

"Oh, excuse me," and Yvonne left to get some more towels but the woman raised her voice, "My girl from Little Rock doesn't ever leave me until she's finished fixing my hair."

Yvonne just kept on walking away, speaking to herself. "That woman is giving me a hissy-fit. I'd like to tell her what I think of her and I wouldn't even care how she took it. She could take it to China for all I care."

But then when she saw Thurston, standing over Mildred Shealy massaging in a hot oil treatment, looking upset, she went right back to the woman from Little Rock, whistling a tune, carrying a basket of sanitized hair curlers.

The woman immediately started in with, "That roller don't go there," and then built up to, "You aren't rolling both sides back, are you?" after Yvonne had already rolled them back and had fourteen more rolled the same way on the top of her head. And it was a blessing indeed when Yvonne put that woman under the dryer, and on a low speed to keep her there for a long time.

But now the woman was back, pushing at her hair, saying, "That is not enough teasing."

She's trying to break me, thought Yvonne. "Yes ma'am, it is enough teasing."

"Aren't you going to tease some more?"

"No I am not going to tease anymore. You are lucky to have anyone available to tease your hair at all."

"What are you talking about?"

"Well, most people don't even give shampoo-and-sets anymore."

"Why, what on earth else would they do here?" asked the lady.

"Blowdrys, curling irons, you know," said Yvonne.

"No, I don't know. I've never heard of such a thing. What are all these blacks doing here?" She was talking about the one black woman Thurston had waiting on him while he rinsed Mildred's conditioner for chemically damaged hair out.

"Oh didn't you know? Black hair is where the money is these days. Like I was saying, there are hairdressers that will refuse to do sets."

"I've never heard of such a thing. They don't have that kind of shop in Arkansas."

"Well, it'll get to Arkansas. Progress is moving that way."

Yvonne sprayed Paula Payne Hair Spray all over the woman's hair.

"I've never heard of such a thing," she repeated. "I'm getting my hair set until I die."

"Well, that's not where hair is going now."

Yvonne looked the woman over. Despite what she had looked like when she had first come in, she was actually a nicely dressed woman. "People come out of the beauty schools now and don't even know what a set is," Yvonne told her. "They can't even do them."

41

"I'm going to always wear a set." The lady took her big hands and flattened the teasing that was still wet from the hairspray. "This isn't right. It's separating. My girl from Little Rock never lets it separate. You'd better do it over."

"Whoever heard of such a thing? I'm not doing it over. It's separating because you're poking at it. Besides, I'm not your girl from Little Rock." Yvonne pushed the woman's hands away. "Quit poking at it, why don't you."

"My girl from Little Rock doesn't ever take this long to fix my hair," the woman said.

So Yvonne poofed and pushed and picked at the lady's hair and sent her my-girl-from-Little-Rock-ing all the way up to the front desk with a ticket that made her eyes widen and made her cuss Miss Ruby out.

onder had told Miss Ruby that she was willing to do just about anything if Miss Ruby would only take her back. When Miss Ruby had said manicures, Ronder had said that would be fine. And when Miss Ruby had said pedicures, Ronder had sucked in her breath and said okay to that too. Nothing could be worse than giving a pedicure but Ronder wanted her job back more than anything. And then when Ronder thought the worst was over, Miss Ruby threw her the low pitch way out on the outside corner. "Honey, if you're going to come back into this shop," said Ruby, "you're going to have to do bikini waxings."

Ronder's heart fell. She could think of nothing more horrifying than taking the hair off of a bunch of forty year olds' upper inner thighs.

She sat up on the couch and said, "Buckkkk, turn that TV down. You're joking, right Miss Ruby?"

And that's when Miss Ruby had told her that she had already booked her for seven whole bikini waxes the following Tuesday.

"Seven?! Well Miss Ruby, I'm not so sure I can do that."

And so Ronder said she'd have to talk it over with Buck and call her back.

Buck could have cared less. The minute *Wheel of Fortune* had gone off the air, he had gone out for a pizza and left Ronder sitting at the same spot she'd been sitting all morning.

She would just have to try to call Gladys Bessinger again to see if she could go to work for her. No matter what a prude Ronder thought Gladys was, she knew that if Miss Ruby found out that she was working for Gladys, Miss Ruby would do anything to get her back. Probably even offer her a full salary and insurance. She'd be sorry then that she'd ever made Ronder Jeffcoat beg.

But all Ronder kept getting was Gladys' answering machine, telling her to leave a message at the sound of the beep.

Thurston had turned Mildred away from the mirror, trying not to worry about her botched up hair, trying to fix it up with the Sweet Cream temporary rinse. He was running the Atlanta Hair Show through his head instead. This is the way he saw it: First he would have to convince Miss Ruby how truly important it would be in the war against Gladys for Yvonne to be kept off the stage. Once that was done, the sky would be the limit. Once that was done, he knew he could talk Miss Ruby into buying all sorts of flashy new clothes and jewelry for him to wear to the competition. He thought something in a fuschia silk would be nice. Or even one of those Bob Mackie things with all the sequined buttons on it. And his model could wear the same thing.

Thurston's head was just swirling with ideas—swirling right into the future, when, after he returned to Stuckey with his new title, his name would be replacing that ugly old THE CELEBRITY STYLING SHOP sign. He could see it all so clearly. He'd redecorate the whole shop, pulling up the faded aqua throw rug in the waiting room and putting down a plush peach carpet in its place, to go under the new Victorian winged-back chairs he would order. The rest of the floors he would simply do in a black mirrored tile, to match the new black shampoo basins which he would order to replace those flesh colored ones Miss Ruby had been using since God first made beauty shops.

Thurston couldn't wait to remove the small window units and put in central heating and air, so that when he danced and styled, he wouldn't sweat. And he'd put bird cages in every corner and fill them with exotic talking birds, which he would teach to say, "Darling, you look lovely. Darling you look devine. We love Thurston." And you'd almost have to use a machete to get through the scheffleras, ficus and corn plants that would line the walls.

Miss Ruby would be his partner, of course—his silent partner—backing him financially and coming in on Saturdays to have her hair done. And he could hire Duran to be manager and keep Yvonne in line by getting her to dress better and teaching her all the new hairstyles for a change.

Thurston was getting excited. He began dancing around Mildred as he squirted the rinse through her hair, thinking about how great it was going to be to get rid of those old Bonat automatic hair dryers once and for all, and then the thought of Duran came swooping back down on him like a hawk on a field mouse.

Up until now Thurston had assumed that his only problem would be finding the perfect model for the Hair Show, and getting Yvonne off the stage and out of that uniform. But now there was another, more immediate, problem. The idea of telling Ruby, who had never seen a prisoner before, that she was going to have to hire one, made him weak all over. And on top of that, he would have to tell her that he was gay. And on top of that, that he was black. Prisoner, gay, black: not one or two, but all three. Even Gladys Bessinger, with all her exotic European gigolos, had never gone that far. Even when Gladys had hired that DeoCampo boy with the four earrings, she hadn't gone that far. And DeoCampo didn't own a bright yellow '63 Convertible Fin Tail El Dorado, customized into a stretch, with a bar and stereo deck in the back, either. But Duran did and it was the reason why he was doing time. One day he had walked out of Brice's Barber Supply and found a guy running a key across the side of "El Dog," and he broke the boy's nose. It wasn't just any boy's nose, either. It belonged to the twenty-four-year-old son of a county councilman, and the judge thought about three months in prison would be the right amount of time to cool Duran down.

Thurston couldn't quit thinking about Duran. He was such a flirt. He was probably having the best time of his life in that jail with all those men.

"Ohhh Duran Duran Duran," he breathed aloud.

Mildred looked up. "What? What did you say?"

"Nothing, baby, just nothing."

"Oh, I thought you said something," she said, wiping the sides of her face where the temporary rinse had dripped. "Thurston, this stuff smells funny. What is it? You've never used this stuff before. Let me see." Mildred tried to turn to the mirror but Thurston spread a towel over her face and held it against her eyes. "It's another conditioner, sweetie. This one makes the color last longer."

"Another one?"

"Yes. It makes the color last longer," he said, rolling his eyes. He kept one hand firm on the towel, the other busy with the color. Once he got the color in, everything would be all right. Until then, his heart felt like it was about to jump right out of his body.

He went back to thinking about Duran in jail. Then, just as fast, he decided not to think about Duran in jail, locked up with all those men. Alone. Without himself, Thurston, there beside him to keep his wandering eye in check. The last time he had seen Duran outside of those four walls with all those men grabbing through the bars for him, Duran had threatened to leave him for someone new because Thurston had refused to marry him. Thurston shook his head clear and decided to think about something else, something happier, something, anything, or somebody that he could do something about—somebody like Yvonne. He looked around the room for her. As soon as he blew Mildred's hair dry, which was finally looking like something she could walk outside in, he was going to have just enough time to take that Yvonne Tisdale out back and tell her a few hard facts.

6

But Thurston was not going to tell Yvonne anything, because behind his back she had snuck off across town and was now standing at the Franklin-Levy Funeral Parlor with a little portable dryer by her side.

"Don't you put me in a room with several of them," she said.

"Don't worry," said the attendant. "She's all alone."

He opened a door to a small room, and before she was even ready for it, he had pulled the sheet back from Bebe Pointer's face and Yvonne was staring right into it.

"I used to think I could never be in a room with a bunch of them either," he said. "That it would scare me to death. But you know, after a while it's just like any other job. My dates love it."

"Oh," said Yvonne.

She was still staring at Bebe.

Thurston was wrong thinking she'd never seen a dead person before. When she was little, she had gone to her grandfather's funeral and they had him all laid out and bald in his coffin.

Yvonne could remember wanting to do hair even that far back in her life. At the time, she was nine and the aunts who had raised her had about a hundred wigs and Yvonne would spend hours brushing and styling them. But looking at her grandfather was the first time she'd ever gotten a close up look at a bald head and Yvonne was more intrigued with that than the fact that he was dead. His head shined like it had been buffed with a shoe rag. And right where he should have had bangs, he had soft little white hairs like Yvonne had on her arms.

When no one was looking she reached down and touched it. It felt just like the hair on a caterpillar's back.

"You can do the neck and the sides," said the attendant, "but you've got to stop at the back. You just have to skip that unless you want to move the whole body."

Moving the body was not what Yvonne had in mind.

The attendant was a greasy boy of nineteen or twenty with a gap between his front teeth wide enough to fit a quarter in. His suit looked as if it had been stitched on it was so tight.

"We're lucky," he said. "We almost didn't get her teeth in in time. You've got to get them false ones in quick or else it's too late. The cheeks sink in."

He looked at Yvonne and licked his lips. "Notice how we sewed the eyes and lips together with those tiny stitches? That's in order so that the makeup can be applied just right."

Yvonne just stared at him.

"Yeah, see, most places glue the eyes and lips shut. We tried it one time, but this woman came in to do her sister's makeup and the glue wasn't dry, and when she tried to put the lipstick on her, well . . . Let's just say that woman had a fit. She screamed for hours. Normally we do the makeup ourselves unless somebody requests differently. Don't you think I did a nice job?"

He stood back and stuck his skinny little chest out proudly.

Yvonne nodded her head.

"Yes, I think so too. One of my best yet."

He set up a stool by Bebe and motioned for Yvonne to sit down.

"Did you know that when you die you lose twenty ounces right off the bat? It's scientific," he said. "They've measured people that have died and they know for a fact it's true. It's supposed to be your soul going up to heaven."

"Oh." Yvonne nodded her head slowly. "Listen, do you mind if I do this alone?" she asked.

"Not at all. You know, last week a lady brought in a pair of diamond earrings for her mother to wear but we couldn't get them through her holes. It was a surprise to me. Did you know that when you die, your skin freezes up? I didn't. That's what's nice about working here. You learn something new every day. Anyway, we told her we could only do clip ons. You can't wear pierced earrings unless you die with them on."

He began to laugh and Yvonne's ears began to ring.

"So if you ever start to feel like you're about to croak, you'd better slip those earrings in fast," and he left laughing, leaving Yvonne staring at Bebe.

Had she known, Bebe would've hated not having the back of her hair done. That was the place that was always worrying her the most. And Yvonne wished she was anyplace but where she was sitting right then, but she was convinced now, that Bebe must've been sick and not in her right mind when she rewrote that will. And she was equally convinced that she owed it to Bebe not to let Thurston work his evil ways on her.

By the looks of things Bebe hadn't had a set in a week.

Yvonne reached down to touch her hair and her fingers accidently brushed against her forehead. It made Yvonne's skin crawl. It was rubbery and as cold as ice.

She sighed. "Well I'm just going to have to get with the program. I know how much you hate to be kept waiting," she said to Bebe.

Thank goodness Bebe wasn't already in the coffin. Instead she was laid out on a surgical table, dressed in her best outfit. Well, not to Yvonne it wasn't. "Bebe, I hate to tell you this, hon, but that has got to be the worst dress you own. It makes you look fat."

Bebe just lay there with her head resting on a pedestal —the kind they decorate large wedding cakes on.

Yvonne began to apply the solvent that the attendant had left with her all over Bebe's hair. It smelled like lighter fluid. "This is one product that would not go over well in the shop, Bebe. It sort of smells like those old timey perms we used to give back in the old days, doesn't it?" asked Yvonne as she combed it through.

"Which reminds me. Remember old Mrs. Foster? Remember how she went out for groceries last week and never came back? Well they found her. She was down in Brunswick, Georgia, with not an idea as to where she had been." Yvonne laughed and slapped her knees. "Ha! I told you she was crazy. I told you I told you I told you! Oh, and look, I brought your Black Rage. Of course it's just a temporary rinse but that'll do for now. Where you're going you'll probably never have to worry about getting your old hair dyed again. Probably you'll just wake up every morning and say 'blonde' and zap! you're a blonde."

Yvonne shook the bottle of Black Rage and squirted some slowly around Bebe's temples so it would run backward into the rest of her hair. "This stuff is murder to get out of your pillow cases, isn't it? Oh and you'll never believe this, Bebe. Things are changing now. Miss Ruby is hiring a bikini waxer. And from what I hear, she'll be doing all kinds of shapes. Christmas trees, hearts, diamond shapes, any kind of shape you want. I couldn't do it, myself. I wouldn't want to be looking at anyone's noonie for that long. She's going to dye them too, Bebe. Red, purple, green. I still remember when it was considered wild to wear red fingernail polish."

Yvonne reached down and took a brush roller from the basket in her suitcase and pulled a long strand of hair off of it before she put it in Bebe's hair. "Of course, Thurston can't wait. He loves anything that has to do with sex."

She picked up another roller and stuck it in. She didn't even have to use clips, Bebe's head was so still.

"It used to be they stayed in the closet. Now they get married and divorced and married again. Shoot, they even wear wedding rings. Oh?" Yvonne sat back and looked at Bebe, surprised. "Do you mean to tell me that you did not know that? Why Bebe Pointer. I can't believe it! That means you didn't know a thing about Duran wanting to marry Thurston?!"

Yvonne went back to work as if Bebe had just finished shaking her head in total shock.

"Well, honey, let me tell you, Thurston's been married four different times. And he has a diamond for each time. Four of them. And I guess I can understand why he wouldn't want to start in on number five."

She reached around to see just how far she could roll Bebe's hair. "I guess you wouldn't have gone to him had you known about it, huh? Wouldn't have written me out of your will?"

Yvonne carefully spread a hairnet over Bebe's rollers for the last time. "Yeah, well, it's okay, sugar. I know all about it. I understand the whole thing completely. A gay wants to be a woman and that's all there is to it. Of course, there's no way of him ever fulfilling that on this earth. I guess you're glad I came down to fix your hair after all."

She reached in the back and tied the hairnet into a knot. "You know, you never did have much of a neck did you, Bebe?"

Miss Ruby waved good night to Thurston and watched him walk out the front door. He stopped and lit up a cigarette out on the sidewalk, then headed out across the square, where two statues looked like they were waving at each other. One was the General Robert E. Lee on horseback and the other was a woman waving a flag. One of her arms was missing. Miss Ruby watched Thurston pat Robert E. Lee's boot as he walked passed him with some purpose in mind.

Then she was all alone, doing exactly what she always caught Yvonne doing when Yvonne thought no one was looking. She was feeling the furniture, running her hands across the counter, touching the old Bonat hair dryers. She walked into the dispensary and pushed aside the new Zotos perms and reached into the back and pulled out one of the old Miss Charmette's. She held on to it as she walked back up front and looked around, and looked around, then went back to where Thurston's and Yvonne's little individual stations were and looked around some more.

It never ceased to amaze her, the difference between those two.

Yvonne had brush rollers, double prong curl clips, Dippity-Do, Happy Hair, and everything was in its place, had always been in its place for the last twenty years, up to and including the hairnets that hung down from her mirrors.

Thurston, on the other hand, had vent brushes, blending shears, styling shears, air guns, curling irons, crimping irons—all in fashion colors—four 1600 watt hand dryers, a pair of T-edges, and all the mousse anyone would ever need for a year. Miss Ruby never saw the same product in the same place from week to week, because every week a different product came in, replacing the old.

She cupped the little bottle of Miss Charmette and kissed it absentmindedly, and sat down in one of the dryer chairs, with its hood turned back carefully to the right as it had always been, lined up in a neat little row with the other five dryers—just one of those little things Yvonne had always done before she left the shop.

Miss Ruby cried. She didn't make a sound, but she cried just enough that the Miss Charmette became wet and the label began to slide down to the bottom of the bottle. But Miss Ruby didn't notice. She was looking at her little shop for the last time. After today, nothing would ever be the same. She had called the contractors and set everything up. They were coming in the morning and by Monday most of the work would be done. By Monday, the old Celebrity Styling Shop would be just a shadow of itself.

Miss Ruby got up again and went back over to Yvonne's station and put the little Miss Charmette carefully beside the Barbicide jar. She looked at all the combs disinfecting in there and tried to remember the last time she'd ever seen Thurston clean a comb. She never had. And neither had she ever held anything back from Yvonne. But she had today. She had watched Yvonne turning those dryers just so before she had left and hadn't even bothered to tell her that when she came back, those dryers would be gone—

replaced by a newer, brighter dryer that wouldn't require hairnets because they wouldn't suck the hair up in them like these old ones did.

She looked out the window and felt just awful about not telling Yvonne. So guilty it was hard to breathe.

And that's when she saw the light. Well at least she thought she'd seen a light. It looked like it came from the back of Gladys' shop, but she couldn't be sure. Ruby ran to the front and opened up a drawer, grabbing out her binoculars, then rushed back to the window. She drew the blinds shut and wedged the binoculars in between two slats and stayed in that position for at least twenty minutes. When she finally emerged, it was only because the sky was getting dark and she couldn't see past the Robert E. Lee statue. She had to rub her eyes to adjust to the shop's light.

She knew Gladys was in there. She knew she was up to something because her car was over there, but it was parked behind the Dempsy-Dumpster. She had seen the little red ball sticking up from the antenna. What Ruby would have liked to have known was why it was so all fired important for Gladys Bessinger to even hide her car, unless, of course, she was up to no good.

It was a good thing those contractors were coming, and not a moment too soon, she thought, as she jotted down important things on her long list of things to do for the shop: design paper bags for customer products, look into getting own name brand shampoo, buy a wreath for Bebe Pointer's funeral.

8

The rain was pounding down as everyone left the church and headed across the back to Bebe's burial site. It was only a hundred yards but it seemed like a thousand. Every few steps the girls' high heels would stick in the clay and they would have to stop.

Miss Ruby's shoe came off in the mud. When Thurston reached down to pull it out, it made a thick sucking noise. Ruby grabbed the gold slipper with the tiny heel and said, "My hair's going to be ruint." She looked behind her and saw a little track of holes that led from where they had left to where they were now. "Damn! It can't be. Is that Ronder walking with Yvonne?" she asked, holding the muddy slipper gingerly in the air between two fingers.

Thurston saw the two women slipping and holding on to each other. There was no question that one of them was Yvonne. She was wearing a snood, and over that, one of those plastic rain hats with the little red hearts all over it that could be folded up into the size of a pill box.

"I don't know if it's Ronder, but it's definitely Yvonne," said Thurston. The other woman kept stopping to pull her spiked heels out of the mud. He had never seen her before.

Miss Ruby was holding on to Thurston as she slipped her shoe back on. "That's Ronder, all right. Nobody wears heels that high anymore."

Ronder was stuck in the mud and Yvonne was helping to pull her out. Miss Ruby kept heading for the tent. "If she thinks she's going to talk me out of doing those bikini waxings, she's got another think coming."

That was exactly what Ronder had in mind. She was trying to hurry and catch up with Miss Ruby. She knew that if she could just sit by her then everything could be worked out. But her heels kept getting sucked into the mud. Yvonne wasn't much help because she had to keep stopping to blow her nose. She was carrying on about Bebe, as if they were mother and daughter instead of beautician and patron.

"I can't believe she's gone," wailed Yvonne for the tenth time, wiping away the tears. "This is my darkest hour."

Once again Ronder rolled her eyes and patted her on the back. "There, there, Yvonne."

Ronder knew Miss Ruby was the type to sit at a funeral and feel sorry for herself and wish for the good old days. If Ronder could just sit by her, she'd just pat Miss Ruby's hand the way she was patting Yvonne's back now, and remind her of the good times they used to have, and she'd forget all about those horrible bikini waxings. Ronder took her heels off and was standing in her stocking feet. "Dammit, Yvonne, hurry!"

While Ronder waited for Yvonne, Miss Ruby passed the standing spray of pink carnations she had sent and took a seat next to Riley Pointer, still not believing that there, right there in front of her, rested Bebe's coffin, draped with the largest blanket of roses man ever made.

She knew Gladys had sent the roses, because when the casket had rolled down the aisle during the church service, everyone had gasped and a woman behind Ruby had hissed, "Those must be the flowers Gladys sent."

And another woman had whispered, "Five hundred dollars' worth. Can you imagine? Five hundred!"

"Well," said the first woman, "it's only because she's had such a crush on Riley for so long."

Miss Ruby hadn't even moved when she had heard that. She hadn't moved even to breathe. She had just dug her fingernails into the palms of her hands, like she was doing now, sitting right in front of those roses, close enough to count the bugs on the petals. Of course, she didn't need to sit close to see what that big golden banner had written on it. It loomed up out of those roses like a cigarette advertisement, saying: BEBE POINTER'S HOMECOMING DAY.

When Ronder finally walked up, her high heels caked in red clay up to the instep, she was too late. Louise Stokes had just wiggled her bottom into the last folding chair and was reaching across Ruby's lap to pat Riley's hand.

"There, there," Louise said. Then she straightened up and sat back, and when she did, her hands flew to her chest. "My word! Would you look at that!" She was pointing to the banner. Then she leaned over and laughed to Miss Ruby, "All I sent was a potted plant."

A woman from behind tapped Louise on the shoulder and said, "Honey, if you think that's something, Gladys has catered the whole reception. Food, drinks, everything."

Miss Ruby tightened her thighs and looked over at her standing spray, which seemed to be getting smaller and smaller with each clap of thunder, while out of the corner of her eye she could see Riley just staring straight ahead, not looking at much of anything. Out of her other eye, Ruby saw Louise's white streak of hair, wet and plastered to her head like a skunk.

Then the minister began his sermon. It was a short sermon and no one could even hear him over the pouring rain, it was so loud, or see him for Gladys' banner. Miss Ruby tried to get her mind off of Gladys. She tried to concentrate on Riley instead. But all that came to mind were the sad things. There would be no more Tuesday afternoons when he would hear Bebe's car come up the gravel drive, jump up, turn off the TV and put a shirt on in time for her to breeze on through their back door with her beauty shop gossip while taking a steak out of the freezer for him. No longer would he watch her tall hair as she made him mashed potatoes and told him about the presents she had bought for the girls who had gotten married, pregnant or divorced. From now on, he could take the plastic cover off the couch and stick his feet up on it whenever he wanted because Bebe would no longer be there to tell him no. Miss Ruby bet it would be a long time before that cover came off. It would be a long time before Bebe's presence left that house. She was a strong one, that Bebe Pointer. Which led Miss Ruby to believe that if Bebe had been there now, where they were sitting right now, she would have walked right up and ripped that banner down without a moment's hesitation.

Miss Ruby glared at the banner and the rain began to drip through the tent onto the back of her neck, reminding her that Ronder was somewhere nearby waiting to wear her down. With each drop of rain that ran down her neck, she tried moving to the right and then the left. But it was no use. She watched the minister's lips move and she began counting. She counted twenty-three, twenty-four, twenty-five ice cold drops that soaked her to the skin before the sermon was finally over.

On the way back to Riley's house, Ronder tried to get next to Miss Ruby again. But it was no use. Thurston had taken it upon himself to act as her bodyguard, as if she, not Riley, were the grieving one.

"I swear, Yvonne," said Ronder, flipping a strand of wet hair over her shoulder, "you'd think she was Elizabeth Taylor, the way she's wearing those dark glasses and carrying on so."

She watched Thurston's black coat swish around Miss Ruby's back as they made their way across the red clay, where all the little holes that the high heels had made were now filled up with water.

Thurston had to drive Miss Ruby around the town square five times before he could get her to settle down. Five times he drove around the General Robert E. Lee statue and the statue of the one armed woman still waving her flag, and five times Miss Ruby grabbed at her chest and said, "Thurston, I think I'm having a heart attack. As a matter of fact, I know I am."

On the sixth time around the square, they stopped so she could breathe into a paper bag.

"Slow, deep breaths," said Thurston. "Slow now, slow."

She held it up to her face, breathing faster and faster, talking right into it. "Did you see that limousine Gladys rented for him? Now where did she get that? It must have cost a hundred dollars an hour."

"Slow deep breaths, baby. Take slow deep breaths."

Ruby panted. "And that cute little . . . chauffeur . . . with the black miniskirt and . . . leather gloves . . ." she panted, "standing beside him . . . with her hands crossed . . . ohhh!" Miss Ruby wailed, pulling the bag away.

Then she held her breath.

Suddenly a great calmness washed over her as she stared out the car window looking defeated.

Everything was quiet.

Everything except for the rain hitting the roof of Thurston's car, sounding like little dogs running across linoleum.

She looked at her shop, and then across the square at Gladys'. There was something in the way the steam was rising from the street that made her think about Bebe, and how, now, she should know the answer to why most women just felt so miserable for no apparent reason. It reminded her of how miserable she felt now, and she let out another wail that sent Thurston reaching for the bag again.

"Try again, Miss Ruby. Long, deep breaths."

She was breathing faster than ever now, like a small dog in a hot car. "Oh Thurston! What am I going to do?"

"Hey," he said, massaging the back of her neck, "I've got a great idea!"

"What?" asked Miss Ruby, looking at him out of the corner of her eye, the paper bag still tight over her mouth.

"Why not invite Riley to Atlanta with us?"

"Are you kidding?" she asked. She inhaled so deeply that the bag crumpled in on itself. Then she exhaled and said,

"The last thing I want is to have him tagging along talking about the Civil War all the time."

"Yeah, I see what you mean," said Thurston, tucking some of Miss Ruby's hair back into her updo. "But just think how jealous Gladys would be."

"Jealous? You think?"

"Jealous with a capital J. Gladys is crazy about him."

Miss Ruby dropped the bag and turned to Thurston, grabbing his face and kissing his cheeks over and over again. "Thurston, you are brilliant. Just brilliant! Get me to Riley's house, fast. I've got to get there before Gladys gets her dirty little paws on him."

This time it was Thurston who stared straight ahead. "On one condition."

"What's that, hon?" asked Miss Ruby, all excited now.

"You let me fix your hair first."

So without even going in the shop, he pulled out a comb and repaired her hair right there in the car, even applying a lovely plum blusher and matching lipstick to Miss Ruby's already flushed face.

Yvonne was just making it around the square when Ronder spotted Miss Ruby's car. "Yvonne, can you make this thing go any faster?" she asked, pushing and pulling on the dashboard, craning her neck to see through the window, the trees, the statues, the rain.

Yvonne was so short it was hard to see anything but her knuckles from outside the car as she peered through the steering wheel of her Dodge Dart. She was taking the corner at a snail's pace, holding up half the funeral procession. The speed limit sign in the square said 15 miles an hour, and 15 miles an hour it would be.

A car from behind honked and Ronder groaned, sinking just a little lower in her seat, watching Yvonne never taking her eyes off the road, never ever looking in the rearview mirror.

"Yvonne, would you like for me to drive?"

"Shhh," hissed Yvonne, slamming on her brakes and gripping the wheel even tighter. "Don't talk to me right now. This intersection makes me so nervous."

Another car honked and Ronder started picking at her nails. The scene that lay ahead was going to be grim. She just had to catch up with Miss Ruby before her name was spread all over as the town's first bikini waxer. She was tapping her foot as fast as she could. "Yvonne baby, you've got a green light."

10

The first ham had arrived at nine o'clock. By noon there were nine more, glazed and laid out all over Riley Pointer's dining table. Riley was greeting women from all over town that he didn't even know existed. He couldn't figure out where they all came from, or how they all seemed to know him.

When Ruby and Thurston pulled up, they found Riley caught between two of them. One had on a black feathered hat to match her black feathered dress, which matched her black feathered shoes. She wore giant black earbobs and carried a ham platter. It was Earline Maddox.

The other wore a simple linen suit with just a touch of brass jewelry that seemed to offset the white streak that swirled in her hair like an expensive frosting on a cake. This was Louise Stokes, formerly Miss Greenville. She still walked as if she were wearing high heels and a bathing suit. "Earline," Louise said, scanning Earline's outfit, "I told you time and again not to wear that feathery monstrosity. It makes you look *huge*." She handed her a ballpoint pen and pointed to the register. "Sign this, dear," she said, then turned away in disapproval.

But Earline wasn't signing anything. She had already moved in on Riley, her feathers tickling his skin, her heavy perfume soaking into his every pore. He was just dying to wipe her sticky grape lipstick off his face, only she wouldn't let go of his hands. "Oh, Riley," she said, "it seems like I'm related to everyone lately, but I only claim the ones I like, and I sure did like Bebe."

"Well," said Thurston, walking up and taking the pen from her. He signed his name in big, swirling letters. "It just goes to prove, you didn't have to be smart to like Bebe."

Miss Ruby signed the register next, putting Celebrity Styling next to her name. She flipped through the pages to see if there was any trace of Gladys.

Louise whispered over her shoulder. "Don't bother, hon. You won't find *her* anywhere in there."

Miss Ruby tried to act suprised, as if she had no earthly idea what Louise Stokes was talking about. But no one was paying Ruby any attention. All eyes were focused on a roasted pig that was being carried through the front door, manteled on a shining gold platter, garnished with a baked apple in its mouth.

"Oh my!" said Earline.

"It's from Gladys Bessinger," said Louise, who had taken it upon herself to check all the food in, putting little pieces of numbered tape on all the plates that arrived.

Miss Ruby couldn't believe it. Everything was happening too fast. Gladys wasn't even in the room but the room was full of Gladys. She wasn't even giving anyone else a chance with Riley. Ruby had to make her next move count.

"Now you know, Riley," she said, firming up her shoulders, "you can't go burying yourself in this house just because Bebe is no longer with us." She was talking too loud, overcompensating for how small she felt. She stepped in front of Earline and continued, "Now, I know it's kind of soon to be thinking about what you're going to be doing next, but it's just like I always say, there's no time like the present. Isn't that right, Thurston?"

Thurston was imitating Miss Ruby, fanning his hands, shooing away Louise and Earline as if they were flies on his food. "That's what she always says, Riley, old boy."

Ruby said, "I mean, what I mean to say is that you've got to pick up where you left off and start over again."

Thurston rolled his eyes. He knew that this was the place where Miss Ruby was going to go into one of her famous "Grab Life and Live It" speeches. He looked hard at Riley, to see if his eyes were glazing over yet, but it was hard to tell just exactly what it was he was thinking.

Thurston himself was thinking the exact same thing that Louise and Earline were thinking as they all stood there sizing Riley up while Miss Ruby droned on. They were all wondering how a man as attractive as Riley had ended up with someone like Bebe.

It wasn't that they thought Bebe was all that bad. It's just that she had carried all that extra weight around with her for such a long time. Thurston shuddered when he thought of the annoying habit she had of just plopping herself down in his chair and not even bothering to close her legs. Well, Thurston thought any man deserved a better break than that. A man who looked as good as Riley deserved a few nights with someone wonderful. Someone like himself. So when Miss Ruby got off her soap box and started talking about the Atlanta Hair Show, inviting Riley along, Thurston's heart began to beat hard.

"Well, I hadn't ever been to Atlanta before," said Riley, his eyes bright as coins, "but I always did want to go and see that Civil War monument they have there. I like to consider myself a virtuoso in history. Did you know that they first started canning tuna fish during the Civil War?"

Earline was astonished. "Tuna fish?! But that was so long ago."

"I know. Can you imagine that?" he said, looking at her, nodding his head.

"So you'll go?" asked Miss Ruby, delighted.

"Why it'd be my honor, Miss Ruby. I swear it would."

Riley's face was glowing and Thurston thought he was so cute he might die. "How about you going as my Rhett Butler, darling?" he asked, looking Riley over as if he wanted to devour every little bit of him.

Suddenly the widows looked more attractive, less smothering, to Riley. He turned back to Earline. "You know, I believe they even started canning lemonade back then too."

"Lemonade?" she asked, bringing her black feathered gloves up to straighten her black feathered hat. "Well I'll be."

"You want to see my rifle collection?" he asked. Both of the ladies lit up, nodding their heads eagerly as they followed him across the room.

"This," said Yvonne, walking up and grabbing Miss Ruby's arm, "is the saddest day of my life. Poor, poor Bebe."

It was the first time Thurston had ever seen Yvonne when she wasn't in uniform and it was worse than he had expected.

She had on a tannish-pinkish dress, not unlike the color of Pepto Bismol, made of chenille on the body part and chiffon on the arms. Somehow the designer had even managed to throw in a few giant flowers, all combined to make what Thurston considered the worst fashion disaster since the elephant pants.

Her shoes were brown wedgies.

"Ugh," he said. "If you're looking for something to wear to that Atlanta Hair Show, sweetie, that may be your ticket right there."

"Miss Ruby, she just looked so small laying there," cried Yvonne, ignoring Thurston.

"Bebe? Small?" asked Thurston. "Hardly."

"Ohhhh, it's the saddest day of my life," Yvonne wailed, squeezing Ruby's arm tighter.

"You already said that, darling," Thurston said. He pulled out his pink handkerchief and held it up to her nose. "Blow hard. You know it's too bad it was closed casket Miss Ruby," he said. "You should have seen her. You should have seen that hair."

"Shut up Thurston," said Yvonne, knocking his hand away.

"It was the Aunt Bee Express!" he said, waving his hands in the air like a preacher. "That's one hairdo that's sure to shoot Bebe Pointer straight up to heaven."

"What on earth are you talking about Thurston?" asked Miss Ruby.

"I said shut up, Thurston!" Yvonne stamped her shoe.

"Mayberry R.F.D! You should have seen her! There was barely enough room left in that coffin once they got her hair in there."

Miss Ruby knew she shouldn't laugh, but she just couldn't help herself and soon she was in tears, trying to compose herself desperately and patting Yvonne on the back, but laughing hysterically.

"Thurston, that is not funny!" yelled Yvonne, jerking away. "And for your information buster . . ."

"Don't stamp your wedgies too hard, darling," said Thurston. "They might go through the floor."

This broke Miss Ruby up even more.

"Does somebody around here want to tell me what is so funny?" It was Ronder, laughing and offering everyone a tray of cold cuts and bourbon balls. She was dressed to the nines, impressing even Thurston. She had just heard about Gladys Bessinger's nervous breakdown and was nervous herself about facing Miss Ruby.

On seeing Ronder, Miss Ruby immediately stopped laughing, and turned her head away with her nose up in the air as if she were posing for another silhouette.

"Oh come on, Miss Ruby, don't act like that," pleaded Ronder.

But Miss Ruby was not about to act any other way.

So there was dead silence until Thurston broke the ice, imitating himself on the phone. "I'm sorry," he said in a nasal tone, "but she's busy buying jewels now. She can't come to the phone. Can she call you back? Can she call you back? Can she call you back?"

Ronder slapped his arm, laughing. "You devil. So you're the one. I didn't know who that was, I swear I didn't. Are you a beautician too?"

"Thurston's the name, men's the game. But baby, don't you ever call me a beautician. *That*," he said, pointing to Yvonne, "is a beautician. I'm a hair designer." He held out his hand to be kissed and Ronder kissed it, curtsying.

"So, dear, are you ready to do those bikini waxings on Tuesday?" asked Miss Ruby, whipping around, not wanting to lose control of the moment.

"Yukaroo!" said Thurston. "So you're the one doing those horrid things?"

"Let's get something straight here, Miss Ruby. I didn't say I would do them yet. I said I'd think about it. Remember?"

Miss Ruby turned away again.

"Ah come on, Miss Ruby," begged Ronder. "Don't be like that. I can still cut hair and I'm good and you know it. I like to do that. I like to cut hair, Miss Ruby."

Miss Ruby didn't budge.

"Why, I'll be," said Ronder, handing Thurston the tray of cold cuts and wiping her hands in the air. "There's old Louise Stokes. I've been trying to get in touch with that old fool for days." She walked away, just like that, infuriating Miss Ruby, happy to get away from her and on to Louise.

Louise was just as happy to see Ronder. "Ronder!" she squealed. She pulled her into the bathroom, along with a woman named Millie Loudermilk. Ronder had never met her, but like a true beautician, the first thing she noticed was her hair. It looked horrible. It looked like she had slept in pink dimestore sponge rollers and then not bothered to brush out the roller marks.

"Honey!" Louise squealed again, slamming the door and

clutching Ronder's hands. "Did somebody tell me right? Are you really going back to work?"

"That's what you heard all right," said Ronder, proudly.

"Well let me ask you this," Louise said, lowering her voice, "you and Buck aren't having any marital troubles now, are you?" Her gold rings glinted as she squeezed Ronder's hands even tighter.

"Buck and me?" laughed Ronder. "Absolutely not! Where'd you ever get an idea like that?"

"Well," said Louise, dropping her hands and pulling a tube of lipstick out of her purse. She began circling her lips with it. "That's not what Earline said. She said you were practically divorced." She pulled the lipstick away from her mouth and focused in hard on Ronder as she said the word "divorced."

"Ha! Buck and me, divorced?" Ronder laughed a small, hollow laugh. "You have got to be kidding. She said that?"

Louise's head bounced up and down, eager for the news, her eyes sparkling like her rings.

"Hon," said Ronder, flipping her hand at Louise, "put your mind to rest. We're doing just fine. As a matter of fact, Buck's taking me to Myrtle Beach the next free minute he's got."

"Well, from what Earline tells me," said Louise, pressing her newly painted lips together, "I understand he's got all the free time in the world right now." She popped her lips right in front of Ronder's face. "Hand me that Kleenex Millie, hon, would you?" asked Louise, pushing her purse at Millie to hold. "According to Earline," she said, "he fell off a ladder and hasn't painted since."

Louise took the Kleenex from Millie without even looking at her, pushing her away from the mirror so she could blot her lips.

"Oh, Louise," said Ronder, "it was just a tiny accident. He'll be back to work this week."

Someone knocked on the bathroom door and Louise shouted, "*SOME*one is *IN* here! Millie, hon, reach in my pocketbook and hand me my powder, will you?" She began powdering the back of her neck and said, "Is that so? That isn't what I heard."

"Rest assured, Louise, we're doing just fine." Suddenly Ronder couldn't breathe. She had to get out of the bathroom. She opened the door to leave, but Louise snapped her compact shut, grabbed her purse and darted out ahead of her all in the same motion, past a line of women all waiting to use the bathroom.

With Louise, it was Louise first, always.

"Well, well," said Earline, who had been standing in line but was now descending on Ronder like a bad nightmare, her feathers rustling as she patted Ronder on the back, "some little angel told me that Buck didn't come home the other night."

"Some little angel told you wrong," Ronder said, walking away. She couldn't take one more bad news Buck line.

"Let's not talk about Buck," said Louise, picking up on this, motioning for Earline to follow, leaving Millie behind. "Let him drag his own name through the mud. What I want to know about is this Gladys Bessinger thing. Some story, isn't it?"

They went over to the food and began filling their paper plates with green bean casserole, three bean salad, cole slaw, honey baked ham, and other entrées and side dishes. Ronder listened to Louise go on and on about Gladys while she watched Earline eat a little of her cole slaw and then a little of her ham and then just enough of her mashed potatoes until they were leveled and in even proportion to everything else. Then she watched her go around her plate one more time with the same precision, careful to keep her feathers out of her food.

Louise, on the other hand, was eating all of one thing before she started in on another.

"But the real Gladys story," said Louise, finishing her green beans, "is that she closed down her shop because she was on drugs."

"Louise, that can't be true," said Ronder. "Gladys? I just couldn't believe that."

"Well believe it," said Earline, coming in with her two cents worth, taking another bite of ham. "I know for a fact that she went to the doctor's and he gave her some pills to help her lose weight. She just started taking them all the time."

"That's right," said Louise, dabbing at the corner of her lips with the corner of her napkin. "She got to the point where she was always talking, talking, talking, so fast you could barely understand her. You couldn't get a word in edgewise."

Earline had one eye on her mashed potatoes and one eye on Millie, sitting across the room with Riley. "Just look at her, would you," she said, interrupting, "she's got him pulling out his swords now."

"He must be in heaven," said Louise.

A woman they didn't know walked up to the table and everyone quit talking. The woman, who had come up for a whole plate of food, felt so uncomfortable by their silence that she just picked up a small brownie and left.

Earline eyed the woman's hips as she left and said, not particularly whispering, "Honey, you'd have done better with some of that cole slaw."

Ronder, who had just taken a sip of her Coke, almost choked. "You are so funny, Earline," she said, wiping her mouth.

"She is though, isn't she?" said Louise, not laughing.

Ronder looked over at Millie, who seemed to be making great progress with Riley. He had her on the couch now and they were looking at a big coffee table book together.

"Isn't that something," said Earline, still trying to make Ronder laugh. "I've seen that book three times now and all it is is a bunch of black and white pictures of a bunch of soldiers standing around."

Ronder pointed her plastic fork over at Millie. "Well, if you ask me, she sure looks like she's enjoying it."

"She's like a little dog," said Earline. "She follows anyone around who pays her the slightest bit of attention. Which reminds me," she said, putting down her plate and digging in her pocketbook and pulling out an 8½ by 11 pink flyer with hand drawn flowers bordering the edges. "How about this?" She held it up for everybody to read:

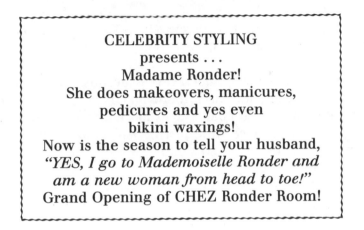

CELEBRITY STYLING
presents . . .
Madame Ronder!
She does makeovers, manicures,
pedicures and yes even
bikini waxings!
Now is the season to tell your husband,
*"YES, I go to Mademoiselle Ronder and
am a new woman from head to toe!"*
Grand Opening of CHEZ Ronder Room!

Ronder took a deep breath and grabbed the announcement. "Umm, can I have this?" She didn't even wait for a reply.

She found Miss Ruby in front of the Blueberry Bundt Cake that Millie Loudermilk had brought, examining the piece she had just sliced.

"Miss Ruby," she said, furious. She was waving the flyer at her. "Miss Ruby, I didn't tell you I was coming back yet. How could you? How could you, Miss Ruby? I am so embarrassed!"

"I don't know who made this cake but it isn't even near ready. Would you take a look at this," said Miss Ruby, pointing to the gray pastey looking dough in the middle of the cake. Then she looked up at Ronder and saw the tears. "Oh don't go getting all sensitive about it dear. Just think of the money you're going to be making. And did I tell you?" Miss

Ruby put her arm around Ronder and they walked together. "We are going to be expanding, and not only that, we're going to Atlanta to that famous Hair Show. I'm paying everybody's way and we're going to have a real good time. Here here, don't cry now."

She gave Ronder a handkerchief that had the silhouette of her updo monogrammed on it. "Wipe your eyes now." They stopped walking and she pulled Ronder's head onto her massive chest. "I'll tell you what. We'll get us a penthouse suite and live it up just the way we used to. Would you like that?"

Miss Ruby had always been very generous with her girls. Every Christmas she gave them elaborate gifts. Lockets with diamonds, gold chains with lockets, rings with opals and pearls, and these were just the stocking stuffers. The big present came when Miss Ruby rented out the fanciest suite there was at the downtown Thunderbird Motor Inn and pretended that she and her girls were far away at some exotic place. Once she'd even decorated a suite to look like a Las Vegas Casino and brought in a roulette wheel and Ruby and her girls gambled all night long.

Ronder missed those times more than anything, and before she knew it, Buck was fuzzing out of her head, being replaced with the good old Miss Ruby days, and she was nodding her head and drying her eyes.

That's when all the commotion began.

Someone yelled, "It's Gladys! It's got to be Gladys!"

Then someone else said, "That wasn't Gladys. It just looked like Gladys."

"Come on," said Thurston, "who else do you know that drives a little red Corvette?"

On hearing this, Miss Ruby flounced to the front door and saw the tail end of what she was sure was Gladys' tiny sports car drive by.

"That was Gladys, all right," said Ronder, who was looking over her shoulder. "That was her plain as day."

"All she had to do was talk to me and tell me what was going on. I would've gladly helped her," said Louise.

Earline took Ruby's arm. "Miss Ruby, I bought her the cutest little birthday present, I swear I did. Just a darling little scarf, but you know what I'm going to do? I'm going to give it to you instead. I'll bring it my next appointment."

Miss Ruby pushed at her hair and picked at her stomach and, in her best celebrity posture, she began walking around Riley's house comforting all of Bebe Pointer's friends. Not so much comforting them about Bebe, though, as about Gladys, who had, they all felt, abandoned them. And as she did so, Miss Ruby went off into a daydream. She knew that right now, right this very minute, the contractors were in her shop working away like busy little ants. She had this perfect image of what her place was going to look like when Tuesday rolled around. Never again would these women ever have to worry about going some other place to have their hair done. From now on, the world of hair was going to belong to Ruby McSwain, and only to Ruby McSwain.

A small woman in a forest green pant suit tapped Miss Ruby right out of her dream, saying, "If I didn't know any better, Miss Ruby, I'd think somebody ordered this weather for the funeral. The rain has just ruined my hair!"

"I guarantee it," said an even smaller woman dressed in a seersucker suit. "You know, I remember a time when I was on a business trip and my boss and I were coming in out of the rain, on our way to a very important dinner meeting, I must add. And when we got in the elevator, his eyes got real big and he said, 'What happened to you?!' He was horrified. You should have seen his face. So I got to the ladies room as fast as I could, and the first thing I saw was my Red Flame temporary rinse running all down my neck, soaking into my collar and my shirt, straight through. Imagine how embarrassing that was." She nodded knowing everyone else knew exactly what she was talking about.

"Since then," she continued, "I've gotten a little grayer and switched to White Minx, but I swear, if my girl puts too much on, even that will rub off on my pillowcases at night."

"Ain't it the truth!" joined in another woman. "And another thing about these rinses. They may make us look good, but have you ever noticed how when you go to the beach, that salt water makes that rinse get all sticky?"

"No, hon, that's the hairspray," said Thurston, walking up to them, trying to drum up some business. "Hairspray always does that. Now mousse, mousse is where it's at."

The woman who had told the business trip story started laughing and said, "Now isn't this just something? Wouldn't Bebe just love to know that we were all sitting around in her living room talking about hair? It would be just like her, wouldn't it, to want to talk about her hair at her own funeral?"

11

Next to Saturday, Tuesday is the busiest day in the hair business, because that way women can get their hair done and it will last until the malls close on Saturday. On Sunday they can just wear a hat to church. Like Broadway, hair shops are dark on Mondays.

Ruby McSwain used the time between the funeral and Monday to have three new stations built, six new hair dryers moved in, and the stockroom changed into what would now be billed as the new Chez Ronder Room. By the time Thurston made his exotic entrance Tuesday morning, it was into an even busier shop than before. For once the women weren't even paying him any attention. Conversation was buzzing and Miss Ruby was erasing and penciling in appointments as fast as she could. She had purposefully left the blinds open, letting in the too bright morning sun, so that when Gladys Bessinger looked across the square through the trees, through her binoculars, she'd have a good shot at what was going on.

Miss Ruby knew for a fact that Gladys had a pair of binoculars, because one day when she was looking through hers, she had spotted Gladys looking through hers.

The first thing Ruby had done after she had walked into her newly renovated shop was to peer through her slats and see what Gladys was up to in her still closed Tres Chic. Gladys had moved her throne to the window and was now sitting and waiting and watching. Ruby couldn't resist making her wait. She couldn't resist making all the women wait, just a little longer, standing out front in a long line so Gladys would have something to see.

It seemed like everybody in town wanted a bikini wax. And even though most women were too shy to really get one, Ronder felt that by ten o'clock that morning the whole town had sat down in front of her and spread their legs, giggling and said, "You are going to cover me up, aren't you, because honestly, I don't think I can do this any other way," as if she, Ronder, could.

"You can't go in there, Thurston," said Yvonne, when he walked in and went peeking through the Chez Ronder curtains.

"Oh disgusting," he said, shuddering. "Do you actually think I'd want to?" Then in a low voice, he asked, "Yvonne, have you ever had that done to you?"

Yvonne looked around to see if anyone was listening. "No, but I've been keeping an eye on what's going on, and it looks like it hurts to me."

Ronder confirmed this when she emerged at lunchtime, not at all hungry. She washed her hands in the shampoo basin and then washed them three more times. "Well Thurston," she said, "let me just put it to you this way. They sit down in that chair and spread their legs and tell you they want to look good on the beach." She was shaking her head. "And it hurts. It really hurts. Especially when you get that wax caught on that long hair and pull and they go '*Owwwww.*' Personally I think you can get just as close with a Gillette and a blade for what the human eye is going to be seeing on the beach."

She flung the water off her hands, then grabbed a towel.

By now Miss Ruby had joined Thurston and a few patrons and everybody was hanging on to her every word. Ronder said, "That hot wax pulling a whole strip of hair and you know it hurts. It causes welts too. And with those panties rubbing all day long, well, I just don't see the point." She took the corner of her towel and tried to get under her fingernails. "And in the end you have a trash can full of pubic hair, which you have to empty. Yuck, gross!"

Now it was Ronder who was shuddering and who declined a fried chicken basket for lunch, courtesy of Miss Ruby. "Thanks, hon, but honestly, if I saw a hair sticking out of a chicken wing right now I'd go into a coma, I swear I would. I think I'll eat me a salad instead." Her nose itched but she rubbed it with her arm because her hands still felt dirty. "Did Buck happen to call yet?"

"No, hon," said Miss Ruby, "but everybody else did. You're booked."

Miss Ruby couldn't believe what a wonderful business sense she had. Creating the Chez Ronder Room, with its peach colored curtains, low lights and two velvet chaise lounges, was the best move she'd ever made. It was sure to put her shop miles above anything Gladys Bessinger could ever touch. Women were just dying to have anything done to them as long as it could be done in there. And Miss Ruby hadn't stopped there, either. She had called the Women's Section of the local paper and gotten them to write up an article about the Chez Ronder room.

While Ruby was watching Gladys watch Ruby's shop, Ronder was taking a cigarette break, drinking coffee, thinking about Buck. She wondered why he hadn't called. There used to be a time when Buck called two or three times a day. But things were different now. Now she knew why he wasn't calling. All the signs were there plain as day. The late nights. The phone calls. The hang ups. The way Buck was dressing different. He'd even started laying his clothes out before he went to bed. No, she was not a stupid woman, and things like that didn't get past her. Ronder wondered who the woman was. She just couldn't figure that part out. Stuckey was such a small town; only two hair shops, four gas stations, a Hardee's. Why it could even be one of the women in the shop. She looked around, but it was hard to tell with all the curlers in the hair just who could be Buck's type, but she thought none. Everyone here had thick ankles. Buck hated that.

"Smile!" Thurston had jumped out of nowhere and was now aiming a camera at her face.

"Don't, Thurston. I'm so dirty," said Ronder, crossing her arms over her face.

"Come on, I need practice. Look what I've done," he said, spreading snapshots all over the backroom wig counter, of clients' befores and afters. "Look at this one." Thurston pointed at a woman who had gone from having one of Yvonne's famous updos to one of his new style air waves.

"Gorgeous, eh?!" he asked, shuffling a few more around, pointing out the differences, and Ronder couldn't help but notice how long his fingernails were.

She remembered Yvonne telling her earlier that Thurston had looked at her nails and said, "Yvonne, my nails are as long as yours."

"I went home that night and cut them all off," Yvonne had said. And Ronder remembered that Yvonne had also said, "Sometimes he even wears polish."

Ronder looked a little closer and noticed some leftover something near his cuticles, a pink polish maybe, or a buff.

Yvonne had the answers for why Thurston was gay. "They work around women all day and they become feminine. It's just the opposite of being a construction worker, where you work around men and become manly. Oh Ronder, and when he starts talking that sex talk, well, that's about as exciting to me as a bat."

Ronder let Yvonne's words spin around in her head a little

longer while she drank her coffee and Thurston showed her his pictures.

"Once," Yvonne had said, "he took a drag off of my cigarette, and you know what I did? I dropped it in my coffee."

Ronder looked at her own cigarette, the one Thurston had picked up and begun smoking, and she wondered if she could smoke after him.

"I see his hands," Yvonne had said, "and I think, 'Ooooh, this is the way I do it.' "

"Oh what the heck," Ronder said now. "Thurston, let me have some of that cigarette."

"Sure, and look at this, darling," he said, pushing the camera away from his chest and unrolling a poster which showed an enormous camera shot of himself sprawled across a huge bed. He was wearing his rhinestone boots and a floor length fur. And he was drinking a daiquiri. The caption read HAIR DESIGNER OF THE YEAR.

Ronder started to laugh. "Thurston, this is hilarious!"

Thurston held the poster against the wall and smoothed it down. "Don't you just love it? The boots, darling, it's the boots that give it the effect, don't you think?" He ran his fingers along the lines of the boots and smiled. "I'm going to hang it up in the front where everybody can walk in and see it."

"Thurston, does Miss Ruby know about this?" asked Ronder, who could no more see that poster at the front of the shop than in the back.

"Does Miss Ruby know about it? Honey, Miss Ruby took this picture. Look at the bed. Don't you recognize the bed?"

All of a sudden it dawned on Ronder. The balled fringed bedspread, the jungle throw, the satin pillows were all in place. Ronder couldn't believe she hadn't recognized Miss Ruby's bed right off. First of all, it was the biggest bed she'd ever seen. If there was ever such a thing as a king sized king size, Ronder was looking at it now. The second reason Ronder should have known it was because it was this very bed she had been dreaming about for months now. The one where she had daydreamed of snuggling up close to Miss Ruby, far away from Buck and all his lies and all his promises.

Ronder just couldn't believe Miss Ruby had let Thurston into her bedroom, on to her bed. "Thurston," she said, "it isn't like Miss Ruby to let a man in her house."

"Oh I know what you're thinking, but honey, believe you me, nothing went on. You know how I am."

"Still, it's just not like her." Ronder put her empty coffee cup down on top of one of Thurston's before and after pictures.

Thurston thought about moving it but decided against it, since it was only a picture of Mildred Shealy, and as far as he was concerned there wasn't an after picture in the cards for old Mildred. She was meant to be a before, always.

"Well," he said, "at first we were going to do this at my place, but if you think Miss Ruby's bad about having men in her apartment, it's nothing compared to the way she feels about stepping into a bachelor's pad. She wouldn't do it." Thurston began to roll the poster back up. "But when I explained to her that we had to have the right bed for the effect we were trying to get, she just kind of gave in."

Ronder wondered what kind of effect he was talking about.

"Oh, by the way," he said, stretching a rubberband carefully around the poster and tucking it under his arm, "I forgot to tell you. Your one-thirty is here."

"My one-thirty? I didn't know I had a one-thirty. Do you have any idea who it is?"

Thurston began walking away. "Harriet Simpson. Big woman," he said, holding his hands out in front of him like he was hugging a barrel. "Big as an old Ford."

"Oh my lucky day. Wait, Thurston," Ronder said, hiding behind his long, long labcoat, walking with him up to the front. She just had to look to make sure. Maybe it was a mistake. But sure enough there slept Harriet Simpson, her head on her shoulder, her book at her side.

"Look, Thurston, look at her ankles," whispered Ronder. "They're shaped like Peanut Logs and I'm going to have to massage them."

"Nasty. She looks like she was squeezed into those shoes," he said, staring at Harriet's feet.

"I got in more trouble with her once," said Ronder, laughing. "But she caught me at it. Ask Yvonne. I was in the back mixing a color and Yvonne came back there, and I was so mad at Harriet because with her it's always 'Get me this and get me that, light my cigarette and blah blah blah,' and I was about up to my ears with being her slave. And then Yvonne comes back and says, 'Harriet told me to tell you that she wants a Diet Dr Pepper.' "

Ronder looked up at Thurston to make sure she had his full attention, and then she continued. "Thurston, I was so busy that day. It was one of those days where I had two or three perms going at once and a frosting under the lights, you know, *busy*." Ronder saw Harriet shift so she lowered her voice. "So I ran to the A&P and got her that stupid Diet Dr Pepper and shook it all the way back. When she opened it, it exploded all over her. It was so funny, and Yvonne and I laughed about it all afternoon. That is until we saw the old bag herself, standing there listening."

Thurston looked shocked. "And you're going to give her a pedicure? Yuck. I shudder to think about it."

Ronder nodded her head. "Me too! And she's mean, Thurston. She's the head nurse at the loony bin. She's got the graveyard shift and it gets a little wild up there at that time of night. Harriet's the only one that can calm them down."

"Well, I can believe that. Thank God I've never seen her in here before," said Thurston. "She's a disgrace to her gender, baby."

Ronder woke Harriet Simpson up, rolled her hair, and stuck her under the dryer and was now filing her toenails into a square shape to prevent ingrowth.

"Oh that just feels delightful," squealed Harriet, wiggling her toes. "I just love for people to play with my feet. It seems like I'm always standing and I get corns, you know. They are so painful." She wiggled and curled her toes again, which made them seem even bigger to Ronder than they already were, and that's when Miss Ruby came up.

"How's it going, honey?" Miss Ruby asked.

Ronder looked up and smiled, although she was having a horrible time. She couldn't even hold Harriet's ankle with one hand, and the stubble from where she had shaved days ago just pricked her palms.

Miss Ruby smiled back and crossed her arms. "Gladys has been sitting in that damn throne all day. She hasn't moved."

"What are you talking about?" asked Ronder.

"She's been spying on us since morning," said Ruby. "Didn't even leave to get lunch."

Ronder didn't say anything else; she just kept on filing Harriet's toenails.

The dryer was humming and Harriet's head was pushing against the hood, letting some of the hot air escape right on to Ronder's face, making Ronder nauseated. Harriet smiled with her eyes closed. She didn't even know Miss Ruby was there.

For Harriet, it was just Ronder and Harriet and her feet. "I can't seem to see my feet anymore these days," she said. "It must be those midnight snacks." She giggled a horrible giggle, sending shock waves from Ronder's wrists all the way up to her neck. Ronder just knew Harriet had to have picked that laugh up from one of her patients.

"Better go ahead and clip the corners, hon," said Harriet, reaching down and pointing at her feet with her eyes still closed. "I don't want my hose to snag."

"Harriet?" said Miss Ruby, touching her knee, interrupting her. "Hey, Harriet, we haven't seen you in here for a while."

But Harriet didn't want to be disturbed. "What is it that you want?" she snapped, jerking the hood of the dryer up.

Miss Ruby was taken aback. She pressed at her collar

bone and said, "Hon, I was just saying that we haven't seen you in here for such a long time." Her throat was closing up and she forgot what she was trying to say.

"Well," said Harriet Simpson, "I heard Ronder was back, and frankly, that's the only reason I would even think of coming back to this place. Besides, I couldn't get anyone at Gladys' to do my feet."

Miss Ruby stood there with the same smile as before, only now it felt heavy as lead. She wondered exactly how long she should remain standing there smiling like that before she could walk away gracefully.

"Harriet, dear," said Ronder, standing up, trying not to laugh at Ruby, "you'd better let these soak a bit." She stuck Harriet's feet in a little portable tub that had a vibrator with three speeds. Then she set it on the third speed, the highest speed, since it was the best bet for getting rid of any dirt.

While Harriet was soaking, Thurston was in the dispensary with the color bottles and perm solutions trying desperately to think of things that would make him cry. He had started with his favorite dog, a French Toy Poodle named Lillette, who had run away, and then he went right on down the line, thinking about all the people he had loved who had either died or dumped him.

It was working; the tears were finally coming. When they reached full force, he yelled for Miss Ruby to come back.

He had stayed up all night rehearsing what he was about to say, and when he started in with the part about having to leave the shop, he looked at Miss Ruby and saw the exact response he wanted—horror.

His plan was working so well that he had to quickly think of his little Lillette again or else he would break into a smile. So he was quiet and then the tears came pouring down again, and that's when he told Miss Ruby all about Duran.

"Someone," he said, "will have to be there to help him when he gets out of prison. And I thought maybe we would try and open our own hair shop together, or something. But I hate leaving you, Miss Ruby, I swear I do. There's never been anyone like you in my life." And Thurston bawled all over the dispensary.

"There, there, Thurston," said Miss Ruby, patting him on the back. "Did you say he was a beautician, too?"

"A hair designer. But there's another problem, Miss Ruby. A bigger problem." And here, right here, Thurston let out the biggest moan of all. "He's black."

She stared at him, worried, rubbing her hands together, and he could see her scrolling her long list of clients rapidly through her brain to determine who might go for this and who might not. That's when he played his hole card, his ace. "Miss Ruby, don't feel like you have to say yes because you like me. I mean, even if we can't make it on our own, Gladys said she'd be more than glad to open up a slot at her place for us."

Miss Ruby's nostrils flared and her eyebrows pinched tight. It had backfired on him, he could tell.

"Well," she said, looking twice as large as she did when she was being nice, "Gladys has had a nervous breakdown in case you didn't notice. And her shop is closed. So good luck." And she started for the door.

"But," said Thurston grabbing her arm, "I was just talking to her this morning when I was out emptying the trash. She came out of her shop and said that if she were you, she wouldn't ever make me empty garbage."

"She said that?"

Thurston nodded his head, fast, like a little boy. "She also said she'd be willing to open her shop again if Duran and me would come to work for her. She said that what she needed were two men like us to run her business. Now Miss Ruby, you know I love you, but . . ."

"Cut the crap, Thurston. Let me think about this for a minute."

But it didn't even take a minute before Miss Ruby moved back in with all the answers. Not only was Duran set, but

Miss Ruby threw in a raise for Thurston and a higher commission on his shampoo sales.

It had been easier than sin; he almost felt guilty. He thanked Miss Ruby, and secretly he thanked his little Lillette. And when they walked up front together, Miss Ruby insisted they do so arm in arm so that Gladys could see the whole thing through her binoculars.

When Yvonne heard the news, she let out a gasp. "Assist? You want me to assist a black man? A prisoner? Thurston's wife?"

"He's not my wife. We aren't married," said Thurston.

Ronder, who was up front going through the appointment book, started laughing.

Miss Ruby said, "Yvonne, from what Thurston tells me, this Duran has got a much bigger clientele than you do. And let's face it, hon, you aren't exactly bringing in the money you used to."

"A gay prisoner?" Yvonne was in a state of shock. "Black?"

"It's only hair, Yvonne," laughed Ronder, and then Miss Ruby gave Ronder her news

Ronder looked stricken. "What?! Harriet Simpson?! A bikini wax?! Come on, Miss Ruby, surely you're kidding?"

"Nope," said Miss Ruby. "It was the very first thing she asked for when she got here.

"A bikini waxing for Harriet Simpson?" Ronder repeated, dazed.

Yvonne smiled. "It's only hair, Ronder."

12

Ronder looked up and up and up Harriet Simpson's
leg. It was going to be a long afternoon. Harriet was asleep
under the dryer, still holding her glasses backward, only
now they had slipped from her face to her chest and the
book she had been reading had fallen next to the tub her
feet were soaking in. Ronder had told Harriet that she was
soaking in Antonio's Special European bath, but what it
really was was a combination of Clorox, Pine Sol and cheap
Coconut Shampoo. Sometimes on a bad day Ronder would
also add lotions and conditioners and whatever else she
could find back in the dispensary. Today it had been Comet,
and Ronder had told Harriet it was Antonio's new special
European Apricot Scrub, and now the skin on Harriet's feet
was not only shriveled and pruney, but grainy as well, and
Ronder would have to remember not to ever do that again.

She took Harriet's leg and began to massage it with lotion
and tried not to think about what lay ahead but she just
couldn't help it. She just kept coming back and back and
back to that stupid bikini wax. She pictured Harriet, sitting
back with her legs spread wide and her panties—oh what

kind of panties? thought Ronder. Probably something nylon and loose—pulled up high, with bushy black hair sticking out of the sides like Groucho Marx eyebrows.

Then Miss Ruby came back to inform her that Louise and Earline had called and were on their way in.

"They asked for the Chez Ronder Room," said Miss Ruby, bending down to whisper in her ear. "You know what that means, don't you?"

Ronder glared at Miss Ruby. Of course she knew what it meant. No matter what those little flyers had said about makeovers and manicures, skin toning and facials, that room had been used for only one thing and one thing only.

Harriet's book was still on the floor, but she had put her glasses back into their jeweled case and she was smiling now, ignoring Ruby. The smile worried Ronder, as well it should have, because Harriet, not being able to hear herself talk under the dryer, yelled the most devastating thing, which could be heard all the way across the shop, "Ronder, I hear that new husband of yours has been sleeping around on you already!"

If you take how fast news travels normally and then multiply it by five, then you come up with the speed of gossip in the beauty shop. Ronder could see Louise's and Earline's heavy hands at work here. "I know it's true," continued Harriet, stretching her toes taut at Ronder, "because I've seen him look at me before like he was ready to draw the blinds and pull down the sheets. He's real cute, though. I'll give him that. Hon, I think I'm ready for more of that massage now." Harriet was still yelling, lifting the hood of the dryer, letting the hot air escape right on to Ronder's face as Ronder massaged those grainy legs and smelled the sweet smell of Harriet's Shalimar scent as it mixed with the chemical fumes of the shop.

For a minute Ronder thought she would faint and never come back to life, it was so hot. But before she knew it, she was applying a nice shade of Coral Gables on to Harriet Simpson's toenails, and Harriet was adding more and more to the list of things Ronder didn't want to hear. Ronder wasn't paying a bit of attention to what she was doing, which was applying way too thick a coat on Harriet's toes, and when Harriet got home and removed her stockings that night, they'd be stuck to her toenails and she'd have to tear them to get them off.

Louise Stokes breezed in through the Chez Ronder beads and stood by the Chez Ronder mirror, watching Harriet, a woman she had never liked, and never would like, ever, getting dressed from her fresh bikini wax. It was only after Harriet left that Louise removed her skirt. "Darling, do you have a towel?" she asked.

Ronder shook out a small shampoo towel and spread it across the seat of the chair. Louise sat down. "Thanks, dear. I just hate sitting on somebody else's hot seat."

Ronder had already started putting the hot wax on one of Louise's upper inner thighs when Earline flounced in. She plopped onto the other Chez Ronder chaise lounge and picked up a tube of mascara, working the brush in and out of the tube.

Ronder tapped Louise and whispered, "I wonder what she thinks that is," pointing to the mascara brush.

Louise didn't laugh. She was too busy watching what Ronder was doing.

What Ronder was doing was this: She put some gauze over the wax that was on Louise's thigh, pressed it hard, waited for it to dry, and when it dried, she ripped it off so fast and so hard that Louise almost hit the ceiling it hurt so bad. *"Ohweee ohweee ohweee!"* she yelled, and one thing was for sure, she wasn't anything like Harriet Simpson, who had seemed to enjoy it.

"Now don't you pull it so fast this time, hon," said Louise, watching Ronder press the gauze onto her other thigh. "That caused pain."

Ronder pressed the gauze and pressed the gauze until she was sure the wax was good and hard.

"Now don't forget, I said pull it slowly," repeated Louise.

"Hon, it's going to really hurt if I pull this thing off slow."

But Louise sucked in her breath and flared her nostrils and Ronder didn't have any other choice except to pull slowly. She pulled slowly, a little bit at a time, and Louise tensed up and Ronder pulled even slower until finally Louise herself had her hands down there right on top of Ronder's and was yanking that strip of wax off as fast as she could. It was at this point that Miss Ruby called out, "Ronder, hon, the phone's for you. It's Buck."

"Oh Lord, I wonder what he wants," said Earline, who was now taking her skirt off, getting ready for her turn. "Probably some money or something."

"Maybe a divorce," said Louise, fanning her thigh, blowing on it. "No, he's got it too good with Ronder. I think you're right. It must be the money."

These were the words that rang through Ronder's head as she went to pick up the phone. And that's when she looked outside and noticed her car wasn't parked right under the window, underneath the begonias, anymore.

Her heart stopped beating and she remembered something. She had forgotten to put on her emergency brake and her car had probably rolled down the hill, bashed right into Louise Stokes' big cream colored L.T.D. or Earline Maddox's powder blue one, and then kept on going until it took off the other arm of the statue of the one armed woman in the square.

"Hold on, Buck, I'll be right back!" Ronder yelled into the phone without even picking it up. She ran out the door with her heart beating in her ears. Thank goodness she had gotten her insurance mailed in last week, she thought. What if it had lapsed? Well, she just couldn't think that way. It was stupid to even worry about things like that, and just look at Louise's and Earline's cars, she thought, sitting so pretty, as if they were in a commercial, with the sunlight sparkling off the chrome like a knife flashing in the sun. And the statue in the square still safely waved her one arm toward Robert E. Lee as he charged up some Civil War hill on his great horse, Traveler.

Ronder put her hand to her chest and began to talk to her heart out loud. "Calm down, buddy. Just calm down now. You're beginning to hurt a little bit, just calm down. Where in the fuck is my car?!"

This she said, not to her heart, but out loud, loud enough for everyone to hear. For a minute she thought Buck must have taken it. But then she remembered he didn't have the keys anymore. She had taken them away the last time he had come home drunk.

She ran back inside, as fast as she had run out, and grabbed the phone. "Buck, Buck! My car's been stolen, baby. It's gone!"

Gasps came from all around the shop. Louise and Earline were both standing at Ronder's side in their slips, covering themselves from the eyes of Thurston, the only man in the shop. The only man who could've cared less.

Miss Ruby sat behind the desk, biting her nails, flushed with excitement over the publicity possibilities that this would bring to Celebrity Styling.

Yvonne closed her eyes and prayed silently with a comb in her hand, while all of her patrons just stood around with curlers in their hair looking dazed.

This was real news, not just beauty shop news.

This was news that they could actually take home and tell their husbands.

Not in a million years would Ronder Jeffcoat have ever expected to hear what came over those Southern Bell wires next: "Ronder, it was me," said Buck. "I wrecked your car, honey."

Miss Ruby hadn't seen that strange look spread across Ronder's face since the day she had stomped out of the shop leaving Louise and Earline under the dryer so she could go off and elope with Buck. Louise and Earline saw it too and leaned in closer to hear what they could hear.

"Ronder, you there?" asked Buck.

"I just walked outside and it was gone, Buck. Gone without even a tire mark or an oil spot left to prove it was ever here. Gone, baby." Ronder wanted to say something else, something mean, but she either couldn't believe it was happening or she just didn't want anyone to know or she didn't know what, but she just kept on. "Honey, it's just not out there. What am I going to do?"

"Ronder," continued Buck, "it's like this, baby. I was driving down the road and there was this little squirrel, and what could I do? It was froze, Ronder, froze in the middle of the road. I'm sorry, baby, your car is totaled. Smashed up, sugar."

While Buck described what the car now looked like, Ronder put her hand over the receiver. She looked at all the women who had said, "Oh you don't want to marry him. He's going to be nothing but trouble." They all looked so desperate for the worst possible news. It took every drop of blood and muscle she had to do what she did next.

She sat down and twirled the cord around her arm like a bracelet. She smiled and played with the pencils on the desk and said, "That is so funny! Well, honey, just let me know next time. I thought something horrible had happened."

"What! Ronder, are you okay? Ronder, let me speak to Miss Ruby, baby. Get Miss Ruby on the phone," said Buck, who was frantic now.

"And I love you, too," she said, winking at Louise and Earline, who were standing so close, looking so disappointed.

"Ronder, there's something else. Something worse," he said. "I didn't mail in that insurance money like I said I did, Ronder. I spent it at the pool hall and I was going to pay you back, Ronder, next week, but Ronder, what I'm trying to tell you is that your car wasn't covered like you thought. Ronder? Sugar? Are you there? Are you there, babe?"

Every little bit of Ronder Jeffcoat was right there, tied up in knots, clinging to that phone, choking the wire, choking on his words.

"Where are you, darling?" asked Ronder, still smiling for the women in the shop, wrapping the phone cord all the way up to her elbow.

Buck said, "It was a squirrel, Ronder, just like your Rocky." Rocky was a stuffed animal Buck had won at the fair for her by shooting baskets. "He was so cute, but listen, baby, I've got to get off now, Ronder. Ronder, can you come and get me?"

Ronder was furious. Using her free hand, she had already written on a pad four times: DON'T GET MAD DON'T GET MAD DON'T GET MAD DON'T GET MAD.

"How, hon? How do you propose that I do that?" she asked as she colored in the holes in the letters she'd just written, keeping a smile on her face. "And where? Where are you?"

"Ronder, I'm in jail. They put me in here and I need you to come and get me, Ronder. And Ronder, it was a baby squirrel, too. Ronder, Ronder, are you still there? Are you okay, baby?"

For the rest of the afternoon the problem with Ronder and Buck rated higher than Gladys Bessinger's breakdown. But the women were still coming to Ruby, bearing gifts and saying, "I *knew* when I first met Gladys that I couldn't trust her as far as I could spit" and "That's because I told you that. I was the one that said there was something fishy about her. Like the way she always wears those miniskirts, and at *that* age!"

Ruby knew exactly what they were talking about. Leave it up to Gladys; the minute a new hemline hit the newsstand, she was wearing it that night, no matter how ridiculous it looked.

"I've never *seen* a woman carry on so, as if she were twenty years old instead of fifty-five!" said another patron, making Ruby cringe, since Ruby was a year older than Gladys.

"But anyway, Miss Ruby, we are here to *stay*. You'll have to sandblast us to get us to leave." It was finally Louise Stokes who said it all, "Ruby, I wouldn't be caught *dead* in that shop of hers now." Then she changed directions. "Hey listen, is it true what they're saying about Ronder?" she asked, pressing at the white streak in her hair which was looking wilder than ever.

"You mean about Buck?" asked Miss Ruby.

"Yes," said Earline. "The way I heard, he dumped her for another woman and now he's in jail for adultery."

This little declaration sent even more gasps sailing through the shop. Hands went up to hearts, fingers to lips, and every woman at the Celebrity ran through a list of where her husband had spent the night before and the last forty-eight hours before that.

Ronder came back from the bathroom where she had been recovering from Buck's news. Miss Ruby pinched her cheek and Ronder smiled at her.

"She's a brave girl," said Miss Ruby, "isn't she? If anyone should know about adultery, it would be me. Now listen to this. My husband gave me a rabbit fur coat the first month we were married, then he gave me a Mix Master that cost him $13.95 in December, and in May he left me. Now doesn't that make you feel better, Ronder?"

Everyone had surrounded Miss Ruby while she was saying this, and everyone was now laughing the old basic beauty shop "Honey, we have all been there before" laugh. Not one to let an audience down, Miss Ruby went on to tell another one of her famous stories, but not before first pulling the blinds open wider so Gladys could see how many clients were in the shop, hovering around her, laughing.

"One day," she said, "after Bob had been on one of his all nighters, I moved out while he was at work. I left him with nothing but a box of *Playboy*s sitting in the middle of the floor and a phone. When I finally came back for the phone, I found him sitting there with a W.W.II Bayonet, of all things, about to cut his wrists, and I said, 'Oh no, don't you go and do that for me, honey.'" Ruby stopped and patted Ronder's shoulder and added, "Honey, it's just the way men are. Why, we used to have a woman who lived above us and she'd have Bob pacing up and down for her. She'd take

96

a shower and so would he. She'd leave, and he'd go to the store. The only difference between you and me is that the last time he went to the store, he came back and found his clothes and his Lazy-Boy out on the front lawn."

Everybody laughed again, and Ruby turned to the window and posed. She knew Gladys was still watching, because she had stationed Thurston by the window at his station, with orders to let her know if there was any change in Gladys' position. So far, Thurston had not signalled her once.

Where Ruby was jolly, Ronder was absolutely miserable. She knew Miss Ruby was trying to break her down, trying to get her to admit she'd been wrong about Buck all along. Just when Ronder was sure she wasn't going to let anyone get to her though, a fat woman whom she didn't like the looks of at all came running in through the front door, all out of breath, and said, "He ran over a man's legs!"

"Who?" screamed Miss Ruby.

"That husband of that woman who works in here." The woman was panting, leaning against the front desk, squeezing herself, "Poor thing. She must have gone home very upset."

Miss Ruby put her arm around Ronder, "No, here she is."

"Buck ran over a man's legs?" asked Ronder. "Will he ever walk again?" Her head was ringing like a phone.

"Well," said another lady who'd also just arrived, "that's not what I heard. My husband happens to know her husband and he said, he told me, he said that he was in jail because he *killed* the man."

"What?" Now it was Miss Ruby whose head was ringing. "Buck killed a man? Oh Ronder."

Yvonne opened her Bible, trying to find the right passage to read, while Ronder just sat down, stunned. "I didn't even think to ask if there was anyone else involved," she said to herself.

"That's the most outrageous thing I have ever heard," said Earline Maddox, who just minutes before had slipped her skirt back on, then slipped over to the A&P to use their phone to find out what was going on. She had dashed back as fast as she could to tell the news, only as she neared the shop she had made a point of stopping, then walking back into the Celebrity Styling looking cool and unaffected. She stood at the door now, repairing her lipstick in a way that told everyone there that Earline Maddox was the one with the real inside story.

"Well Earline, is it true?" asked Miss Ruby.

"Come on, Earline, give," said Louise.

Earline snapped her compact open and powdered her lips. Everyone waited until she spoke.

"D.U.I.," she said. "Plain and simple. And yes, Ronder, for your information, there was somebody else involved." Earline made a big thing out of the word "involved" and a bigger thing out of snapping her little powder compact shut and mouthing the words "Another woman."

"But you're sure he didn't hit anyone?" whispered Ronder, pulling Earline into the Chez Ronder Room.

"Just a tree. Of course, the woman was nowhere to be found."

"Uh huh! A woman. You see there! I knew it," said Louise.

"D.U.I?" asked Miss Ruby, following after them. "I said that man was going to be money out of your pocket and I meant it."

Miss Ruby was upset. A murder was one thing, because not everyone's husband did that. But this! "A D.U.I. is about as white trash as white trash can get!" she yelled. "A D.U.I.," she huffed, stomping off.

She found Thurston standing at the front desk with a loaf of Merita bread. He had four slices out and was rolling them into little balls and eating them.

"What are you doing?!" asked Miss Ruby, furious. "Why aren't you watching Gladys?"

He pinched three Merita balls together, then threw them up in the air and caught them in his mouth.

"Well," asked Miss Ruby, "what's she doing?"

"I don't know."

"You don't know?"

"I don't know."

"Why didn't you call me?" asked Miss Ruby, putting her hands to her forehead.

"Calm down, sugar," said Thurston. "She must have sat in that throne for six hours without moving. Now she's sitting on the floor looking at the phone. Just sitting there staring at it."

"Let me see those binoculars." Miss Ruby took them and peered through the front window.

Thurston was right. Gladys was sitting in the middle of the shop, on the floor, looking at the phone.

"Thurston, call her up and see if she'll answer."

"What am I supposed to say if she does?" he asked, rolling his last slice of bread into ten even balls.

"I don't know. Make an appointment or something."

"Miss Ruby," Thurston was getting irritated, "my three thirty is dripping back there. I don't have time for this."

Miss Ruby's eyes hadn't left the binoculars. "Thurston, there's an extra ten dollars in it for you. And whatever you do, don't let her know who you are."

Thurston picked up the phone and dialed. He didn't even have to look Gladys' number up, because Ruby had it written all over the desk blotter, over and over again.

"Miss Ruby, why, if you never call Gladys, is her number written everywhere?"

"Shhhh!" said Miss Ruby, waving her hand behind her as she continued to peer across the square.

A man was walking around it and stopped to admire the one armed woman, who was waving a battle torn flag at Robert E. Lee.

"Damn! Get out of the way," hissed Miss Ruby. The man was standing directly in front of the one spot where she could see Gladys.

"It's ringing," said Thurston. "One ringy-dingy, two ringy-dingy. Hello? Hello? Yes, this is the great Thurston from

Celebrity Styling. I'd like to make an appointment to have my hair done."

"No!" hissed Miss Ruby, who was dying a thousand deaths, reaching over to hang up on Gladys. "Oh! How could you, Thurston!" she wailed. "You weren't supposed to tell her who you were."

"I couldn't help it. I got stuck."

"Oh Thurston!"

Thurston could see that Miss Ruby was about to cry. "I'm just fooling around, Ruby old girl. Don't get upset. She didn't even pick up the phone, Miss Ruby. Like I said, she's acting real weird."

Miss Ruby didn't know whether to believe him or not, now.

"Watch," said Thurston. "Go on back to the window and just watch her sit there while I call again."

So he did it all over again, but this time the man in the square wasn't blocking her view and Ruby watched Gladys as she picked up the phone. But she didn't say anything.

Miss Ruby studied her for a minute and then turned to Thurston. "What's going on?" she mouthed.

He shrugged his shoulders and mouthed the words "She's not saying anything."

Miss Ruby mouthed back "Make an appointment or something." She went back to looking through the binoculars again.

Thurston was trying to think of exactly what to say, when Yvonne came running up yelling, "Miss Ruby, could you come look at this color? I could use a second opinion."

The last word Gladys could have heard over the phone was the word "color" because Thurston had hung up. But she'd heard enough for Miss Ruby to see that Gladys had put down her phone and was now standing up, looking out her window at the Celebrity Styling Shop.

It was a lucky thing for Miss Ruby that Gladys wasn't using her binoculars. It was embarrassing enough to be caught calling her on the phone without having to face the equal humiliation of being caught spying. It was a spooky thing indeed for Miss Ruby to see those haunting eyes staring across the street at the shop.

While the Gladys incident was in full swing, Ronder had started in on Earline's bikini wax, pretending that each strip of hair she removed was Buck. Somehow it made it easier.

"I want it shaved into a heart shape," said Earline. "Can you do a heart shape?" she asked as Ronder pulled up the last strip of hair.

"A heart shape?" asked Louise, who was fanning her recently bikini waxed area. It was burning. "At your age? You've got to be kidding."

"Why, Earline," said Ronder, "I think that would be just about the cutest thing." She hoped she sounded carefree enough so that everyone would think that everything was just fine with old Ronder Jeffcoat. Under no circumstances would she let Miss Ruby or anyone else see just how upset she was. But she was getting more upset by the minute, because she couldn't even draw a stupid heart on a paper with a pencil, much less on Earline Maddox's pubic bone. And it wasn't like Earline was the firmest person in the world either, and her skin kept pulling this way and that, and Ronder was beginning to whittle down more hair and more hair, trying to get it even, trying to get it right, until there was barely any hair left—just the tiniest most crooked heart.

Then Earline said, "Pink. I think I want it dyed pink. You know, to match my lipstick."

Ronder stood up slowly and walked the long walk back to the dispensary where all the hair dyes were, thinking about the first day she had ever met Buck. She was over at a friend's house and he had just breezed on in with those big sexy ways of his and sat down without saying a word, and watched Ronder cut her friend's hair. And when she was through, Ronder's friend went to the bathroom to put her makeup on, and Buck asked if Ronder would cut his hair. And before Ronder knew it, she was cutting Buck's hair and he was saying, "I can just imagine you cutting my hair with your boobs out."

That was all it had taken.

It wasn't what he had said, it was how he had said it. Like he knew it was nasty, but he also knew that the smile that went with it was the smile that could break a woman's heart.

Ronder had never done it before, and she would never do it again, but that night she walked right out of that apartment with that poor girl's date—Buck—and went straight to his trailer to finish up that haircut. When she thought about it now, it seemed like she was always walking out on somebody on account of him.

When Ronder returned to the Chez Ronder Room with a bottle of hair color in one hand and some extra towels in the other, Louise fanned herself harder and said, "I'm on fire!"

After Louise cooled down and the heart was dyed pink, Earline asked Ronder to remove "this tee-niny little mustache," as she called it, from around her upper lip. While Ronder waxed, she tried to get up the courage to ask Miss Ruby for the keys to her Cadillac.

Yvonne, on the other hand, sat in the dispensary with the color bottles. She was reading her Bible, making her final plan, shook up over the news about being Duran's assistant, and waiting for her last client to get out from under the dryer. It had been a slow afternoon for Yvonne despite all the excitement. The new dryers had taken their toll and the whole shop was hot. Especially up front, where Miss Ruby was fanning herself with one of the pamphlets on the Atlanta Hair Show that lay spread out before her.

Thurston was ringing up his last client. When she gave him a dollar tip, he held it in the air as if it smelled bad. "I'm going into the hospital soon, Libby," he said, still holding the dollar up.

"Oh my!" said Libby, a thin client of his who wore so

many bracelets they jingled as she reached to touch his arm. "Thurston, when did this happen? Are you okay?"

"Headaches, darling, headaches," he whispered to her. "I might be very ill. There's talk of a brain tumor. The doctors say it's only a matter of time, but don't tell anyone. I want it to be graceful, you understand."

Libby assured Thurston his secret was safe with her, and tipped him an extra five-dollar bill. Then she made her next week's appointment, saying, "I'll understand if you can't make it, Thurston," and left, touching her bangs, worrying about who was going to do her hair after Thurston was gone.

"You're horrible, Thurston," said Yvonne, who had overheard everything. She had just walked up to the front of the shop with her suitcase packed full of hairnets and rollers. Yvonne had finally decided that it was time to leave Celebrity Styling for good, just as soon as she combed out Mrs. Pike.

"But I do have headaches, darling, and I think I feel one coming on right now," said Thurston as he grabbed his head with both of his hands and squeezed tight. "Oh oh oh," he said, stomping his boots.

Yvonne ignored him and said, "That is not funny. Here." She handed him a broom and said, "It's your turn to sweep."

Thurston looked at Yvonne as if she had just offered him a dead bird. "Moi? Sweep?"

"Yes, and when you're through with that, you can fold some towels for a change. I myself am not doing one more thing. For your information, today is my last day. So here," she said, jamming the broom at him again. "Take it."

"Your last day?" he asked.

Miss Ruby coughed and cleared her throat and said, "Yvonne, come here and help me please. I have got a major decision to make and I really need your help."

This time when Yvonne pushed the broom at Thurston, he took it and watched her walk away, calling out after her, "Hon, you don't want to quit, sugar. We need you here where you belong." Had Yvonne turned around, she would have seen a tear rolling down Thurston's cheek—a genuine tear.

Thurston loved Yvonne like a sister and he felt like he'd known her all his life. And maybe he had been a little too rough on her, but she should have known he was only playing. He felt horrible. He'd just have to talk to her was all. He'd tell her that he would turn over a new leaf—turn over some of his patrons to her. After all, he was getting a little overworked and with Duran coming and all, he could use the free time. If it was Duran who was the problem, well he could fix that too. He'd just have a little heart to heart with Miss Ruby and get her to hire another assistant. The tricky part was going to be talking any of his clients into going to Yvonne. The ones who used to go to her would never go back, and he couldn't begin to imagine any of his regulars wearing one of Yvonne's old timey updos. He shook his head back and forth.

"Don't worry about it, Thurston," said Miss Ruby. "She isn't going anywhere. Now look here, Yvonne." Miss Ruby showed her a picture of a limousine. "Do you think we should go in this black one here? Or how about this white one?"

"Go where?" asked Yvonne, jutting her jaw out, then looking up and squinting at Miss Ruby. "Oh, I get it. Now you listen here, Miss Ruby. Don't you think for a minute that you can talk me out of it this time because my mind is definitely made up. I am leaving."

"I won't talk you out of anything, dear," said Miss Ruby. "I promise. But do tell me, what do you think? Black or white?"

Yvonne stood there, clutching her suitcase in front of her with both hands good and tight. By now Thurston had really worked himself up. This time he didn't even need to think about his little Lillette up in heaven. All he had to do was look at the back of Yvonne and see those tiny shoulders hunched over the front desk—look at the back of that hair, at those petal curls that must have taken an hour just to pin up—see those scuffed up nurse's shoes and that support hose. That's all it took to send him walking off in tears, to sit in the back room next to Mrs. Pike, who was asleep under the dryer.

If Thurston only knew what Miss Ruby knew: Yvonne threatened to quit any time anything ever went wrong. Since that was almost every week, every week Yvonne came up front and stood there with that blue cardboard suitcase with HAZEL'S BEAUTY SCHOOL stamped on the side, squeezing the handle tight, clenching her teeth, announcing that she was going over to Gladys' to work. But she never meant it. Miss Ruby knew it was just a way for her to get attention. And Lord knew Yvonne deserved some. If someone had told Ruby McSwain that she'd have to work for a gay black inmate, she'd be shook up too. Hell, one out of three of that choice would be enough to shake her up for years.

"I thought you were going to fly to Atlanta," said Yvonne, squeezing her suitcase handle even tighter.

Miss Ruby knew she was going to have to hold that dumb lost look on her face no matter what it took. Yvonne might not mean what she said, but Yvonne didn't know that. She was liable to walk right out of that front door if Miss Ruby didn't play her cards just right.

"Well, what do you think, Yvonne? Fly or drive? I was sort of thinking it would be fun to drive on down and maybe have a roadside picnic. Get us a handsome chauffeur with white gloves. Wouldn't that be cute? And we'd have champagne and a color TV in the back. Now wouldn't that be fun?"

Miss Ruby's next line was going to be the tough one to deliver. It was going to have to be just smooth enough to glide over Yvonne's common sense so Yvonne wouldn't know she was being manipulated. "But, well, without you there," said Miss Ruby shaking her head, "without you there I guess we'll just go on ahead and fly. No need to drive if it's not going to be a party."

Then Miss Ruby let out a deep, long sigh and began gathering up the brochures. But Yvonne stopped her. "Don't you be silly, Ruby. You can still have a party without me."

"Well I sure don't think so. Thurston!" she yelled. "Come out here a minute."

Thurston had been crying, watching Mrs. Pike. He was amazed at how much she resembled Yvonne. It seemed like all of Yvonne's patrons looked like her; they even dressed like her.

He went up for the bad news and Miss Ruby asked, "Thurston, can we have a party without Yvonne?"

"No. No parties without you, baby." And he snapped his fingers and did his usual twirl and for once Yvonne didn't mind. For once it almost made her feel good, because once she walked out of the Celebrity Styling Shop there wouldn't be a place in town for her to go to, because Gladys' CLOSED sign was still hanging in the door. The only other shop in town was a black stylon, and Yvonne's clientele would never step foot in a place like that.

So Yvonne decided right then that it was just as well to work in a shop with one black as opposed to a place with four or five of them, no matter if the one she'd be working with was a prisoner *and* a homosexual. Of course, she wasn't going to let Miss Ruby and Thurston off that easy. She'd let them sweat for a while longer and make them beg a whole lot more before she'd hang her little blue labcoat in the back one more time.

Miss Ruby already knew all this and winked at Thurston and they went to work. "You see, Yvonne," she said, "what we'll do is take two limos. Yes, that would be nice, wouldn't it, Thurston? I'll rent the black one and the white one, and you can choose who gets to ride in which car."

"Splendid idea!" said Thurston, who was now doing a twirl after every one of Miss Ruby's splendid ideas. "Not only that," he added, "but you can ride in the lead car. Yes. That's a good idea too, don't you think, Miss Ruby?"

"I wouldn't have it any other way," she said, and she and Thurston kept it up even after Yvonne had left to go into the back to comb out Mrs. Pike.

No sooner had Yvonne left when two women came in and began looking around. "Sugar, have you seen Duran?" asked one of them who was dressed for Soul Train. "I hear he's out of the prison system now." She had on a pink sequined minidress and black zippered spiked heels. Her handbag matched her heels and she was digging around in it for a cigarette while the other one—the one who was wearing the tightest black pants Thurston had ever seen in his life—began to tell them everything she knew about Duran. Every time she said something she thought was funny, she'd flip her wrists just like Thurston, only she had long, long red fingernails that made Miss Ruby jump whenever they came too close.

"Duran, Duran, oh Duran," she squealed. "I can tell you so much about Duran."

The other woman stuck her cigarette into a long gold plated filter and began to smoke away. Her arms were lanky and she reminded Miss Ruby of a spider. Miss Ruby didn't know what it was, but it seemed like every time she saw a black they were either too fat or too skinny. There was never any in between. And these two girls had redefined the word "skinny."

The one with the tight black pants leaned in real close to Thurston, like she was going to kiss him, and said, "That old sugar pie. He's such a scam. Those clothes, that car. You should see that car," she said, stepping back from Thurston and flipping her red fingernails in Miss Ruby's face again. "It's this great big yellow convertible Cadillac, and he's got black tinted windows so you can't see in. Only he's always got the top down so it's like what's the point. He calls it El Dog, you know."

Thurston did know. That car was one of the sore spots in their relationship. The way Duran carried on so much about that car, someone would have thought it was his wife or something. Thurston was actually jealous of it.

He wanted the girls to leave before they said too much more about Duran. Once Miss Ruby met him, everything would be okay, but to hear about him was a whole different ball game. Thurston could see that Miss Ruby had that "What have I gone and done?" look about her.

"Well girls," he said, sounding straight for the first time in years, "he'll be in next week. If you want an appointment I'll put you right down."

"Yessss." The one with the zippered shoes was drawing that "yes" out long and sexy, and smoke was following it right out of her mouth.

The other one wasn't even listening. She was still talking. "One time he cut my hair and I told him, 'Sugar, don't you cut that back now,' because I like my hair touching the back of my neck, you know?"

Miss Ruby nodded as the girl's nails waved in front of her face.

"And Duran," the woman squealed again, "well, do you know what that silly boy went and did?"

"Pray tell," said Miss Ruby, who was shaking her head because she could only imagine.

The girl kept on, "He went and cut it all off in the back and left it long on top. So I started crying, right?" Miss Ruby was nodding to her every word. "And I said, 'Duran, I said I wanted it short on top and long in the back, not the other way around!' And that Duran, he twirled my chair away from the mirror so I couldn't see what was going on, and he picked up those scissors and chop chop chop, and he got that hair on the top of my head short, too, until everybody in town thought I was having chemotherapy treatments."

With this, she placed both of her hands on her hips and looked at Miss Ruby with this "Well what do you think about that?" expression, and Thurston knew exactly what Miss

Ruby thought about that. He was only glad Yvonne hadn't come up to hear any of it.

He got their names: "La Wando," one said, and the other one said, "Shirelle," and he scribbled them down on Duran's side of the book for a time when he thought Yvonne and Miss Ruby might go out to pick up some lunch.

"What did you do?!" asked Miss Ruby, now good and shocked.

Shirelle, the talker, flashed her nails at Ruby again and just laughed. "What do you think I did, honey? I wore it around town and told everybody Duran had done it, and by the next week there wasn't a woman in town who hadn't gone and gotten Duran to cut her hair the same way. He's what I'd call a trend setter. Isn't that right, La Wando?"

La Wando did her smokey "yes" again, and that was all.

"He's crazy," said Shirelle. "Anyway, he gets in these moods and you can almost always see them coming by the clothes he wears. Like if he starts wearing his 1930's suits, then it's an almost sure fire guarantee that he's going to do something truly different to your hair. That Duran," she said laughing, "he is really something else."

"Uh-huh," said La Wando. "He's that all right."

It wasn't until after they had left that Miss Ruby began to weigh the choice of a shop without Thurston versus a shop with Thurston and his Duran. She patted her updo and was thankful to feel it there. The part about cutting that poor girl's hair all off just kept running through Miss Ruby's mind over and over again.

Thurston understood what he had to do next. He had to do something to take Miss Ruby's mind off of things before she had a chance to think too hard. So he dashed to the dispensary and came running back with something about the size of a painting, and it was draped just like a painting underneath a sheet. "Darling," he said, "the moment we've all been waiting for."

Whenever Thurston did anything, he did it with a great flair and this was no exception. He had practiced this little routine in front of his mirror time and time again. "Voilà!" He flung the sheet off the picture like a magician, twirled once, twice, and then again, and came back on the third time, swooping his wrist down and stopping his hand at the name ANNABELLA.

"Just look at her," said Thurston. "Feast your eyes on her. No one can top my beautiful Annabella." The look on his face was unlike anything Miss Ruby had ever seen.

"I needed a model for the Hair Show and so I've decided to bring one down from New York. Isn't she the most devine thing?" Thurston started kissing the glass on the framed poster, kissing Annabella as if she were standing right there in the room with them.

But the woman Ruby McSwain saw was not the same woman Thurston saw. What she saw was an over the hill type who looked as if she should go straight to Atlanta, straight to the Belk Department Store and do a girdle commercial before she got too much older.

"Don't you just love her?" he asked, stroking the hair in the photograph. "Don't you just think she's divine?"

"She's all right, Thurston. She reminds me a little of Lana Turner, but older."

"I know! Isn't she the most beautiful woman? I mean she's got the greatest hair. Don't you just love her hair, Miss Ruby? Isn't she great?"

Then Thurston began to explain all about how he had arranged for her to fly down to South Carolina the day before the Hair Show so that she could go with them to Atlanta. That way she could be there in time for the papers to interview her and him together.

"She'll be the star attraction," he said, spreading his hands in the air in front of him. "All the papers will be after her for interviews. But I'll teach her how to be the elusive one." He tapped Miss Ruby's sleeve and eased down close to her, almost whispering. "How do you like that touch? Elusive."

111

Miss Ruby decided that she didn't like that touch very much at all. If anyone was going to be the star attraction at her Hair Show, it was going to be Ruby McSwain herself, with capital letters.

15

The policeman at the County Jail had been a very nice man who had pointed Ronder to some yellow feet and told her to follow them until she came to some red ones, and there'd she'd be able to find Buck. The feet looked as if they had been cut out of construction paper and were supposed to be sewn on to beach towels, only they weren't even yellow anymore, just a sort of dullish beige with some of the toes either peeling up or torn off.

Deep in the cell block the place smelled worse than any perm Ronder had ever given. When she reached the red feet, she saw Buck, all hunched over himself like somebody had beaten him on the back of the neck with a club.

Buck felt bad. He tried to talk to Ronder but found that whenever he spoke, two words came out in place of one, and everything that did come out echoed and rattled around in his head. This accounted for him holding his head in his hands.

"Well, buddy," asked Ronder as she stood with her arms crossed over her tight new pink blouse, "are you proud of yourself now?"

She had left work early to stop off at the Mall on the way over because she had heard they were having a sale. She figured it wouldn't do Buck a bit of harm to let him sweat it out in jail a little longer. But there was another, more womanly reason for her shopping spree. It was Ronder's philosophy that whenever Buck did something wrong, she should always look her best so that he would go crazy for her and feel extra guilty.

Sometimes Buck wouldn't even know what he'd done, but he'd still be right there at her feet promising the world to her and apologizing for everything on earth, because if there was one thing that drove him insane, it was when she was dressed like she was now.

She knew she'd done the right thing.

The blouse wasn't only tight and pink, but it was a little bit see-through and she had worn a black lacy bra underneath. And boy did it work as she uncrossed her arms and posted them on her hips and repeated, "Well, buddy, I bet you're proud of yourself now."

That was going to be all she'd say. She had practiced the whole thing on the way over. She'd even written out her lines on the back of a placemat as she drank her Orange Julius at the Mall and then rehearsed her speech one final time. Then she had repeated it all out loud in the car until she had finally narrowed it down to the exact words that her favorite star, Farrah Fawcett, would use—star quality words.

"Where are your glasses, Ronder?" was the first thing Buck had asked.

"Glasses? Buck sugar, we're not talking glasses here. We're talking about your future. And you'd just better remember that."

God, he always did that. Always went and brought up her glasses, or something she was equally embarrassed about, to throw her off guard. Well she couldn't let that happen this time. Too much planning had gone into this little visit to let any of Buck's old tricks get in her way. Nevertheless, she could feel her eyeglasses in her pocketbook, haunting her. She drew herself up.

"Well, I asked if you had anything to say for yourself?" she asked again.

"Ronder, I think you should wear your glasses. If you're dressed like that without wearing your glasses, then that accounts for why you're dressed like that," said Buck.

"What on earth are you talking about?" asked Ronder, but then she saw the look on Buck's face, which told her she'd opened up the conversation too much and if she didn't close it up now, Buck would be all over her, turning everything around, making everything her fault.

"No," she said, holding her hand up in the air, "don't you even answer that. Buck Jeffcoat, I hope you're proud of yourself, going off and wrecking my car. And by the way, when did you happen to get a set of my car keys? Now there's a question. Boy, if you want a good question, that is one for you. Huh? Did you do that when I was sleeping? Is that the kind of thing you do when your wife turns her back?"

"You see," said Buck, "you could get raped in here dressed like that. I can only assume that you didn't know that, didn't even think about it. Yep, you must have been dressing without being able to see again. Unless, of course, you wanted people to think you were a hooker or something."

He could see that he had her right where he wanted her. She was cooling down now. Not only would he be out of jail in time for dinner, but he'd be in the warm arms of his little Ronder for all night long.

"Hooker? Buck Jeffcoat, did you call me a hooker?"

"Calm down, honey. I didn't call you that. I just said that people might get the wrong idea. Men are always getting the wrong idea, Ronder. If you only knew how pretty you looked right now, standing there. Oh Ronder, baby, I can't stand it. Get me out of here. I've got to be with you."

There it was, that look on her face. She was coming around and she'd be in his arms tonight for sure. Heaven sweet heaven he could smell that sweet perfume she wore

115

behind her ears, see that cute little silk nightie she had, wrapped around her silky skin, and all of a sudden his hangover was going away.

"Pretty? Buck, do you really think I look pretty? You haven't said that to me in months."

"I know I hadn't, sugar. I hadn't said a lot of things. But let me tell you, pretty isn't the word for you. I don't think there's a word on this earth that could explain just how beautiful you are."

He was up now and holding on to the bars, and he was reaching out, buttoning her blouse up one button higher. "You're the kind of pretty I don't want to share with anybody."

Ronder patted the button and smiled at him and then she began to dig around in her pocketbook.

"You are such a good wife, Ronder. And you know what, honey?"

"What is that, Buck?" she asked, digging around.

"I've decided that I'm going to start going to church with you every Sunday from now on. Would you like that, baby?"

Ronder looked up, the tears brimming over the rims of her eyes. "Buck, do you mean it?"

"Yes, honey, and there's something else. I've decided that I'm going to get a job, a full time job, and then you and I are going to start going out to the movies and stuff. Maybe dinner, too. Would you like that, Ronder? Dinner?"

Ronder raised her knee and pushed her large pink pocketbook against it and kept digging around. "Oh no, honey. I can't find that money. It was right here a minute ago. Oh, good, here it is," she said, sighing with one hand on her chest.

Buck let out a deep breath, too. He couldn't wait to get out, and he really did want to take Ronder to the movies and make up to her. "Ronder, it'll be just like it was in the beginning, only better. Movies, dinner—hey, we can even start cooking out like you've always wanted. We'll invite

116

Miss Ruby and I'll do the steaks. Would you like that, baby? Cooking out? The movies?"

"Oh Buck! I would love that."

He had her now, right where he wanted her. She had stopped crying and started looking sweet again. He was getting ready for the home stretch and it was just a matter of minutes before he'd be heading away from this place.

"Hon," she said, "I would love that so much." She was pulling her hand out of her pocketbook now, and all he could think about was that long shower he was going to be taking.

"Hon," said Ronder, "just as soon as you get out of here, I'd like that a lot. But for right now, I just came to get a shot of you for our divorce lawyer." She pulled out an Instamatic and took a picture of Buck, still holding on to the bars with one hand, trying to hide his face from the flash with his other. When she was sure he could see again, she wiggled her shoulders at him like a go-go dancer, the same way she had rehearsed in the department store dressing room mirror. "Hey," she said, doing that cute little jerk with her hair that she'd seen so many times on *American Bandstand*, "maybe you can give Riley Pointer a call. He might could get you out of here."

And Ronder Jeffcoat, in her infinite wisdom, unbuttoned the button that Buck had just buttoned, flipped her hair one more time and walked away, doing a little thing with her walk that just really drove Buck crazy.

16

illie Loudermilk had never been one to go to a beauty shop. In fact she had only been once in her entire life and that was when she had turned thirteen and her Grandmother Lillian had decided she needed a more mature look. One perm, one haircut and half a can of hairspray later, Millie Loudermilk walked out of that beauty shop looking exactly like her Grandmother Lillian, and oh how her mother had cried.

That was years ago, and now, years later, she was working the counter at the corner pharmacy and Louise Stokes and Earline Maddox were there telling her it was time to do it all over again.

"If I had hair like yours," said Louise, pushing at her own white streak, "I'd want to get it looked at by a professional."

"Me too," said Earline.

"Come here, sugar," said Louise, guiding Millie over to the Revlon counter and pushing the top of her head right up to the mirror. "Let me show you something." She worked the part apart at Millie's scalp and said, "You see that line of color?"

Millie looked up as hard as she could before she started seeing spots and then said, "I can't see that far up, Louise."

"Well, anyway," Louise said, motioning for Earline to come and look, "you see that line, don't you, hon?"

Earline's head bobbed up and down.

"Well, you can just imagine then that out there in that sun, it just jumps right out at you."

Louise kept pushing around in Millie's hair, pushing her right on up to the mirror. "Do you see it, Millie? See it now?"

"Ouch! Stop! You're breaking my neck, Louiiise!"

But Louise wasn't ready to let Millie go. "Honey," she said, "if you'd just let Ronder fix it then it would look so much better."

Now the reason Louise and Earline wanted Millie to get her hair fixed was a complicated one indeed. It had a lot to do with Riley. Louise thought that if Millie looked good, then Riley wouldn't look at Earline. And Earline thought the same thing about Louise. They'd been competing like that since elementary school. Neither one of them worried about Millie turning Riley's head. At the same time, Louise and Earline wanted Millie to have her hair done because they just couldn't stand seeing a woman, any woman, looking her worst. And if the smartest man in the world had come and tried to work out what made Louise and Earline tick, he'd just as soon tell you, "Women don't always have to have a reason to do anything," as to tell you anything else.

But the smartest man in the world wasn't there. It was just Louise and Earline, confusing Millie and working the mirrors and hovering over her until she didn't know what to do but to agree.

"All right," said Millie. "I'll do it, but I don't want to."

Millie still looked confused and then Earline came in with her pitch. It was a better pitch even than Louise's, because instead of trying to talk Millie into the decision through positive reinforcement, she made Millie feel that there was much, much more wrong with her than just her hair.

"It's not just your hair we're talking about either, hon," she said. "It's your clothes, your posture, your makeup, everything. Have you taken a good long look at your face lately?"

Millie bent down and peered into the mirror. She pushed her hair away, pushed at her cheeks, and asked, "What's wrong with my face?"

"Oh forget it," said Earline. "I told you she was a lost cause, Louise."

"Nonsense," said Louise. "Come on, yall."

And before Millie even had time to take off her drugstore smock, but just enough time to clock out, they had pulled her into the department store across the street and were showing her the more expensive lines of cosmetics.

"Do you know what Ronder told me about this eye makeup?" asked Louise as she held up a glittering green eyeshadow. "She said the reason it sparkles is because it has ground up pearls in it, but that the stuff they sell in the drugstore has fish scales instead. Now, knowing that, which would you rather use?"

This was what Millie Loudermilk's day was like while Ronder was visiting Buck, and Miss Ruby was preparing to close up The Celebrity Styling Shop for the day, and Yvonne was still battling it out with Thurston over Duran. And on it went even as the three women, Millie, Louise and Earline, walked up to Riley's loaded with shopping bags, ringing his doorbell.

Riley was amazed and astonished to see not just one but all three women homing in on him. He'd just sat down to an afternoon of beer and ESPN and now here they were, wanting to visit and discuss recipes and shopping and babies and grandbabies and any other annoying things that go on when a man wants to watch baseball.

Riley had no other choice but to do what he did next.

He hid.

He flattened himself up against the wall and tried to reach the remote control by foot. It was just inches away, inches away from him being free for the rest of the afternoon.

But it was too late.

Louise, with her supersonic hearing, had already heard the TV blaring.

"The TV's on!" she squealed, clapping lightly. "He must be home."

"Not necessarily," said Millie, who felt incredibly strange wearing all the new makeup that the salesgirl had applied so freely to her face. "Some people just leave the TV on so criminals will think they're home."

Riley breathed a short and shallow sigh, thanking Millie Loudermilk and listening to the click click click of their heels as they walked away.

Or as he thought they walked away.

"Hold on," said Earline, "I think I see him in there." She was standing on her tiptoes over the azaleas, peering over the edge of the living room window, saying, "Yes, yes, there he is. Hi! Hi!" she yelled, rapping on the window with her class ring, all excited now, waving and smiling and pointing to the front door to be let in. Riley had no choice except to unflatten himself from the wall, flip off the game and open his home up for an afternoon of gossip.

His beer sat warming up in the living room as he sat cooling down in the den.

Louise and Earline were the first to start the conversation and they kept it going all afternoon.

"Well," said Earline, "after you hear about what happened to Buck, you won't even want to hear about Gladys." She reached over and touched Riley's arm. Riley hated to be touched.

"Well, go ahead, Earl," said Louise, "tell him about Gladys first. No, I'll tell him. You can tell him about Buck."

Riley widened and squinted his eyes whenever they said something, whenever he thought it was appropriate,

121

causing both Louise and Earline to go, "Yes! And if you think that's something, well just listen to this ..." and it wasn't long before Millie came out of her shell and piped in her two cents worth.

Riley just smiled and nodded and wished for a nap.

There was a big difference between being around one woman as opposed to two or three of them.

Earline was all right, he thought, although he couldn't take his eyes off of her upper lip. The skin above it looked red and swollen from her mustache wax, and he couldn't keep from staring.

Louise was funny, but plump, too plump, like Bebe. And she was tall, too tall. Riley liked his women skinnier. And shorter.

Like Millie, only she was a real mess. He didn't know what it was about her exactly—it was the kind of thing that he couldn't quite put his finger on—like she always had a cold or something.

He looked at them separately and then together. It wasn't exactly a top of the line choice. So when the phone rang and it was Buck, calling to ask Riley to get him out of jail, Riley breathed a sigh of relief.

On the way back from jail, Buck talked Riley into stopping off at the Majik Market for a six pack. "This way," he said, "I'll be telling Ronder the truth when I tell her I was out drinking with you. Hell, can you believe she just left me down there? Man, don't ever get married." Buck took a swig of his beer and rubbed his nose with his sleeve. "Man, you must feel like you're the only free guy left in the world," said Buck, thinking how wonderful that would be right at that moment.

Riley felt free, all right, but more like available. Too available, he thought as he drove around, not quite knowing where to go, but not wanting to go back to his house yet where all those women were waiting for him.

"Yep," said Buck, chucking Riley's shoulder, "it's Riley this and Riley that and, man, what is it that you've got with these broads?"

Buck smiled, looking over at Riley, noticing that he looked all drawn and uncomfortable. "Oh man, I'm sorry. I guess it's not the right time." Now it was Buck who felt uncomfortable. "I know we hardly know each other, and I never

123

really did get a chance to get to know Bebe, but I heard she was a good woman."

Buck didn't know how to deal with death at all. He had absolutely refused to go to Bebe's burial, and Ronder had to threaten him with divorce to get him to go to the wake, which was one of the reasons he had gone out for pizza instead and not come back. He just couldn't stand funerals.

He looked over at Riley again as Riley drove mindlessly about, and he started to suggest going over to his house. But then he pictured Ronder, standing at the front door, holding a rolling pin in one hand and a frying pan in the other, just like in Andy Capp. Instead he said, "Let's go shoot some pool, huh buddy?"

Riley, of course, thought this was a grand idea.

While Riley and Buck had even more beer at the pool hall and shot nine games of eight ball, Louise Stokes had practically rearranged Riley's entire living room and was now cleaning out his refrigerator and freezer. There were so many leftover hams and pies and turkeys and cakes. She looked at the cake Millie Loudermilk had brought. It had sat virtually untouched, except for a thin slice that had been stuck back in to make it whole again, and now it rested lopsided on the bottom shelf of the refrigerator, taking up space. This was the sort of thing that made Louise's heart go out to Millie.

She found Millie eating peanuts and looking heart rending. She was always looking heart rending, only this time she was doing it in Riley's Lazy-Boy in her stocking feet, watching a soap opera, and Louise was appalled. "What on earth," she said, "is going on in here? Bebe hasn't been dead a week."

"She's got her sight back but somebody's stole her baby!" Millie said, pointing to a woman on TV. She looked up and smiled at Louise and went right on back to watching the show.

Louise couldn't believe it. She disapproved of soap operas, as a general rule. They were good for only one thing and that was hair. No matter what the situation—rich or poor, dumb or smart—everyone had a million-dollar hairdo. Louise watched a forty-year-old woman kissing a cool, blowdried youth and then she snapped the TV off and crossed her arms, preparing to lecture Millie like she always did, only Millie was up in a flash, turning the TV back on and getting the reception fine tuned.

"Hon," said Millie, "Brad's about to run off with Olivia. Do you have any idea how mad Tara's going to be?"

"Millie, hon, I think it's about time you turned that thing off."

Millie held her hand up in the air. "Shhhh!" and then she said, "Ohhhh, he's going to do it, he's going to do it. I can't believe Olivia convinced him to do it."

Louise decided to give up on Millie and go find Earline, but she didn't have to. Earline came plowing out of the bathroom, tugging at her pantyhose, almost knocking her down. "What did I miss? What did I miss?"

"Did you see that?" asked Millie, not taking her eyes off of the TV even for a second. "Brad ran off with Olivia."

"What? You've got to be kidding!"

"No. It's true. He's taking her to the ranch."

"Ohhhh," said Earline, "Tara's going to be furious." Earline was still working her hose up her legs when Buck and Riley came through the front door.

Riley looked at the TV set and asked, "What's this?"

"Okay, girls," said Louise, smoothing down her white streak, "for the last time, I said turn that thing off." She marched across the room and pulled the plug on the set, feeling like a heroine—knowing that Riley would come running over to her with his deepest gratitude. This was what Louise was thinking, which was why she was so surprised when Riley grabbed the TV cord and plugged it back in.

Riley yelled, "Damn! That was Brad, wasn't it?" and then, "Damn Louise. You can't go turning the TV off like that

125

when people are watching. What's Brad doing with Olivia, anyway?" he asked, turning to Earline. "I thought he and Tara were having a thing?"

And Buck said, "If you were Brad, wouldn't you be with Olivia?" And then as he sat down on the couch next to Earline, casually dropping his arm behind her neck, he looked up at Louise and said, "Hey doll, got any coffee back there? I've got a hangover that won't quit."

It was a week later and Gladys Bessinger was back and in full swing. Overnight her fancy neon TRES CHIC sign had been replaced with an even fancier, multicolored neon sign. This time it read: PELO BONITO, with a beautiful dark haired Spanish woman dancing wildly in red and black around a giant green frond palm tree. And this time it blinked.

Gladys' doors were open and her parking lot was filling up, and the phones were ringing all over town again. Ringing right into Ruby McSwain's head, where she had been dreaming that she was taking her final bow at the Hair Show, holding a trophy in one hand and a ticket to Las Vegas in the other. Tom Jones was by her side. Then suddenly, an alarm went off and the judges rushed up on the stage and took it all away, saying, "I'm sorry. It seems we've made a grave mistake." Ruby could see Tom Jones turning into Gladys, adjusting her dress, patting her hair, getting ready to take her prize, but the lights were so bright and the alarm was ringing so loud, it woke Miss Ruby up.

She looked at the time, seven o'clock, and picked up the phone. It was Ronder, calling to see if she needed her to come over.

"No, I don't think so," said Miss Ruby. "Why? Is something wrong?"

"You bet," said Ronder. "Gladys is back." She began filling Ruby in on the news. Ruby walked the cord into the kitchen and spotted Yvonne peering through the curtains. She was ringing the doorbell with one hand, while holding her little beauty school suitcase with the other.

"Come on, Ruby!" Yvonne shouted. "Open up. We can't let these people get to us."

Miss Ruby was shaking when she hung up on Ronder, and still shaking five minutes later when Yvonne took her into the bathroom and took out all her hair pins and began brushing her hair.

Yvonne was brushing so hard, she was snapping Miss Ruby's neck. Miss Ruby knew that something must be bothering her, too. Then it dawned on her. Not only was Gladys back, but today was the day Duran was coming in, and suddenly Miss Ruby felt all dry and gritty and wrong.

Yvonne said, "Don't worry about a thing, Miss Ruby. It's just like you told me. A couple of old bats like ourselves have got to stick together."

So they did. Yvonne picked out Miss Ruby's clothes and dressed her, while neither woman talked and Miss Ruby shook. Then they drove silently to the shop and went in the back door, with Miss Ruby pressing at the sides of her new updo while Yvonne pulled her along. They passed the dispensary, where Thurston had taken a load of towels out of the dryer so Yvonne could fold them; past the wig room, which was no bigger than a walk in closet, and into a shop that was empty of everything, except Thurston, who was mesmerized, looking in the mirror. He kept making these little gasps, higher and shorter than that of a buzzing bee.

"Oh my God! Male pattern baldness!" he finally yelled. He pressed his hair apart on the top of his head and looked harder and harder and sure enough, right up there on top of his head was a patch of skin.

"It was the first thing Duran noticed when he got out of jail," wailed Thurston. "How big is it, Yvonne?"

"Oh, about the size of an egg. And it's about that same shape. As a matter of fact, if you put an egg in that slot, it would fit there perfectly."

"An egg?!" Thurston squealed.

"Where's Duran?" asked Miss Ruby.

"He took one look at all the people that weren't in here and said he was going back to bed. An egg?!" he cried again.

"Well, where's Ronder?" asked Miss Ruby. "Did she go back to bed, too?" She looked out across the square, wringing her hands, not believing her eyes.

"She went over to look at Gladys' shop," said Thurston, parting his hair faster and faster. His mouth was getting a funny metallic taste in it, and his tongue felt twice as large as normal.

"Are you telling me," Miss Ruby began to yell, "that Ronder Jeffcoat actually went over there? Walked out of this shop and into that one? Why, I'll fire her on the spot, that little bitch."

"Miss Ruby, calm down, pay attention," said Thurston, who was sitting down and standing up and sitting down and standing up again. "I'm the one who's upset here. I don't know what I'm going to do. I'm going bald!"

"Oh shut up, Thurston," said Miss Ruby. "It's just stress. Be still for a minute. There are some things I have to figure out."

Ruby had spent over five thousand dollars renovating the shop, and now with Gladys back, she knew she was in trouble. She was going to be the laughing stock of Stuckey, South Carolina unless she did something fast.

She stood in the middle of her empty reception room at eight o'clock in the morning, and except for Yvonne scuttling around and Thurston moaning, everything was completely silent. Suddenly Ronder blasted through the front door, her face all flushed. "You would not believe what she has done. Gladys has put in sun beds. Oh, honey, you're worse than I thought," she said, taking Ruby's hands in hers.

"Sun beds?" Miss Ruby jerked away and pressed her hand against her stomach, which felt heavy and sick.

"That's right," said Ronder. "The kind you lay down on and get a suntan in, and get this . . ."

"You are fired!" said Miss Ruby, turning her back on Ronder.

"Oh nonsense." Ronder went on, "Not only does she have sun beds, each one of the stations in the shop represents a different European city. There's France and Spain and London and Germany. The French one even has a poster of the Eiffel Tower that goes all the way from the ceiling to the floor. And Miss Ruby, are you paying any attention to me?"

"How could you go over there?" Ruby asked with her back still turned. Ronder could hear her crying.

"Come on, Miss Ruby. How else was I going to find out what she did? You wanted to know, didn't you?" Ronder patted Miss Ruby on the back and walked her into the Chez Ronder Room and sat her down on a chaise lounge. "Okay," she said, "have you gotten a hold of yourself yet?"

Miss Ruby nodded.

"Okay, you sure now?"

She nodded again.

"Okay," said Ronder, "because I've got some plans."

She took some foundation and dotted it onto Miss Ruby's cheeks, throat, forehead and under her eyes, and began to circle it around in light upward strokes as she talked. "You see, Miss Ruby, her place may look real good, and it does, there is no doubting that. But there's something wrong with it. I don't know, it lacks some kind of homey quality or something. Now this place here, it feels like a home. Or else it used to until you went and did all this to it." Ronder spread her arms wide to demonstrate the whole Chez Ronder Room.

Miss Ruby rubbed the right side of her throat and quietly listened.

"Now what we need to do is get back down to the basics. We need to combine the glamour and the glitz with your special down home touch. But first, you're going to need to listen to what Gladys has done over there, so we can come up with an idea of how to work against it."

Ronder picked up an eye shadow compact with Misty Blues and Raspberry Rose shades and proceeded to tell Miss Ruby all about what Gladys had done.

"Okay, remember all that track lighting, all those mirrors?"

Miss Ruby nodded her head.

"Be still," said Ronder, applying a blue shadow from Ruby's eyelid to her brow. "Well, she's still got that. She isn't going to give that away. But she's also put the names of the hairdressers in neon above all the stations. I mean, even if the operator in the French station decided to leave today, and she hired someone else to take his place, the new guy would still be called Raphael."

"Raphael?" asked Miss Ruby, grabbing at a shiver that was running up her neck.

"That's correct. The neon sign reads RAPHAEL." Ronder circled some rose shadow on the outside corner of Miss Ruby's eyes. "Here hon, this will bring your color back some. Anyway, Miss Ruby, you should hear Gladys going on about what a neat idea it is. From now on, no matter who works for her, no matter how much turnover there is, there will always be a Raphael, a Carlos, a Trevor, a Wilhelm, a Tonino and a Lars of Norway."

"Lars of Norway?" Miss Ruby pushed away the makeup brush and stared at Ronder.

Ronder laughed. "Yes, he's quite blond."

"I didn't hear you mentioning any women's names," said Yvonne, coming in and cracking everyone up, because everybody knew that the only time Gladys would ever hire a woman would be if she could hire one right out from under Miss Ruby's nose.

"Well, anyway," said Ronder, turning back to Miss Ruby and applying a thick coat of mascara to her eyelashes, "my idea is this. What you need is to be associated with something. You need to be considered the authority figure on anything that has to do with hair. So I was thinking, what if you went on the radio every day at the same time and talked for five or ten minutes about hair?"

Miss Ruby's eyes opened wide, dotting and smearing her mascara.

"Damn!" said Ronder, laughing. She pulled out a Q-tip and rolled it around on the smeared part, and she and Ruby and Yvonne went to town. They discussed everything, from "Ruby McSwain's Minutes on Hair," to "Dr. Hair," to "The Frizz Hour," and then they moved on to even sillier topics like, "What to Do If the Man You Date Has the Wrong Hair." They were whooping and grabbing at their stomachs, and going down even crazier paths, pretty much knowing they were going to come back to "Ruby McSwain's Minutes on Hair," until Ronder stopped laughing and said, "Wait, wait. I've got it. How about this one. Picture this. A woman drives up to a gas station and will only push her window button down one thirtieth of an inch to slip out her credit card because it is raining outside and she doesn't want her hair to frizz. This will be called . . . called . . . what? Come on. Help me out."

Nobody talked for a few seconds. Yvonne and Ronder and Ruby just sat there and held their breath. Then they all looked at each other and burst out laughing at the same time, harder than ever. Then, right there in that room, in that little hair shop that didn't have one single customer at eight-thirty on a Wednesday morning, they devised the one weapon that was going to be so useful in the war against Gladys.

It was decided, by unanimous decision, except for Thurston who was too busy in the other room doing strand tests on his hair, that Ronder Jeffcoat, starting as soon as was negotiable, would go on the air with the "What Will the Weather Do to Your Hair Today" report.

Suddenly a loud piercing scream came from the back of the shop. They ran out and found Thurston staring in horror at what was supposed to be Duran's new station. "He's on his way in!" he yelled, trying to rip apart what lay before their eyes. "I just saw El Dog circling the square. Duran will be here any minute. Quick, we've got to get this stuff off!"

It was amazing that no one had noticed the station before. It was a bigger than life religious shrine. Stretched across Duran's mirror were dozens of hairnets tied together. Decorating the hairnets were voodoo dolls, hexagons, and Buddhist prayer sticks. Stars of David, crucifixes, African cannibal beads, and everything from every culture that had anything to do with religion was spaced apart in some mystical order, lying against or on or in the brushes, hairsprays and the Barbicide Jar.

So nobody really knew what to do when Duran made his entrance, seconds later. He was all dressed up in a sleek black gangster suit, wearing lizard skin lifts and a shiny silver tie. He turned around once one way, and then he turned around twice the other way. Then on his third turn he stopped flat, holding on to his lapels, and said, "So, how do you like my new suit?"

Everyone was speechless, and Duran held up his finger as if to say wait a minute. Then he did his little routine over again, only this time he ended with a little tap of his boot.

But everyone's faces were still just as blank as before.

Then he saw the shrine.

Thurston started trying to pull the prayer sticks out of the hairnets again, but they just seemed to get more tangled up. It seemed like voodoo dolls were falling from everywhere.

"Yvonne?" asked Miss Ruby, who kept looking cautiously over at Duran. "Do you know anything about this?"

Yvonne stared at it in amazement.

When she had started out planning it, and even when she had begun to erect it, the shrine seemed so little, as if there wasn't going to be enough stuff in it to ward off the impending evil she had foreseen in her dreams. Now it just blazed out across the shop like an angry red scar and for a minute she thought she must be going crazy. "Did I do that?" she asked.

"No, baby, I brought it all the way with me from prison," said Duran, laughing. "You know how blacks are." He began to laugh even harder, only he was laughing alone.

Yvonne and Ronder and Ruby and Thurston were all standing there with tight necks and shoulders, afraid that Yvonne might have reached that fine line where sanity fades and senility takes over.

But Duran had already left once because of an empty shop. He wasn't about to leave again because of some practical joke. As a matter of fact, he placed it right up there with one of the funnier things that had ever happened to him.

"Hey, it reminds me of home," he joked. "You know," he said, picking up a Catholic incense sensor and swinging it around, "I begged and pleaded but they wouldn't let me have one of these in prison. It really made me kind of mad." He circled it around his body and then around Thurston's and then Yvonne's.

After everything that everyone had heard about him, nobody had expected Duran to be what Duran was all about. He was cool and calm and could walk into a room and size

134

a person up and tell immediately whether he could boss that person around or know what kind of promises he would need to promise them. This time it was no different. He said, "I think I'm going to like it here. She's a trip," he said, cracking everyone, but Yvonne, up.

Here's what Yvonne had expected Duran to be like.

Yvonne had woken up the night before with the night sweats. Her chest and even the insides of her elbows were just dripping with sweat. At first she had thought it was those peanut butter crackers that she had eaten right before she went to bed. Then she remembered the scarf and the boots and the gown, all bright pinks and greens and oranges, screaming neon at her in her dreams, wrapping and swirling around Duran as he pranced into the shop blotting his newly painted lips, leaving a scent of women's perfume trailing behind him. It was a bad dream, a horrible dream, and Yvonne couldn't get the way he was flashing and flipping his wrists out of her mind. She hadn't slept a wink all night.

Now, here he was in living color, with nothing swirling about him, just a simple gangster's suit on. And everyone seemed to love him.

The phone rang.

"I'll get it," said Miss Ruby, running to the front. "Let's just hope it's a client."

It was a woman, soliciting for Pelo Bonito, and it took Ruby a few beats before she could get the name oriented in her mind. It was the name of Gladys' new shop.

"Good morning and congratulations!" the merry voice said. "Your name is one of the first names on our list to call. We would like to inform you about our new tanning salon. We are offering a first time free . . ."

Miss Ruby hung up on her. She looked at her empty appointment book, then through the binoculars at Gladys', where she saw Louise and Earline coming out of her shop, dressed exactly alike, looking like two old clowns, the way they were always grinning and talking and never once both-ering to hear one word the other said. That's when the idea came to Miss Ruby like a light bulb flashing over her head just like they do in the comics. It was so simple she couldn't believe she hadn't thought of it sooner.

After fixing hair for over thirty-five years Yvonne didn't think she'd ever really learn anything new again. All those New York styles that were all the rage now, were simply takeoffs from the old days. Yvonne just had to look at the pictures to understand how to do them. But this thing Duran was showing her—this thing about straightening black hair before you curled it—it was all new to her.

And it was all happening so fast. Celebrity Styling was becoming the new black shop in town. Miss Ruby may not have been competition for Gladys, but she was sure giving the Vanity Box a run for its money. It seemed like every head of black hair in town was coming in for a Duran special.

Yvonne had had her mind set on black hair feeling like steel wool, not at all soft, like cotton. And when she told this to Duran, he couldn't stop laughing and began to tell her everything. "Baby, you know in jail there are styles that you wear that tell people that you are the one with power." Duran told her this as he put his marcel iron to his client's head. He was in the mood to talk. "Yeah," he said, looking at Yvonne's eyes as they widened. He laughed. "This one dude had me shave his initials onto the side of his head. And I won't even tell you what those initials spelled out. He was a mean daddy. He told me if I used the same tools on his head that I did on women, that he'd break my face."

Yvonne didn't understand why any man would get upset about something like that, until Duran explained, "No, baby, not that kind of woman. He was talking about men that dress up like women. Like him," said Duran, winking and pointing towards the Chez Ronder Room.

He was pointing at Thurston, who was now hooked on looking into the Chez Ronder mirror, seeing that spot on the top of his head shining out like a silver dollar deciding one moment that it wasn't so bad and the next moment that it was the end of his career, his life.

Ronder looked at Thurston, all hunched over himself, looking pasty and white, looking at himself in the mirror. He looked exactly like she felt.

For days now if it hadn't been one thing it had been another that was breaking Thurston down. First off, there was Annabella. Thurston's New York model had called and said she couldn't make it to the Hair Show. And after she had said yes to more money, she had called back insisting on a first class ticket with Delta and Delta only. Then she called back even again, demanding that a limo be waiting for her at the airport upon her arrival.

Thurston had said yes to everything and stomped around the shop yelling at everyone for the rest of the day, including his clients. Especially Mrs. Krepps, who, when she had asked, "Thurston, are you sure this is the right hairstyle for me?" Thurston had replied by putting his hands on his hips and huffing at her, "Well! I never! Madam, do you question your doctor when he prescribes medicine for you?"

Now, to top it off, there was this thing with going bald. It was a wonder with the way he'd been carrying on so and flinging his arms about, that he had any hair left at all.

After Ronder had told Thurston five times that his little bald spot wasn't so bad, Thurston screamed at her, "What are you saying to me?!"

"I don't know anymore," she said, her hands on her hips. "What is it that you want me to say?"

"Well just don't say it's not *so* bad. It's either bad or not bad. There's no such thing as so bad when you're talking about hair, honey."

"Okay, then, it's bad. You've got a bad little bald patch on top of your head, Thurston."

"Thanks a lot, Ronder. Just thanks a whole hell of a lot!" Thurston stamped out, looking every inch like Buck did the day she had left him in jail.

The thing with Buck had gone something like this: After Ronder had gotten back from the jail, she had put all of Buck's clothes out on the lawn, changed all the locks on the doors and nailed the windows shut. She had shown no mercy. It was dark and raining hard and when Riley had finally driven up with Buck, everything was completely soaked through, and Buck had to stand outside for half an hour, begging to be let back in. Ronder slipped a note through the front of their double wide. Written on it were two choices: (1) Stay outside or (2) Take a job that one of my clients' husbands has offered you. Laying Sheetrock.

He took the job. Then he took her to dinner. And then he took her to bed. And ever since then her stomach had been upset for days, as if she didn't know if the choice he had made was the best one for her.

Thurston spent the rest of the day calling Atlanta and New York, Chicago and L.A. and they all gave him the same old story. They'd have to see him first.

"One woman told me that they could cut my scalp, pull

it tight and then sew it back on like a rug for just under a few thousand dollars," he told Miss Ruby as she walked back into the Celebrity Styling carrying an arm load of bags.

"Well, put your mind at rest," she said, "because I've got something to show you that will take your mind off all your worries."

"Hold on," said Thurston. "Before you show me anything, I have to tell you that I've made a decision and I'm standing firm." He came around from the other side of the desk and grabbed Miss Ruby's elbows. "Miss Ruby, I've decided that we aren't going to the Hair Show this year. I can't stand the thought of anybody seeing me with my hair like this. And of course without me, you have no chance of winning. I'm sorry to let you down, Miss Ruby, truly I am, but there's no other choice."

There, he had said it.

Miss Ruby let out a short laugh. "Of course you're going. Now listen, I have the perfect thing for you. You're going to love it. As a matter of fact the minute you see it, you'll be counting the minutes until we leave for Atlanta."

She handed him one of the bags she was carrying, proudly, and he ripped it open.

And there, hanging in the air by as few of his fingers as possible, as if he were emptying a litter box, was the busiest cowboy suit that had ever left a sewing machine. He turned it around and around, examining the elaborately embroidered flowers, the rhinestones that looked like big pieces of candy that had been sucked and then stuck on, the suede tassels that dangled from the pockets and the sleeves.

Miss Ruby looked so proud of herself, standing there, hugging the other bags. "Don't you just love it, Thurston? Isn't it you? When I first saw it, it just knocked me out. It had Hair Show written all over it."

She waited for Thurston to respond, but he was still studying the chaps and the silver spurs that came with the outfit.

140

The whole get-up looked like something that belonged in a Fast Food Roast Beef Restaurant. Thurston dropped it to the floor and screamed. He kicked it across the room and screamed again. "Ahhhh! Get it away! I can't wear that. It's the ugliest thing I've ever seen."

Miss Ruby took one long look at Thurston and headed for the back of the shop.

20

Thurston found Ruby in the dispensary, curled up in a fetal position in an old chair by the washing machine. She was holding tight to her shopping bags and Yvonne was trying to get her to snap out of whatever was going on. "Come on, Miss Ruby," she said, "come on, tell me what happened."

Yvonne had on rubber gloves that had hair relaxer on them. She tried to pick Miss Ruby up with her wrists, but Miss Ruby wasn't budging.

"What happened to her, Thurston?" Yvonne screamed. "What did you do to her? I'd better call an ambulance."

"No don't. Miss Ruby, it was the chaps, that was all. I just couldn't take the chaps," he said.

Miss Ruby didn't make a move. Yvonne just stared at him.

"Come on Miss Ruby," he said, pulling the bags out of the tight grip she had on them. "Let me see the other stuff you got for me."

He peeked in one of the bags and said, smiling, "Here, Yvonne, quick, go put this on."

"What is it?" she asked.

142

He kept stroking Miss Ruby's forehead. "Don't ask. Just do it." He tried to say loving and cooing things to Ruby, continuing to stroke her forehead, her cheek.

His knees were shaking. He couldn't tell if that was because he was in a strange squatting position trying to soothe her, or if it was because of Yvonne, who was taking a really long time to put her outfit on.

There was a reason for the delay. Yvonne was standing in the bathroom looking at herself in the mirror, wearing almost the same suit that Thurston had kicked across the floor minutes before. Only her cowboy suit was a cowgirl suit. It was a dress; a very short dress. And the first thing Thurston noticed when she walked up was Yvonne's fifty-year-old knees poking out from beneath it.

He turned away and began fanning Miss Ruby with the top of a bleach box which he had torn off. "Miss Ruby, Yvonne's here. Look, she's all dressed up like a little cowgirl."

Miss Ruby looked up and Thurston helped her to stand. "What do you think, darling?"

"Oh," she smiled weakly, "it's better than I thought. She looks so cute. Doesn't she, Thurston? So sweet."

Thurston didn't want to look again, so he turned in Yvonne's direction as fast as he could with his eyes closed. "She's a doll, Miss Ruby. You've outdone yourself this time."

Miss Ruby reached over and touched him. "You really like it? You really like yours? You promise it was just the chaps you didn't like?"

He was so happy to see her happy, he nodded his head up and down and said, "That's all, Ruby baby, just the chaps."

"Well, you know," she said, snapping out of her little tantrum as if it hadn't even taken place, "I was against them, too, at first, but then I couldn't decide. So finally I just decided that with your taste, you'd probably go crazy for them. Isn't that strange how you can be so wrong about a person sometimes?"

Thurston hugged Miss Ruby and said, "Yes, yes," and patted her back. He winked at Yvonne, who was standing by the bleaches, holding her arms down, squeezing her legs as if she were naked.

Miss Ruby looked up at him and said, "Thurston, do me a favor. Please. Please put yours on. I'm just dying to see what it looks like."

It took a little while, ten minutes to be exact, but Thurston finally walked up to the front looking like he was about to try out for the Grand Ole Opry. Miss Ruby was so happy. It didn't even bother her very much when she walked past the Chez Ronder Room and noticed Earline and Louise sitting there, filling Ronder in on more of the Gladys Bessinger gossip.

"Did you know," said Earline, "that Gladys has even got a television in every station?"

"Not only that," said Louise, "but she's also got a clock at each station telling exactly what time it is in that country. If I were getting my hair done over there, I'd sit in Spain. I just love Spain."

Ronder wasn't listening. She was brushing out Louise's hair for it to be shampooed and she was feeling sick. It seemed like she was so nauseated all the time lately, ever since Buck had taken her out late that first night back from jail. At first she thought it had been some bad clams, but now she was thinking stress.

The only thing she was sure about was that she couldn't imagine working with a hot blowdryer now. Just the thought of that heat made her head spin and her stomach turn. Lately, she'd found it a lot easier just to talk women who never should have them into getting shampoo-and-sets so she wouldn't have to worry about the fainting.

"The way I see it," she had told Thurston the day before, "I just roll them up, stick them under the dryer, set the timer for thirty minutes and Presto! It's faster than cooking a TV dinner."

They had laughed about that for an hour, only now it

wasn't so funny. Now Ronder was bending over her Chez Ronder shampoo bowl, sweating and scrubbing Louise's hair while Louise stuck her fingers in her ears and squeezed her eyes shut tight to keep the water out, and continued to talk about Gladys and her new shop, and Buck and his new criminal record.

"If nothing else," she said to Ronder, "it was impressive, dear. Hon, don't forget to get the back of my neck real good. You know, somebody told me that he was in jail for three whole days. Is that right?"

So there Ronder was, sick as a dog, upset that Buck had put her in this situation in the first place, and suddenly she noticed the strangest thing. Louise used a razor on her eyebrows and around her lips. Louise Stokes shaved. Ronder hated Buck more at that moment than she had at any other moment in her life.

"Louise, if people don't quit talking about Buck, I'm going to get upset," she said, squeezing the suds out of her hair too hard.

Louise opened her eyes and looked up, craning her neck to get a better look at Ronder. "Come to think of it, you don't look very well. Are you all right?"

"Well, now that you ask, not really. My stomach's been upset for days."

The water began to run a little cold, but Ronder was leaning against the bowl not paying any attention.

"Well," said Louise as she patted Ronder's hand, motioning for her to get the water hotter, "you do look kind of white. I tell you what. As soon as you comb me out, you should go on home."

Ronder's head was spinning faster, and it felt like she had cotton in her ears, her mouth, her eyes. And she couldn't seem to get her mind off of Buck.

She knew that things were exactly as they appeared in the movies, and even though Buck was working every day now, she knew that she was going to have to keep a sharp eye out on him. This wasn't really hard, since practically everywhere he went he had to get a ride from her due to his D.U.I.

It was no wonder she felt bad. She probably wasn't sick at all, just merely exhausted from running him all over town in that little Japanese rental. It had helped when Buck started getting rides from a friend, but even then she had to drive him to the mall to meet him. And lately he'd gotten into the habit of waking her up real early. A good example of that was this morning, when he had started shaking her at six, saying, "Hurry, hurry hurry!" Before Ronder knew it, she was flying down the road faster than lightning with his feet tapping to beat the band and her, with not an ounce of makeup on, not even her false eyelashes.

"Come on, come on, Ronder. I'm going to miss my ride!" he had yelled, tapping away.

So she had driven even faster and screeched up to the mall, right in front of Sears, and not a soul was there except for her and Buck. And he had looked over at her and said, "You got any money?"

Ronder put a second shampoo onto Louise's hair and remembered it all so clearly. "Buck, when are you going to get paid?" she had asked.

"Soon, Ronder. Real soon," he had said. "I have to work a couple of weeks first before they can give me a check. You know how it is."

So she had given him every red cent of the tips she had made from doing all those bikini waxings, which wasn't much.

"Ronder, is that all you got?"

"Buck!"

"Never mind." He'd had some nerve, just getting out of the car without even a kiss or a goodbye or anything. It had upset her to no end, she thought, squeezing the suds out of Louise's hair a little tighter even than the first rinse.

Louise was frowning.

Well, thought Ronder, at least he's a working man now, and that's no small thing. But Lord, was she ever tired.

"I don't believe it!" yelled Earline, jumping up. "Look what the cat dragged in, will you?" She pulled a wide-eyed Millie Loudermilk through the Chez Ronder hanging beaded curtains.

Millie stopped and stroked the beaded curtains and stared in wonderment at the same posters that Thurston had been begging Miss Ruby to take down ever since the first day he had come into the shop. They were of beautiful women with beautiful smiles and, Millie thought, beautiful updos. She had always wanted her hair fixed that very same way, only she could never afford to get her hair done once a week. But wouldn't it have been a luxury? Her ex-husband would've hated it if she had worn her hair that way. He liked her simple. But he was from the same bottom of the heap that Miss Ruby's ex had come from, and maybe it really was time for Millie to go for the big change. She pointed to one of the posters, showing a smiling woman with a fluffy chignon. "I want my hair done up like that one up there," she said.

"Oh honey, no!" said Louise, who was now getting the back of her hair rolled. "That hairdo is sure to give you jowls."

Millie looked into the Chez Ronder mirror. "I don't have jowls."

"No," said Earline, butting in, "but you will if you wear that. My cousin, you know the one over in Fayettville? She got that exact same haircut just two weeks ago, and is she ever sorry. It looks like she's aged ten years and gained ten pounds."

"Let me see that," said Ronder, moving up to the poster and turning Millie this way and that. "I'm afraid she's right, Millie. With your bone structure you can't wear something on the crown of your head like that. You need more height up front. Let me think on it for a while. We'll come up with something you'll like."

Ronder went back to rolling Louise's hair. She didn't want to think about anything else today. Louise handed her roller clips with one hand and lit up a cigarette with the other. The smoke rose up thick into Ronder's nose, making her sicker than ever. She was still too young for menopause, but all of a sudden she was having Hot Flashes. It was going to be a disaster if she didn't take her mind off of that cigarette.

Ruby was up at the desk, hearing everything about Gladys that was floating out from the Chez Ronder Room while she frantically drew up a new secret plan to get her clients back. Spain or no Spain, TVs in every station or not, she had so much to do in such a short amount of time, she didn't know whether to do this or that first, so she continued to draw while she picked up the phone and dialed her ex-brother-in-law and told him what she needed. He said, "No problem," that four or five of his friends would be over shortly to bring Miss Ruby's dream to life.

Miss Ruby knew that Gladys may have the upper hand now but that soon, real soon, she was going to just die with envy.

After Ronder had written up a ticket for Louise and Earline and sent them talking, talking, still talking about Gladys and Buck, out the front door, she slipped off into the dispensary and slipped into her brand-new Indian costume, complete with a one feathered headband and a belt of colored corn.

"Oh brother," she sighed. "It's so short." But as she tugged at the hem, she noticed Yvonne in her even shorter cowgirl dress. It was the first time Ronder had noticed Yvonne's knees. She looked at her own and then back at Yvonne's and decided not to complain. She couldn't decide whether to wear the feather at the front or the back of her head, and went to ask Miss Ruby, who was handing Thurston his final present—a great big red ten gallon cowboy hat.

"With this on," said Ruby, joking around with him, "nobody will even know you're bald, baby."

Thurston's face dropped. It had come to this. A hat. A cowboy hat. A red cowboy hat. He squared it on his head and looked in the mirror, sadly. Who'd have ever thought that Thurston, a.k.a. Billy Joyner from Spartanburg, South Carolina, would be standing in the middle of a beauty shop, going bald in a red cowboy hat. Ronder decided it would be better to ask about her feather another time. There was no rush. The smell of closing time was heavy in the air.

That's when a woman walked in. She was a big boned woman, a tall woman, and a woman who looked more like a man dressed up like a woman than a woman woman. Or maybe she looked like a high class hooker type. Ronder couldn't figure it out. All she knew was that there was something vaguely familiar about her. But she would have been hard pressed to say just exactly what that was.

Miss Ruby noticed it right off. "Oh my God!" she said, cupping her hand to her mouth.

"Darling," the woman turned to Miss Ruby, "do you happen to know where I can find a Thurston somebody?" She didn't just ask either. She flipped her hair and asked. Hair that Ronder thought was way overdue for a color job.

Thurston, who was underneath his new huge cowboy hat still calling long distance, swung around with the phone still at his ear and said, "I am The Great Thurston."

The woman struck a sexy pose against some invisible object in the middle of the room. "Well, I am Annabella."

The expression on Thurston's face said it all. Those black roots were just glaring out at him and he couldn't get over her age. Something terrible had happened to her on her flight down from New York, he thought. She didn't look a thing like her picture.

"You're not supposed to be here yet," he said, still covering the receiver.

"I decided to catch an earlier flight." She switched to

another pose and began flicking her fingernails, as if she were waiting for something elaborate to happen, and acting like it had better happen fast. "Well?" she asked, scanning Thurston's cowboy outfit, making him feel like he had training wheels on his boots instead of spurs.

Ronder could see every little bit of Thurston's energy draining out of him. She wanted to rush up and protect him. She wanted to bury his head in her breasts just like a mama. But no one could move.

The minutes passed like eternity as he hung up on the San Diego Men's Hair Club, and then it dawned on him just exactly who the woman standing before him looked like. She looked exactly like his mother.

21

Duran found Thurston standing alone studying Annabella's picture, shaking his head back and forth, looking so small under his new red cowboy hat. "I just don't understand, I just don't understand," he kept saying. Over and over again he said, "I just don't understand at all."

"Airbrush and retouch, darling," said Duran. "It goes all the way back to the Egyptians. See how they brought her jaw up?"

While Duran pointed at the high gloss shot of Annabella, the real Annabella was making history in the Celebrity Styling Shop's reception area. She was picking all the shampoos, conditioners and brushes up, and so fast. Something about her didn't sit right with Miss Ruby. She felt like Annabella might start lifting some of the things into her pocketbook or something.

Annabella picked up a bottle of hair conditioner and unscrewed the cap. "This stuff cost as much as it smells?" she asked.

Miss Ruby pulled it away from her and said, "More, darling. Why don't you take a seat. Thurston will be right back."

The thing was, Annabella was a nervous type and drinking made her even more nervous. Annabella had to drink to go South. Somewhere along the way, she had picked up a beefy looking man in a tan suit and now he, too, stood in the middle of the shop looking familiar and nervous. His suit looked as if it had been hung up wrong, and he had all five of Annabella's suitcases either in his hands or at his feet. They both smelled like martinis.

For a minute it ran through Miss Ruby's mind that this was it. That these two strangers who stood before her were people she'd seen plastered up at the Post Office, wanted for murder or rape or both. They both certainly looked the type. Especially Annabella, who had obviously taken great pains in the airplane bathroom applying her foundation, eye makeup, lip liner, gloss and everything else in the book onto her face and around her temples and up her neck. This did not go unnoticed by Miss Ruby, who was mentally scrubbing Annabella's face with a washcloth and cold cream to see what was underneath.

"Oh hey, Harper." Yvonne yelled over the vacuum cleaner as it hummed loudly over the lobby rug. "I thought your appointment was next week."

The man grinned foolishly and Miss Ruby was relieved to see that he was a customer. For a minute there she had thought she was going to be involved in a real live stickup. With that fear over, she went back to mentally reapplying Annabella's makeup, only this time she did it her way. But still, she could see that it was going to be a long long Hair Show for Thurston.

"Oh there you are," Annabella said, turning around to the man Yvonne had called Harper. She eased up close to Miss Ruby, rolled her eyes and gave her a knowing look. "He was following me around the airport. I couldn't get rid of him so I let him carry my bags and give me a ride over."

"You remember me?" he asked Miss Ruby, loosening his tie and scratching his neck.

Miss Ruby looked blankly at him and then looked over at Yvonne.

"He gets his face peeled every other week by Thurston," said Yvonne, turning off the vacuum. "Harper Mack."

"Hello Harper," said Miss Ruby. And Harper held out a sweaty palm.

Yvonne couldn't stand Harper. It always seemed like he was gloating over her. She just knew he must be a homosexual. She couldn't imagine a man going to Thurston and not being one.

The change that had come over Harper when he first spotted Yvonne did not go unnoticed by Annabella. "Whew, thank God! I thought I'd have him tailing me for the rest of my life," she said, reaching over and hitting Ronder on the arm. Ronder just stared at her and absentmindedly played with her belt of corn.

"He's one of those types," continued Annabella, "that you can't ever get rid of even when you tell them to get lost."

The phone rang then and everyone just stood around staring at each other while Miss Ruby answered it. It was another woman soliciting for the brand-new Pelo Bonito.

"Good afternoon, señorita," the woman said. "You have been chosen as one of the five lucky winners of a free French hairstyle. All you have to do is come on by Pelo . . ."

Miss Ruby interrupted, "Honey, believe me, they give the worst haircuts in town at that place. I would never go there myself."

The woman on the other end of the line sounded like she was in a small closet sized room with three other girls all doing the same thing. She said, "Really? Well, they told me I could get my hair cut for free over there if I wanted, but you say I shouldn't?"

"Absolutely not," said Miss Ruby, sitting back enjoying herself. "I used to have the most beautiful hair. It was so long I could sit on it. Then one day I went over there to get it cut. They cut it all off."

The girl let out a gasp. "That's awful!"

"I know," said Miss Ruby. "It didn't even touch my shoulders anymore. The place you should go, if you really want a good hairstyle, is that lovely little shop called The Celebrity Styling Shop. Now they can cut hair over there. And one more thing, make sure to tell all your friends."

From now on, thought Ruby as she hung up, it was war.

Annabella was leaning all over the desk, the chair, everything, like she was at home at six o'clock and waiting for her mother to hurry up and make her something to eat. Miss Ruby knew the type all right. She was the kind of woman who would put ice packs on her face when she woke up in order to get the wrinkles to go down. She'd wear tape shaped like lips between her brows to keep them from pulling together and causing wrinkles. She'd kneel, just like she was now, in those ugly tight Spandex pants, with her legs straddling the chair, in order to keep her thighs toned up.

Miss Ruby was right on the money. Annabella was flexing her thigh muscles tight. She'd read once that if you did that, it would not only get rid of cellulite, but nobody would even be able to tell that's what you were doing. She loved to do anything in secret, especially when she was bored. And she was very bored, wondering why she had bothered to come South a day early. She couldn't get over all these hokey costumes everyone was wearing. She hoped they were costumes and not some strange fashion that had caught on down here. Of course, in New York people wore strange clothes, too. But at least they were familiarly strange. Here, she felt as if she were on some Hollywood set.

Annabella flexed her buttocks ten times on the right side and ten times on the left, and wished she was still at the airport bar, but with that old yahoo Harper off selling shoes or whatever else it was he sold. The only person she even felt like she had anything in common with was Ronder, and the only thing they had in common was that they both had long blond hair. It wasn't much, but it was something.

Annabella sighed. What the hell, she thought, it's just a

few days and two thousand dollars and then it will all be over. Besides, she had never been to Atlanta before and there might be some modelling jobs available for her there. Lord knows they were thin in New York.

"Darling," she said to Harper, "hand me my coat, will you." Another thing that she had read was that a woman should never get too cold because it caused the skin to dry up and the blood to run sluggish, and from now on, for the rest of her life, she was going to have to think of wrinkles, always.

While a lot of nothing was going on up front, Thurston was in the back talking to Duran, who was leaning against one of the dryers listening to his every word. He had nothing to say to Thurston except "I told you so."

"I told you so," he said. "I have done major motion picture productions and I know all about it. Honey, I can spot a failure a mile off. I told you she wasn't the thing you wanted."

Miss Ruby had come back to see what in the world was taking Thurston so long. When she heard Duran say the word "movies," her ears pricked up. "What movies? You worked in the movies?!"

"Naturally," said Duran, nodding his head with his eyes closed. "I know everybody in Hollywood."

Miss Ruby's mouth dropped open. "Did you know Elizabeth Taylor? Everyone tells me I look and act just like her."

"Know her? Honey, I was her makeup man for years," said Duran, opening his eyes.

Miss Ruby's hands went to her breasts. "Her makeup man! Duran, oh, I can not believe this. Are her eyes really that color?"

Duran nodded. "Not only that, but she has the most devine hair I've ever put my fingers into. Do you know that that woman doesn't even dye her hair? It just colors like that naturally. I was the one that got her off the food."

Miss Ruby was amazed. "No!"

"Yes. I put her on my famous water and banana diet."

Thurston had heard it all before and knew for a fact that the closest Duran had ever gotten to a star was once, when he had done the makeup for Jim Nabors when he had ridden through town for a parade. But Thurston just let Duran go on and on about Robert Redford and Joanne Woodward and all the other big names, because he had fish of his own to fry.

Thurston was now talking to Annabella's picture, using his hands and trying to explain to her that something had come up, that he had gotten somebody else, or that he had come down with a virus. Something, anything. Annabella came back just as he had got to the words "Annabella, you are a very pretty woman but . . ."

She broke in. "But what? You know I can't sit around here all day. I've got to get some beauty rest."

The fact that she reminded Thurston of his mother was probably the reason he didn't say any of the things he had planned. Instead, he took her by the arm and out the front door to the Thunderbird Motor Inn, even though she said, "You told me I'd be staying at the nicest place in town."

"This is the nicest place in town." He would have preferred to drop her back off at the airport and start all over again, or stay back at work and ignore her, or watch Duran come out of the dispensary in his brand-new Indian head-dress and pretend she didn't exist at all. For a fleeting moment he even considered marrying Duran, if somebody would just get this Annabella out of his hair. But the possibilities looked grim. She was already in the door of her room waiting for him to bring in the rest of her baggage.

Meanwhile, Ronder was getting home earlier than usual, trying to figure out what she could do to make her Indian outfit look a little better. She didn't mind being an Indian but she wanted to be a sexy one. So she decided the first thing she was going to do was take out her sewing machine, lower the cleavage, and catch the end of *One Life to Live*.

But when Ronder opened her front door she found Buck watching it instead. He'd obviously been there all day long, and not alone. Bags of pretzels and potato chips lay open on the couch, and beer cans were all lined up on the coffee table like big soldiers and little soldiers.

"Buck?"

"Ronder, can't you see I'm watching something?"

"Buck, why aren't you at work?"

Buck didn't answer and Ronder felt a sinking feeling in the pit of her stomach.

"Buck, how long have you been without a job?"

"A few days now, Ronder."

"And Buck, you made me rush you to the mall every day this week and you didn't even have a job?"

"Yes Ronder, I guess I did."

He got up and went to the bathroom, leaving her alone to watch a woman on TV who was supposed to have amnesia and because of this she was a bum with no family, no money, no home; only she had an expensive Winsome Wheat rinse on her hair. Ronder heard Buck running some water in the bathroom. And he was singing in his low strong voice and his singing made her sad. It made her even more sad that he hadn't even noticed she was dressed like an Indian.

It seemed like everything was upsetting her lately. She knew that the best thing for her would be to get away to the Atlanta Hair Show, only now she wished she didn't have to take Buck. But it was too late. She'd look like a fool if he didn't come now. She had told everyone at work some elaborate story covering up for his D.U.I., making him look like some kind of hero. Now everyone figured they had the best marriage in town.

She was a fool for taking up with him. She could just look around the room and tell that he'd been with another woman. For one thing, her couch smelled like Estée Lauder.

There was only one thing left to do. She was going to have to get Buck back so she could dump him on her own terms. Forget the sewing machine and the Indian suit. That could come later. For now, Buck was going to be her next and only project. She'd think of it the same way she'd think of planning the Hair Show. First there would be a step A and then a step B and before she knew it there would be a step C-D-E and then he'd be out the door and down the road to screw up somebody else's life.

Buck was still singing, only now the water had stopped running. Ronder stared straight ahead. She sat on the edge of the sofa trying to smoke a cigarette, but it was making her stomach ache. With each passing second her stomach hurt worse and worse, to the point where she could feel the pain spreading up into her arms and down into her legs. She dropped her cigarette into one of Buck's empty beer cans and as it sizzled she remembered reading about something called biorhythms. The rule was, when you were upset you were supposed to focus on one small object in the room and breath through your nose and exhale out through your mouth. Ronder held tight to her cramping stomach and focused in on a little desk calendar that was on top of the TV. It was the one that they had given her at the furniture rental place. Since she was near-sighted, she had to bend over real close to study it. Suddenly it was like someone had slapped her right in the face.

Everything came to light.

She jumped up and burst into the bathroom where Buck was taking a bubble bath, holding a mirror up to his face, trimming his nose hairs. "Get out of here!" he yelled, waving his tiny scissors in the air.

"Buck, I'll be right back. Don't you go anywhere. Do you hear me? Anywhere!" And she headed out the door, still in her Indian outfit, and jumped into her new little Japanese rental car and drove as fast as she could to the Revco to pick up a pregnancy test.

Buck was still in the bathtub when she squealed back up the drive. After she had checked to make sure he hadn't left, she ran back into the kitchen and pulled out the directions, shaking like a leaf, trying to read them. They said that if the results were positive then the results would be 99% accurate and a pretty brown ring would form. The directions actually used the word pretty.

Now in some circumstances that little brown ring would be real pretty, maybe even beautiful, but from where Ronder was standing, she would be glad if she never saw one for the rest of her life.

There were also some pills that had something to do

with rabbits, although she couldn't tell what, but she read that she was supposed to mix them in a tube with some urine and wait an hour to see if that pretty brown ring formed.

"How long are you going to be in there, Buck?" she asked, knocking on the door. There was no answer so she knocked louder. Buck came to the door with a towel wrapped around his waist, wearing some socks.

"Do you mind?" he asked. "I've got to shave." He shut the door in her face.

Ronder went out the trailer to the back, hunkering down behind the bushes. She looked to the left of her and then the right, and then went to the bathroom in a little plastic cup. She brought it back inside and after pouring some into an eyedropper, she mixed two little drops of it, along with the rabbit pills, into a tube, then set the whole thing on the kitchen table very carefully.

She sat at the table and waited. She could hear Buck still in the bathroom, but now he was drying his hair, using all three of her professional blowdryers, putting them on all the speeds. He went from hot heat to warm heat to style, and then he switched over to her Conair and used the cool speed. It was the last slap in her face. It was the final slap in her face, because when they were the happiest couple in the world and he was seeing only her, he had always just worn a cap.

After the bathroom door opened and the steam came swirling out, there stood Buck, still wearing his towel. He asked her what she was doing and looked real hard and real long at the box. She didn't say a word. They both stood there for what seemed like forever to Ronder, looking at that box, with Ronder thinking, well, it could be worse. At least he knows what's going on now. At least we'll be going through something together for a change.

And then Buck broke the spell. He pointed to the box and

said, "You aren't going to be doing somebody's hair or something this afternoon, are you? I'm hungry."

Ronder took off her Indian headdress with the feather in it, and got out some frozen hamburger and began scraping off the meat to make Buck three patties. She scraped and scraped, sticking the meat under the hot water some of the time, then scraping some more.

The smell of the meat was making everything worse. She wanted to call Miss Ruby. She wanted to call Yvonne. She wanted to call somebody and cry, but all she could do was salt the meat and fry it.

About twenty minutes later she put Buck's dinner on a tray and stuck it on his lap.

"Where's the ketchup?" he asked, holding the top of the bun in the air, looking at the hamburger.

"Hold on," and she went to get the ketchup, but instead she noticed that there was no brown ring forming in her little pregnancy test. It was way past an hour. It was time for her and Buck to have a long, long talk.

Mostly what he did was not talk. She talked and he listened. But he listened with eyes as cold as icebergs, holding his hamburger bun still in the air to let her know he wanted to eat. Then she told him she wanted a divorce.

Buck put the cold bun down and his eyes warmed up and he said, "Ronder, I will never treat you bad again. I swear I won't." He reached for her hand and gave her all he had. "Please, please, Ronder. Just one more chance. Give me just one more chance. I'll change. I promise I will. I'll be a new man."

Even though it was the same thing he had been saying since the day they were married, she was too tired for any big changes. She didn't want to move and she didn't want to pack his things again. All she wanted was some peace. And his eyes were getting even warmer and his hair was looking even prettier and she was even a little sad that she wasn't pregnant with his baby, who, between the two of

161

them would have the nicest hair in the world. Before Ronder knew what had happened to her, Buck had talked her into removing her Indian outfit and putting on the little pink thing with the matching gloves. This time Buck noticed and this time the TV set stayed off for the rest of the night.

There's a certain period in the morning, when the air is wet and smells like new car seats, and the sky looks as though it can't decide whether it should go back to being dark or not, that beauticians crawl out of their Thunderbirds, rubbing their sleepy eyes lighting their second cigarette of the morning to face another day at the shop. It was during this time that Ronder and Yvonne both got out of their cars, slamming their doors, and looked up to find a new sign replacing THE CELEBRITY STYLING SHOP sign. It was big and it blinked against the cold gray of the dawn. Some sparrows swooped above and below it and Ronder put her arm around Yvonne's shoulder and neither one of them said a word. The smoke from Ronder's cigarette swirled around Yvonne's face, just like the red neon swirled around like a lasso, spelling out THE *O.K.* HAIR CORRAL. The *O.K.* was written in cursive, lying at a slant, while the letters in THE HAIR CORRAL stood up stark, looking like fence posts.

The lights inside looked different, too, more yellow instead of the usual glaring fluorescent tubes. Ronder looked at Yvonne. Yvonne looked at Ronder. Ronder dropped her cigarette and stubbed it out with one of her Indian moccasins. She couldn't help wondering if maybe some other shoes besides Yvonne's orthopedic ones might not make her cowgirl suit look a little better. They opened the front door and the thought fled from her mind like one of the early morning sparrows.

Everything had changed. Drastically. The front desk now looked like a saloon bar, all shiny dark wood with brass circling its every move. The phone was one of those old timey jobs where the mouth piece and the ear piece are two different units. There were even specials written up on the backbar mirror, just like in a real bar, only instead of offering fancy drinks, there were fancy hair names: The Wild Bill Hickok Cut, The Buffalo Bill Perm, The Annie Oakley Bob and The Billy the Kid Frosting Special.

As Ronder shut the front door behind her, some Western Swing came belting out over the speakers, sounding like something out of Abilene, and Miss Ruby came banging through the new swinging saloon doors. She wore a lacy buxom, black and rose, satiny Las Vegas show gown, with the skirt pinched up to the knee displaying black fish net hose and high heels. A pink colored boa wrapped around her neck and a tall plumaged hat swayed on top of her head. She looked like Kitty on *Gunsmoke*.

Miss Ruby tried out a couple of poses then flounced into the nearest chair, which was one of those tight red leather arm chairs with the gold studs circling the fabric. All the chairs were like that, up to and including the wooden stools that hugged the bar.

"Howdy girls," she said. "Ronder, remember when you told me to make it warm and down home in here? Well here it is. Home home on the range!"

It made Yvonne itch all over, but Ronder told Miss Ruby the Western touch was the funniest thing. "Well Miss Ruby," she said, "the only thing that's missing is some old cows' skulls."

Miss Ruby raised her right eyebrow and held up a finger

and said, "Just wait. Wait for Thurston and Duran to get here and I'll show you the rest of the place."

It didn't take long. Miss Ruby had left strict orders on their answering machine that they were to get into the shop early, or else. "And whatever you do," she had told them, "don't forget to wear your outfits."

But when they walked in, Duran wasn't wearing his, because his was still in the back on the dryer. After he and Thurston got over their initial shock, they all walked together to the back, and that's where they all stopped again. It was the same story as the front, just more of it. Saddles and wagon wheels lined the walls, and all of Thurston's hand held dryers now looked like guns.

The piped in music switched over to "Happy Trails" as Duran dragged in from the dispensary wearing his new full Indian headdress, moccasins and gunny sack pants. His chest was bare except for a thin vest of the same gunny sack material, tied in three different places by crooked leather strings. He felt like an idiot.

Ronder was still laughing. She was the only one laughing. Everybody else was looking around. The general reaction was horror.

The first few customers walked in and almost left but Ronder convinced them "to come on back in" and served them some of Miss Ruby's new Sassafrass tea. Only one woman loved the new shop. The others felt out of place the minute they sat down at the shampoo bowl.

Yvonne just couldn't give as good a shampoo as before because her skirt kept riding up her legs and all she could think about was Thurston, somewhere nearby, looking at them. She kept trying to pull it back down.

Miss Ruby herself was in a state of bliss at the front of the shop, calling the Peachtree Plaza in Atlanta, where the Hair Show was being held, making reservations for a couple of suites under the name of Miss Ruby and her Rodeo Hairstylists.

"Your what?" asked Thurston, who was drinking coffee

as fast as he could, trying to wake up in order to get a better grip on what lay before him. He'd had nightmares all night long, and it seemed like he'd just moved from one right into another. Not one of his customers was ever going to be caught dead in a place like this. Already his three nine-thirties had called to cancel. News like this traveled fast in Stuckey. Even Louise and Earline had called in with headaches.

Nobody really knew why the clients weren't coming in. Miss Ruby had called every radio station in town and surrounding towns the night before, hoping they'd give her an advertising spot at such short notice. And the idea was so wild, they had. That, on top of her ex-brother-in-law putting flyers on every car he could find, should have brought a stampede of new women into the new *O.K.* Hair Corral. But it didn't. A few came and looked. Only a few of Thurston's regulars stuck it out. Duran's clients were the only real traffic, but they kept saying things like: "This place won't make it over night, baby" and "Glory, glory, this place seems like the place you used to go to to get those old helmut do's" and "Lord hon, if it weren't for you, I wouldn't be caught dead in a place like this. It's just too tacky to believe." Duran patted their arms and just kept cutting, trying to keep his full headdress out of the way of his scissors.

"Where's your cowboy hat, Thurston?" asked Miss Ruby, covering the receiver. "You didn't leave it at home, did you?"

"No Miss Ruby, it's right over there on the chair, see? It's too early in the morning for me to wear that heavy thing. I'll get a headache."

"Well, see that you put it on, will you?" she said and went right on back to talking to Atlanta.

Thurston's feelings were bruised. Miss Ruby had never sounded so snooty before. He couldn't believe she had the nerve to talk to him like that. He picked up his hat and walked off sulking.

"Hon." She covered the phone again and yelled after him

as he went through the new swinging Western doors. "That Harper fellow is coming in this morning to get his face peeled."

Miss Ruby was mad at Thurston for calling her four times during the night wanting to talk about Annabella. And she wasn't the only one mad at Thurston.

Duran was positively livid. He had actually walked up to Miss Ruby and demanded that she fix him coffee and bring it to his station right away. In her thirty-five years in the hair business, that had never happened to her once. Something was going on. Thurston had been pouting around the shop, and there was an air of a fight between the two, and if coffee could keep the peace, coffee it would be.

After she hung up, she went over to Yvonne's old silver set and made a note to change it to a Western style. She dished out one sugar, two sugars, three, as Agnes Collins, the one client who loved the new look of the shop, breezed through the swinging doors as if she owned the place and took the cup of coffee right out of Ruby's hands.

"Thanks, hon," she said. "Where's Yvonne? Is she sick?" she asked, hoping she was, blowing on the coffee as she stirred it. She didn't wish anything bad on Yvonne, just a sick aunt across the state, or an uncle in time of need—something to take away the pain of having to tell her that she was going to leave her for Thurston.

"I don't know," said Miss Ruby, making Duran another cup of coffee. "Is there something wrong with her?"

Yvonne was in the back folding towels. And there certainly was something wrong with her. She didn't want to have much of anything to do with the Hair Show. If it had been the last thing on earth left to do, she probably would have skipped it. But Miss Ruby had told her this morning that today was the day to pick a model, and being from the old school, Yvonne would respect the wishes of her boss, only it didn't mean she had to be pleasant about it. What Miss Ruby didn't know was that Yvonne was also in the back taking a razor blade to her hemline, letting out the length. She was not going to walk around the shop looking like a teenager anymore.

When Miss Ruby dropped Duran's coffee off and found Yvonne, Yvonne had hid the razor blade underneath the folded towels and brushed her legs off. She began to fold towels again and Miss Ruby folded some, too. They folded in silence for a few minutes and then Miss Ruby said, "Agnes is up front," and Yvonne said nothing. And then Miss Ruby asked, "How about taking her as your model?" and Yvonne said nothing again. Then Miss Ruby said, "Why, I think she'd be perfect," so Yvonne said, "I guess I'll ask her then," and left.

She walked right past Harper, who had a green mud mask up his neck and on his face. Thurston sat beside him, filing Harper's nails while his mask dried. Even under all that mud, it was transparent how eager Harper was to see Yvonne. He kind of jumped whenever she walked by. But Yvonne couldn't stand him. He was always washing his hands and folding his handkerchief into a neat square. Frankly, she didn't see how he kept his hands still long enough to get a manicure.

"Have a seat, Agnes, hon," said Yvonne. "It's going to be a long day."

This was exactly the way Agnes saw it. Today was the day, the only day, that she would ever be able to make her move. It was now or never. Her genes had been programmed so that at the age of forty-two, at nine o'clock, she would be destined to sit where she sat today, trying to figure out some way to tell Yvonne that she would have to leave her for Thurston.

Thurston had wiped off Harper's green mud mask and set him up with a clear one that pulled and wrinkled up as it dried. At the same time Harper was getting worked on, Thurston had two ladies going and both had hair like fashion models—slick and shiny and short and it shook when-

168

ever they turned their heads. Agnes could tell they loved it, and her mouth just watered whenever she saw one of them bend her head back and run her fingers through her hair. It was the kind of hair that you could take with you anywhere: to the beach, the garden club, the bridge club, the mall. And never again would you have to sleep with your head hanging off the side of the bed in order not to mess up your updo. They were styles that belonged to a different world—a younger world—a world where you could get into the shower without a shower cap on. A world where you could wash your hair whenever you felt like it, five times a day if you wanted to.

"Well, hon," said Yvonne, rubbing her hands together, "today's the day we're going to try something a little different. Isn't that right?" she asked, reaching for a smaller, tighter roller.

"Come again?" asked Agnes.

"Remember? You said you wanted to try a little extra height? Remember? You said last week that you wanted it higher, but just don't make it big like Bebe Pointer wore hers. Remember?"

It would have been better to say "I never said that" or "Well that's just because I thought that was what you wanted me to say" or anything else other than "oh yeah," which is exactly what Agnes ended up saying. But it is a hard business, this hair business, and not only for the hairstylists. Here Agnes was, so mad at Yvonne, and she couldn't even tell her about it. She felt guilty for being mad. And she felt mad for feeling guilty and it was just a vicious circle. It wasn't like she owed Yvonne a thing. It wasn't like Yvonne was a sister or daughter or anything like that. She was just a tired old beautician whom Agnes had been coming to for the last twenty years. Agnes shifted around in her seat while Yvonne rolled her hair and prattled on.

"That Harper," pointed out Yvonne, "the man Thurston's doing? I think he's one of them." Yvonne combed some extra setting gel into Agnes crown area. "I just don't think a normal man would come into a shop full of women and have his nails done."

Agnes was burning up inside she was so mad. Normally she would have understood perfectly well what Yvonne was saying, but today she was about to scream at Yvonne for being so narrow minded. As far as Agnes was concerned, this business about men hairstylists all being gay was baloney. One only had to look at Thurston to see that he enjoyed women. He cooed over them and primped them and blew them little kisses and let them enter into his wonderful world. Oh it just made Agnes so mad, and she would have said right at that second, "I've got something to tell you, Yvonne," if Yvonne hadn't spoken first.

"Agnes, honey, I've got something to ask you." Yvonne was making pin curls to frame Agnes' face, and was about to ask her to go to Atlanta as her model for the Hair Show when Ronder came up and interrupted.

"Hon, I've got to talk to you," she said. "I think I'm going mad." Ronder pulled her over to the side. "Listen, hon, this morning that Annabella woman rang me up real early and asked me to come over." Ronder looked around to make sure no one was listening. "So I did, you know. What else could I do, right?"

Yvonne nodded. "What time was it?"

Ronder waved her hands in front of her. "Six, but that's not important. When I got over there, she pulled these evening gowns out of the closet, and you should have seen them." Ronder rolled her eyes. "Yvonne, they must have cost a fortune. We've got to do something."

"Wait, let me guess," said Yvonne. "She's going to wear them to the Hair Show, right?"

"Exactly."

"Do you mean to tell me that this woman has actually brought her evening gowns all the way from New York just so she can have her hair fixed in them?"

"No. Worse." Ronder looked around again. And then she

hooked her head toward Thurston. "*He* had them sent to her from L.A. And honey, I am here to tell you those things are originals. Original whats, I don't know, but they are one of a kind and Annabella is walking the walls trying to figure out what to do with them."

Miss Ruby was perched up on one of the bar stools focusing her binoculars on Gladys' shop, and she had heard just enough of the tail end of their conversation to say, "Oh no they're not. Thurston and his model are wearing their cowboy suits or else they aren't going. Besides, he really loves that outfit. He told me so."

Ronder and Yvonne looked at each other, then Ronder pulled Yvonne farther away from Ruby and Yvonne smiled and nodded at Agnes as if to say, "Be right with you, hon."

Agnes just glared at her.

"You see," continued Ronder, making sure Miss Ruby couldn't hear them now, "he has one for before the contest and one for after the contest, and hon, the price tags on those things are not to be believed. In other words, they aren't refundable. And listen at this. Annabella refuses to wear them. Would you just look at that poor dear?" She nodded at Thurston. "My heart just bleeds for him. He's been talking Hair Show for a month, and now his whole world is falling apart. And did you know that he and Duran had a fight last night?"

Yvonne had heard about it, had been the first to hear about it as a matter of fact, from one of her patrons, since her first patron of the morning had been Thurston's and Duran's landlord. Yvonne had spread the word to Miss Ruby, who in turn had called Ronder with the news and now Ronder was telling the whole story back to Yvonne, only Yvonne wasn't about to interrupt her just in case Ronder had heard a better version of it. Of course, Ronder had a better version because she had had more time to elaborate on it.

This is what had happened according to Ronder:

According to Ronder, Thurston had gotten mad at Duran over something, and it really wasn't quite clear about what, but Thurston ended up locking Duran outside of the apartment. Duran was left screaming to be let back in. He screamed all night until Thurston finally opened the door and then one could only speculate on what took place after that.

But what had really happened was this:

There was screaming all right, but it was Thurston who had been the one locked out. The thing with Annabella had gotten to him, so he had taken it out on Duran. They had come home from work the night before and started supper, and Thurston had immediately started in on the Hair Show. Duran couldn't stand seeing him so miserable, so he began to make little jokes, including one that he himself thought was particularly funny, about Thurston's cowboy outfit. But it hadn't worked and it sent Thurston into another one of his long monologues. Duran hadn't minded listening to the whining so much, but when three o'clock in the morning rolled around and Thurston reached over him to call Miss Ruby for the fourth time that night, Duran pulled out a pair of his hair scissors and clipped the cord. Thurston was so mad he had stomped out to call Miss Ruby from a pay phone. But when he came back, he found that the door had been bolted from the inside.

"Duran, let me in, baby," he had said. But Duran didn't let him in.

"Duran, open up," said Thurston as he jiggled the lock and pushed against the door.

"Duran," said Thurston, pounding on the door, "this isn't funny. Come on, Duran, please let me in."

It had gone on all night long like that until finally Duran had yelled through the door, and the whole neighborhood had heard it, "Get lost, cunt!"

In the morning Thurston had found himself sleeping against the doorjamb. Duran had let him in and fried him some eggs and shown him a new way to wear his hair so that it would appear at least a little thicker. Only to Ronder,

who was looking at it while Yvonne filled her in on her side
of the story, Thurston's hair looked worse, flatter. It looked
like something out of an old French movie. She felt so bad
for Thurston.

Thurston peeled Harper's mask off and dabbed some
Witch Hazel onto his face with some cotton swabs. Then
he covered his face with steaming towels, wondering if it
would help Annabella if he tried this trick on her. Duran
had said, "Just make sure she gets a lot of sleep and she
should do just fine." But Thurston wasn't so sure about that.
He thought maybe he'd call her later and invite her in for
a whole series of facials.

Annabella was way ahead of him, smoking up a storm in
her hotel room, wearing banana all over her face. She was
also wearing a turquoise blue strapless sequined dress, cut
to her navel in the front and down to her bikini dimples in
the back. To move in it was impossible, and what was even
worse was that it came with a man's matching suit. She
hadn't known it was a man's suit at first. She had thought
maybe it was something she was supposed to wear on the
ride down. But then she had tried it on and realized immediately that she was not going to be alone in this little
venture of bad taste. Instead, Thurston was going to be right
there at her side, matching her. She had removed his suit
and put the slinky dress back on. If this little fashion event
didn't make headlines up in New York, nothing would. Annabella looked at the sequined top hat and tossed it onto
the chair across the room. The thing was, these outfits were
better than the other ones that Thurston had sent over. She
didn't even dare think about them. She had long since
stuffed those boxes into the back of the closet and was waiting for room service to bring up that bottle of champagne.

When it got right down to it, the whole thing was just so funny. She figured she might as well relax and have a good time.

While Annabella was taking her first sip of champagne, Yvonne was finishing up Agnes' hair. She didn't know it, but precisely at that time, Agnes was trying to get up enough courage to tell Yvonne that she was leaving. But right as the words were about to leave her mouth, Harper came walking up, grinning from ear to ear with his newly peeled pink and shiny face. Never had Agnes seen so many little red blood vessels before. And the way he just hung around as if he had some business there really got on her nerves.

He reminded her of a dog. A nice dog, but one that, once you gave him a little pat on his little head, he would follow you home and sit outside your door for the rest of your life.

When Miss Ruby came back in distress, upset that she couldn't find a driver for her limousines, Harper shot his arm straight up in the air like a school boy and begged Miss Ruby to let him drive. He had that eager look about him that indicated his brain was calculating the Greyhound bus schedule, and the hours until the competitions would begin in Atlanta, so that he could work out time enough to double back for the second limousine. But then Ronder came breezing through the room overhearing Miss Ruby's dilemma, and in a flash she was begging for her to let Buck drive. The thought of letting Buck drive was more than Miss Ruby could stand, but there was nothing she could do but say yes.

So there they were, Harper, Ronder, Miss Ruby and all of Miss Ruby's problems, standing in front of Agnes, standing in the way of her being able to tell Yvonne that after twenty years of her hair service, she was ready to try something else, someone new, The Great Thurston.

Now supposing, just supposing, Yvonne had heard this news. She would have handled it exactly as Agnes had imagined. She would have finished spraying Agnes' hair and picked the sides with the end of her rattail comb to add lift and airiness, just like she always had. Then she would have said, "Well, Agnes, if you think that's best." Agnes could have handled the whole thing a whole lot better if she knew that Yvonne would just go ahead and yell at her. But it would never happen.

She'd been watching Yvonne ever since Thurston had come to work. Watching her pick towels off the floor from around his legs, and bringing her ex-patrons coffee with sugar and cream, as if they were still her clients and not Thurston's. Agnes was no fool. She didn't think for a minute she'd be any different than the others. Yvonne would come in and offer her a Sanka along with those cheese and wheat crackers she loved so much, and act as if Agnes had never done her wrong.

When Yvonne finally got around to asking, "Now what was that you wanted to tell me, dear?" Agnes just wilted like a flower. Her shoulders slumped and all she could say was, "Maybe if you could just make me some more bangs."

"Bangs? Why, honey, why didn't you just say so?" Yvonne was whipping her some bangs in no time, while Harper looked on with love and admiration pouring out of his soul, making Yvonne wish he would leave. If there was one thing she couldn't stand, it was a man in a beauty shop.

She nudged Agnes' shoulder and said, "Look, Agnes, it's just like a gay to want to act like a woman. I bet he's hanging around to copy us."

What Yvonne didn't know was that Harper wasn't gay at all. All he was, was in love with her. He'd been in love with her since the first day she had shampooed his hair and massaged the back of his neck in the process. All that driving around, day after day, could make a poor salesman's neck raw. And demonstrating those Hoover vacuum cleaners, day after day to women who didn't care to watch could take a toll on a man's neck, and Yvonne just had the hands of an angel.

Harper watched Yvonne's little hands working around Agnes' hair, wrapping Agnes' hair around those little rollers with her tiny little fingers, and he felt like leaning over and putting those little fingers in his mouth.

He was making Yvonne itch all over. She wished he would leave. Maybe she could get him to go on some long errand for her. "Oh, I've got to get to the bank before lunch," she said. "Harper, do you happen to know what time it is?" She eyed his sports watch.

"I give up," he said. "What time is it?"

She rolled her eyes. He was chuckling, but she didn't want to encourage his behavior. "Harper," she asked, "how about if you go on down to the bank for me?"

Harper would have gone to the moon for Yvonne. But before he left, he asked every single person in the shop if they wanted anything. Nobody did, except Thurston, who wanted Harper to stop by his apartment and check his answering machine to see if the New York modelling agency had happened to call with the news of their mistake. After much heavy thought he had come to the conclusion that Annabella was not the same woman he had ordered.

"Hon," said Ruby, "if they were going to call, they would have called here."

"Well it won't hurt to see," said Thurston, pushing Harper to the front door, handing him his apartment keys.

Ruby checked her watch. "Ronder? Where are you?" she shouted, following Thurston to the front of the shop.

Ronder was on the phone talking to Buck, kissing him and sounding like a little girl.

"Ronder, hon," said Miss Ruby, "get off the phone. It's almost time for you to go on radio."

Ronder turned her back on Ruby and blew Buck a few more kisses into the phone before she hung up.

"Now," said Miss Ruby, "you do remember all that you're going to say, right?"

Ronder nodded.

"Got it all in your head?"

176

"It's in there like a picture, Miss Ruby," said Ronder. "Now don't forget, it's up to you to call everyone and tell them to turn their radios on. Especially Louise and Earline. They'll be on that phone to Gladys in no time."

"How could I forget? Oh yes, and Ronder," added Miss Ruby, "whatever you do, don't forget to mention that we're going to be competing in the Atlanta Hair Show."

Miss Ruby gave Ronder a good luck kiss on the cheek and Ronder took off out the front door. She decided to walk, since it was only a few blocks away. The air would do her good, calm her nerves. She'd never done anything like this before. As a matter of fact, the closest she'd ever even gotten to being on the radio was once, on the spur of the moment, when a disc jockey had asked his listeners what famous person had discovered the idea of the solar system, saying he'd take the sixth caller. Not only did Ronder know the answer, but she was the sixth caller. They had put her on hold while they did the news and weather, and she ran different names off in her head, trying to decide which one she would use instead of her own, because she sure didn't want anyone knowing it was her. By the time they'd gotten back to her, she'd simply forgotten the answer to the question. She had blatted out, "Newton," sounding like a sick sheep, and the deejay had laughed. She was so embarrassed. And as if that weren't enough, she'd lost out to a skinny sounding redneck who had gotten the answer right but made "Copernicus" sound like a redneck, too.

Ronder had never told that story to anyone, but she laughed about it now, running her fingers through the low leaves of the crepe myrtle trees as she walked through downtown Stuckey.

When she got to the station, she tapped on the window with her fingernails and the deejay came to the door and let her in.

"What a sweet thing you are," he said, "all dressed up like a cute little Indian." He pinched her on the behind and it made her sad, because he was bald except for some side trim and a few sparse hairs that were growing up top, which he had grown just long enough so that he could deep part them and swoop them over to his other ear. The deep part was making its way all the way to the back of his head. Ronder could tell by his complexion that he hadn't broken any records in any high school popularity contests.

It was nine o'clock in the morning. The hair dryers at The *O.K.* Hair Corral and the Pelo Bonito had been turned off. The women who had been having their hair washed were now sitting up and squeezed out, listening as intently as all the other women around town who had turned off their Phil Donahue show and were now waiting for a chance to hear Ronder talk. Or perhaps even hear her mention their hair as a good example of how to look good.

The forecast was calling for hot hot and humid, and Stan Stan the Radio Man told his listeners that the report was being brought to them by Ruby McSwain's brand-new *O.K.* Hair Corral. "And here with us," he said, going into a lower, sexier voice, "is our little Ronder Jeffcoat with 'What will the weather do to our hair today?' "

Ronder couldn't help noticing that he sounded as good as he looked bad. His voice was so soothing that she didn't have any fears about speaking. It was going to be so easy. When he held up his finger, then dropped it, it was her cue and she was ready. Only she had forgotten everything that she and Miss Ruby had planned for her to say. She took in a short breath and stared at her microphone, frightened.

Stan laughed and got her off the hook. "Well doll, what can you say about hair like mine? Got any ideas on how to make it look better?"

Ronder looked over at Stan, but he was bending over going through some albums. His shirt was too tight and the buttons were bulging, and it looked like his pants were about to split.

"How can you improve on hair," said Ronder, starting in slow, her voice shaking, "that looks like Robert Redford's?"

Stan turned to her and smiled, giving her the A-OK. "Hear that out there in radio land? Now you can't get a better looking deejay than that. So, Ronder, what will the weather do to my hair today?" he asked, pinching her arm and leaving her alone in front of the microphone and two turntables.

Ronder decided to go for it. There was no more shaking in her voice. "You heard him, folks. Hot and humid only means one thing. Stay inside. Why ruin your hair? Call up your boss, your lunch date, your mother-in-law, and call whatever it is, off. If you have to see them, have them come over there. If they can't do that, then you get someone to come and pick you up right at your front door with their car air conditioning running on full blast defrost. And for heaven's sake, whatever you do, cover your head up with a nice bright scarf when you run on out and jump in that car. And run just as fast as you can because it takes less than two minutes for that humidity to straighten out a curl or curl up what you just straightened out. Then, don't get out of that car until you are right at the front door of your destination. You hear me?"

Miss Ruby was so proud of Ronder. She was at her post at the Venetian Blinds, watching Gladys listen to every word Ronder said. She knew she was listening because Gladys was holding her hand up in the air to tell everyone to be quiet.

Stan came back in the sound room carrying a 36 ounce

Big Gulp Diet Soda about the size of a flower pot. In the other hand he carried a medium Coke, which he gave to Ronder, along with another A-OK sign. "Wrap it up," he mouthed.

She A-OKed him back and got even closer to the microphone. "Just one more tip. No matter where you go, or what you do, or who you do it with, just remember—whatever's good for your car defrost, it's got to be good for your hair."

"Thank you, Ronder Jeffcoat, from The *O.K.* Hair Corral. You know, I was just talking to your boss this morning, Miss Ruby McSwain, and she said that you all were having a sale today."

"That's right, Stan. Ten dollars off of anything done to your hair. So I'm going to leave on out of here so I can get perming. Yall come on down."

Now Ruby was sure that Gladys had been listening to the same station, because the minute Ronder had announced the sale, all the women sitting at the Pelo Bonito had immediately jumped up and were now discussing things with Gladys, pointing across the street at Ruby's.

"Way to go, Ronder," Miss Ruby said to herself. She put down her binoculars and got up from her place at the blinds. Then she moved over to her place behind the bar, smoothing out her dress, swinging the boa around her neck. She expected a flow of women any minute and she wanted to look the part of a Western hostess.

They all waited, Ruby and her stylists, for the big rush they knew was going to come.

Thurston waited.

Yvonne waited.

Duran waited.

But the shop stayed empty.

All the early morning clients had already left and there had been no others to take their place. Even Agnes and Harper had left, with Harper trying to get information out of Agnes about Yvonne.

"I don't know, Harper," Agnes had said, walking out the

front door, exhausted by everything. "I guess she likes you. She talks about you enough." She had smiled uneasily at Thurston before she left, touching her hair, just knowing that he hated it as much as she did.

Thurston hadn't given it much thought. He was thinking about Atlanta and Annabella and wondering what he could do to get her back up north where she belonged. Duran sat on one of the stools braiding Thurston's long hair, whispering things about getting married, making Thurston more uncomfortable than he already was.

Yvonne stood at the Western bar underlining certain passages in her big paperback Bible with a day-glo hi-lighter, while Miss Ruby just kept playing with her feathered boa and waiting.

After a while, a few people began trickling in. Each time Miss Ruby would jump up and greet them like an expensive madam. But after they saw the shop, they trickled right back out snickering. Miss Ruby just shrugged them off and sat back down until the next time the door opened.

Finally, after what seemed like an hour of curiosity seekers sauntering in and out, Ronder came breezing back in, in a good mood, cracking everybody up with a play by play on everything that had gone on at the radio station. But it was only a temporary lift because soon another inquisitive group ambled in, talking about Gladys this and Gladys that and what a wonderful shop Gladys had, just loud enough for everyone to hear. When they finally spoke to Ruby, they said little phrases like, "Oh what a quaint little place," with not the slightest trace of enthusiasm.

Miss Ruby simply pretended not to hear a word they said. Instead she decided to talk about the Hair Show, because that was one subject that always made her happy.

"What would you all think," she said to her hairdressers, "if I told you that we were going to stay over an extra day to visit Six Flags Over Georgia?"

The clock was ticking away. Nobody was making any money. And since that's the first thing on a hairdresser's mind, Six Flags Over Georgia wasn't sounding all that good. Yvonne and Duran murmured, "That would be wonderful," with about the same excitement as the people who had been visiting the shop. Thurston and Ronder just smiled weak little smiles.

"Where's your sheriff's badge, Thurston?" asked Miss Ruby, coming around the desk. She straightened out his cowboy vest, trying to get him back into the spirit.

"I left it at home."

"Well, whatever you do, don't forget to bring it to Atlanta. I want everyone to know who my top hairstylist is." She winked to let everyone know she wasn't really choosing favorites.

Thurston stood up and began unbraiding the braid that Duran had done. "The last thing," he said in an icy voice, "I'm going to be taking with me to Atlanta is this nasty thing." There, it had slipped out. Just like that and he wasn't even sorry. Because the very last thing he was going to do was show up in Atlanta dressed up like a cowboy. "Well," said Thurston, examining Ruby's face, hard, "you do know that I'm not wearing this, don't you? That I'm not going to be one of your rodeo idiots."

He waited, but Miss Ruby didn't look away and she didn't speak.

"Well, Miss Ruby," he continued, "I can tell you right now that this thing is going to be hanging in the back of my closet when I'm in Atlanta," he paused and took a deep breath, "or else I'm not going."

Miss Ruby held out her hand.

"What?" he asked. "What's that for?"

"Uh-oh, the keys to the shop," said Ronder, who had seen that same move when she had gone off and eloped with Buck.

Thurston glared at Miss Ruby but Ruby kept her hand out. She didn't flinch once. He looked over at Duran, but Duran just shrugged his shoulders. He didn't know what to do either.

183

Suddenly Thurston knew what to do. He was furious. He stormed into the bathroom and came back out with the cowboy suit on a hanger. Then with two long moves that were so smooth they looked choreographed, he hung the suit on the brass bar rail with one hand and handed Miss Ruby the keys and the spurs with the other. Miss Ruby's hand was still out.

There was no turning back for Thurston now. So right there, standing at the front door, with two women standing behind him waiting to come in to see the shop, Thurston, with nothing but his boots and blue jeans on, told Miss Ruby all the things about her shop that she didn't want to hear. About how you'd have to have some kind of bad taste to dream up a shop with the name of The *O.K.* Hair Corral. About how no one in their right mind would ever think of spending time in the place when they could just as easily be over at Gladys' luxuriating in class. And how, if she would just look around her, she'd see what he meant. He'd never seen a shop so dead.

Duran felt real bad about what Thurston had said to Miss Ruby, but he had no choice except to follow.

Miss Ruby watched them both cross the square, Thurston in his blue jeans and Duran still dressed like an Indian. She squeezed the spurs tight, causing pain, hoping it would make the other pain she felt go away.

Ronder picked up the binoculars and watched as they walked arm and arm into Gladys' shop. On seeing them, Gladys threw her hands up to the heavens, then hugged them both. Thurston was immediately given a red satin labcoat that trailed the floor. Duran was put into a shiny knee length red one with royal blue silk pants to match. After that, Gladys led Thurston to the German station, right next to Raphael the Frenchman, while Duran got to be in Switzerland, next to Lars of Norway.

After Thurston and Duran left, even fewer people came into The *O.K.* Hair Corral. Two of Duran's clients stepped in and looked around, but stepped out just as fast, saying they'd come back later. Yvonne kept reading her Bible, looking for scriptural passages that she could quote to Miss Ruby to cheer her up. She finally narrowed it down to Psalms and Proverbs. But when she started to read them to her, she realized she might as well be reading a flight manual for all Miss Ruby was hearing. Miss Ruby was stretched out on the Chez Ronder chaise lounge with her eyes closed and her heart pounding. Her fingers were in her ears. She didn't want to hear anything from anybody ever again.

It was an hour later when Annabella came jogging in. She took one look at the new Western decor, jogged back out to see if she had the right location, then came back in. She found Ronder and Yvonne in the Chez Ronder

Room hovering over Miss Ruby, who was still sprawled out on the chaise lounge with hot compresses on her forehead. It was the only place in the shop that hadn't been Westernized.

"Hey," she said, "I must have jogged around that square twenty times. It seems to be the only place you can run to without running into a railroad track. Boy, this town is really small. Hey, what happened to her?"

They told Annabella all they knew, which wasn't much, and kept on fanning Miss Ruby and rubbing her feet. Annabella jogged over to the A&P, and came back with some cucumbers, bananas, lemons and a plastic knife. "They were out of kiwi, which is perfect at a time like this, but this will do just fine." She sliced up some cucumber and placed two thick slices over Miss Ruby's eyes. Then she mashed up some banana and rubbed it all over her face. The lemon she dabbed behind Ruby's ears. "This always makes me feel better when the stress cuts in. Come on, hon, come on. Snap out of it." Annabella pushed down hard on Miss Ruby's facial pulse points. "Girls, can we get some different music in this place? Come on, sweetie, wake up. Wake up."

What nobody knew was that Miss Ruby hadn't fainted. She could still feel and hear everything that was going on in the room. The banana was beginning to pull on her face, feeling like it was pulling all that was left in her, out. At the same time she was being pushed back and back into an empty void, maybe even death; but there was no shining light at the end of her tunnel, like the ones she had read about from others before her who had died and come back to life.

She tried to fight waking up. She was so tired, all she wanted to do was sleep. But something in her kept trying to jump out, to be brave, to be strong. She didn't want to be brave or strong; she simply wanted to go down into that dark void and never come back out.

But Annabella's sharp New York accent went shrilling down into the void. "What is this piece of shit she's got on? It is absolutely awful."

After Annabella had heard the whole story of the disaster of The *O.K.* Hair Corral, how no one would set foot in the place, and how Thurston and Duran had left, she grabbed Ronder's cigarette. She puffed on it twice. Then, and it was as if she had seen it in the movies, she stabbed it out in an open jar of cream and grabbed Miss Ruby by the elbows, jerking her up.

"Okay woman, up. You've put too much in this now to give up. Come on, walk it off, baby. Walk it off."

Before Miss Ruby knew it, she was walking around the Chez Ronder Room, holding on to Annabella's big arms, thinking they felt like men's arms. She was listening to every word she said, refusing to open her eyes. Annabella talked about getting even, and the New York scene, and gays, and whatever else came to mind, and then she talked about getting even some more, and about how maybe it wouldn't hurt Ruby to show Gladys a thing or two.

Then Ronder picked up where Annabella left off. Then it was Yvonne's turn. Then back to Annabella again. Finally it was Ronder who said, "Miss Ruby, it's just, well listen, there's no easy way of putting this, but Annabella's right. You just can't have your stylists wearing this shit."

She flapped the skirt of her Indian dress up and down. "Now, I'll wear this stuff because I love you, and I need you. But really, Miss Ruby, it's asking too much of Thurston. The whole idea behind being gay is to be feminine. Lord, honey, you have that poor thing looking like John Wayne."

Miss Ruby covered her eyes and moaned, "Ohhhh, what have I done? I've lost him."

"Oh that's nonsense," said Yvonne. "Thurston loves you, Miss Ruby."

"Damn right," said Ronder. "That boy will be back before you know it."

"She's right, sugar," said Annabella, wiping the tears from Ruby's eyes.

"Oh what a fool I've been," Miss Ruby said again. "I should have known that I couldn't beat Gladys at anything. She's always been smarter than me, prettier than me. Oh God, everything."

"Hon, I can't stand to hear you talk that way," said Ronder. "We'll just fix this place up like it used to be and nobody will even know the difference. It'll be like nothing ever happened. Come on, what do you say?"

"I can't do anything without Thurston. He was my only hope in Atlanta. It's all over. I'm a total failure. A total failure. I'm just going to close this old shop down. Go rent a house at the beach and read, somewhere far far away from Gladys Bessinger."

"Hon," said Ronder, "you can't afford the luxury of all this self-pity. Thurston's going to be banging on your door and then what are you going to do? Offer him a job washing your car? You've got to shake out of this and get cracking. You know what day tomorrow is? It's the tenth, and we're leaving for Atlanta. We've got to get ready."

Miss Ruby yanked away from Annabella, who was wiping her face off, and sunk back onto the Chez Ronder chaise lounge. "There's not going to be an Atlanta. I'm calling the whole thing off."

"Come on, Miss Ruby," said Yvonne, moving in for her last try, "we've got to at least go to Atlanta."

"Yeah," said Ronder. "Come on, Miss Ruby, don't cry now. Thurston will be back tonight. Just you wait and see."

"You think?" asked Miss Ruby, who, deep in her heart, just needed someone to repeat what she wanted to hear. "You really think he'll be back?" she asked, looking eagerly up at Ronder.

"I cold damn guarantee it," said Ronder, smiling.

Then Miss Ruby looked over at Annabella and said, "Can you get the rest of this stuff off my face now?"

Annabella winked at Ronder and put her arm around Yvonne and said, "It works every time. That banana starts drying up and pulling those fine hairs and you can't help but get up and do something. Come on, hon. Let's take that crap off."

26

Ronder was right on the money. Thirteen hours and eleven minutes from the time he had crossed the square, Thurston was knocking on Miss Ruby's door and Ruby was pulling him inside.

"Where's Duran?" she asked, looking around.

"Miss Ruby, it's like working in a hornet's nest with all those screaming gays."

He looked like he was going to cry, and she stuck her finger under his chin, lifting his head. "Thurston?"

"Lars of Norway got to him." He stopped and almost couldn't go on. "Ruby, they're going to get married."

"He left you?"

"Walked right out of my life and into his. It was awful, Miss Ruby, just awful. Those boys really are from Europe. Tonino has four earrings in one ear and six in the other, and he's fixing Mildred Shealy's hair now. Can you just picture that old bat getting her hair done over there? But they're real pros. Duran took one look at Lars of Norway and his blond hair and blue eyes and I knew it was over."

"Poor baby. I know how you must feel," she said, sitting him down on her living room sofa. "I haven't slept all night. The girls have their hearts set on going to Atlanta, and I just don't know how to break it to them that we can't go."

Thurston looked at her, shocked. "What do you mean you're not going? Miss Ruby, you have to go. My life depends on it. Your life depends on it. We've got to go to Atlanta."

Miss Ruby played with the tassel on her night robe. "Thurston, there's no way I can win now. We're not prepared."

"Maybe not, but we've got to give it our best shot."

They looked at each other and Thurston took Miss Ruby's hand. "What do you say, old girl?"

He waited.

Then Miss Ruby smiled slyly from the corner of her mouth. "What would you wear if we went?"

"Okay, dammit. I'll wear the damn cowboy suit." Thurston stood up to go, but Miss Ruby grabbed his hand and pulled him back down.

He looked at her puzzled and she said, "Thurston, what do you really want to wear?"

His whole expression changed then. His eyes sparkled. He looked like he could stay up all night and win a hundred Hair Shows.

"I've got just the thing, Miss Ruby," he said. "It's this devine little sapphire jumpsuit, with a zipper that goes all the way from here to here. And sugar foot, there's a matching top hat and gloves that go with it. You're just going to love it."

"It sounds devine, Thurston. You've got to do me a big favor."

"Name it, Ruby. I'll do anything."

"You've got to take Annabella."

"I'll do anything but that."

"Thurston, she's done so much for me. Frankly I don't think I could go without her."

. . .

Ruby and Thurston talked and talked, crying some, laughing some, hugging some. Finally they worked everything out, up to and including the fact that Annabella was going with them to Atlanta. But there was one thing that Thurston didn't dare bring up. While he was at the Pelo Bonito for that one short day, he had learned that Gladys was going to be at the Hair Show, competing. He had decided that he was going to keep this from Ruby for as long as he possibly could.

It was right before the break of dawn, right after Miss Ruby and Thurston had decided to go to sleep and then passed that stage with more talking and were now wide awake again, when Miss Ruby, with much prodding from Thurston, got on the phone and began calling everyone up for a surprise party. She was happy and upbeat and asking everyone if they could come down and help redecorate the place for the Atlanta Hair Show going away party.

Ronder said, "You mean we're going? We're actually going to do it? Way to go, girl! You bet your ass I'll be there. I'll swing by and pick up Yvonne now."

"Good idea!" said Ruby. "And by the way, you all can wear just any damn thing you want. You hear me? Anything! I just want every one of you there by my side. I don't care if we win or lose or whatever happens. We're just going to damn well be there."

All through the dawn they worked, Ruby and her Thurston and her girls, hanging balloons and streamers, stopping every once in a while to let Thurston cry for Duran, then cheering him up again.

Even Buck came by. Ronder sent him off to make a stop at a liquor store he frequented, which was closed, but he banged on their door and woke them up, leaving with three cases of champagne and wine and whiskey and beer. Then he drove halfway down the highway and bought Bottle Rockets and Roman Candles and what looked like ten thousand firecrackers.

When Buck got back to the shop, Miss Ruby asked him if he'd help Thurston take down THE *O.K.* HAIR CORRAL sign. Thurston didn't want to mess up his nails, so Buck made him hold the ladder while he did most of the work. Ronder had never loved Buck so much as she did at that very moment, watching Miss Ruby watch him. Miss Ruby was making sure he always had a cold beer in his hand. It wasn't long before he had the old CELEBRITY STYLING SHOP sign back up and blazing again.

Thurston began to cry. But this time it wasn't for Duran. He just hadn't imagined he'd ever be so glad to see that stupid sign back up there.

Meanwhile, Miss Ruby drove off a few times, always returning with something wild. The wildest thing she brought back was a giant TV screen and a video monitor that she had gotten from her ex-brother-in-law. "Gladys," she said to herself, standing outside, admiring her old sign again, "may have *Another World* playing all over the world in her shop, but I've got something better. I'm going to have my women watching their ownselves when they walk into and out of my shop."

There was something about Miss Ruby that was different. Yvonne thought it was finally the Holy Spirit flowing through her, giving her a new life. She looked better, wilder, all there. She looked smarter, nicer, taller, chic. That was it. She looked chic. She had removed her show girl dress and had slipped back into one of her long evening dresses, the kind she always wore on Fridays and Saturdays, and she was swishing around the shop like she owned all of Stuckey and maybe even part of France.

The Stuckey TV crew consisted solely of Jim Evans, who anchored and did sports, and Julie Brooks, the weather girl–feature writer. They were celebrities in Stuckey, and when they arrived at Ruby's, shortly after the first firecrackers went off, the whole town seemed to swarm to the square.

When Miss Ruby first saw their little Sky-Cam News 13 Van make its way around the first corner, she had said, "Buck, let's see if you can shoot some of those things off the Robert E. Lee statue. Can you point them this way so that they spray in front of the shop?" Then she laughed. "But don't catch anyone's hair on fire."

"No problem," said Buck, and suddenly firecrackers and Roman Candles began popping and snapping and spreading across the sky toward Ruby's.

Riley and Harper got there just in time to join Buck as he moved on to lighting the Bottle Rockets. Even Thurston got with the fireworks, putting a whole string of firecrackers on the sidewalk. He made Ronder light them though, while

Yvonne and Ruby walked around the square, inviting everyone in for breakfast.

By nine-thirty, the shop was packed. Miss Ruby had arranged for the two limousines, one white and one black, to be parked out front, with explicit orders that the engines were to be kept running. Even though she had asked Harper and Riley to drive, she had decided to hire two models just to stand by the doors of the limos, with their little white gloved hands crossed at their waist, making it look official.

The models were all leg, wearing black high heels with black silk hose that had an even blacker seam that went all the way from the tips of their heels to their French Cut Maillots, designed to look like a Tuxedo, tails and all. The tall, skinny one greeted people as they walked by, handing out free haircut, perm and color passes for the next week in the shop; and the taller, skinnier one smiled and offered champagne cocktails, which she kept in the wet bar on the limo's backseat. Jim Evans kept his camera on these girls for a long time before Julie Brooks pulled him inside.

Inside, plates of Eggs Benedict were being passed around with more champagne cocktails. Annabella was serving the drinks, drinking herself, and calling everything she made a Grasshopper because she was in the South now. Ronder and Yvonne were trying to find models to take along, since Yvonne never had gotten around to asking Agnes, and Ronder had never even given it a second thought until now. Thurston was tagging behind Ruby, who was going back and forth from customer to customer, telling them about Atlanta and Las Vegas and her wonderful hairdressers.

That's when Jim Evans moved the camera in close and Julie Brooks stuck her microphone up to Miss Ruby. She said, "I think it's just wonderful that you and your cousin Gladys are going to be representing Stuckey like this. It's no secret that you all have been friendly rivals for so long. Can you give us some tips on how to get along with your competition?"

Ruby didn't say anything. Everybody sucked in their

breath. Thurston put his drink down. Ronder and Yvonne looked at him and then back to Miss Ruby. The customers didn't take their eyes off of Miss Ruby's face. Julie Brooks jiggled the microphone at Miss Ruby, smiling and waiting for her to talk.

Finally, after what seemed like forever, Miss Ruby reached over and took the cocktail that Annabella was holding out to her, sipped it and said, "Well, this is the first I've heard of Gladys going." She paused and took a deep breath and, looking around, she saw all the eager faces in the shop—the faces that were eager to hear tragedy. So she lifted her shoulders up even higher and straighter than before and said, "Why, what a nice surprise! I can only hope we'll be able to see more of each other in Atlanta. It seems like we're always too busy to get together in town." Then for a last impression, Ruby waved to the camera and added, "Yoo-hoo, Gladys. If you're watching, good luck!" She raised her cocktail glass up in the air and everyone started waving their party hats and blowing their horns, popping balloons and spilling their drinks and toasting her.

She toasted them back. The town, the shop, her girls, Thurston, and Las Vegas and Tom Jones and even Gladys Bessinger. She was so happy that she had to leave the room to cry.

The shop was wild and getting wilder. Someone broke a mirror. One woman was going through Yvonne's drawers. Ronder pointed her out to Yvonne and suggested that she might very well make a good Atlanta Hair Show model. But Yvonne ignored her, just like Thurston ignored Annabella, who brushed right past him on her way to the bathroom. But when Annabella came back out, she was wearing the sequined top hat and the pant suit that Thurston had planned to wear for his performance. He decided he couldn't ignore her any longer. She looked great. He put his arm around her for the first time and posed for a picture. They even did a little jig in front of the video monitor, billing themselves as the Dancing Split Ends.

197

By now it seemed like everybody was at The Celebrity Styling Shop. They were either in the door, or coming in the door, or on their way out to get another look at the limos and the models. Then one of those once in a lifetime, quick as a flash type things happened. Gladys Bessinger arrived on the scene. Miss Ruby would never have known it if Ronder hadn't run back screaming, "Oh my God, she's here! Gladys is right up front waiting for you. Come on, Miss Ruby," she said, clutching her, "fix your makeup and come out like a queen."

That's exactly what Miss Ruby did. She dried her eyes and powdered her face and put lipstick on in record time and ran to the front of the shop, but stopped just short of it so she could make an elaborate, flourishing entrance. Then she looked around, saying, "How do you do, I'm so glad you could make it, dear," to every person she saw, never really looking anyone in the eye because she was searching around for her cousin Gladys, who, of course, had already left.

Then the conversation began to buzz.

It was "Gladys said this" and "Gladys said that" and "You should have seen that dress, that marvelous short dress that Gladys had on."

Miss Ruby looked at her own long evening gown and was beginning to feel old and dowdy and scared, when Thurston swept her up into his arms and said, "Dance with me gorgeous. You're the best looking thing in town. We're going to win this Hair Show. Just you watch."

And it was that picture, the one where they were dancing, that made the headlines. They danced right on out the beauty shop door and into the first waiting limos, where everyone was waiting for them, including Earline and Louise and Millie.

"We see that there's plenty of room in there for us," said Louise. And Earline tagged on, "Well, you might as well know it, we've decided to invite ourselves along."

Miss Ruby looked at Ronder and Ronder cracked up and

said, "Well, why the hell not? Yvonne, it looks like we've finally got us some models after all."

So Earline and Louise and Millie all squeezed into the backseat of the last limo, next to Riley, of course, and off they all went, Miss Ruby and her Celebrity Stylers embarking on their tour.

On the way out of town they passed the Thunderbird Motor Inn, where the marquee read:

**Good Luck To Ruby McSwain
and All Her Hairdressers!
Love, Harper.**

Miss Ruby leaned over from the backseat and kissed his cheek while he drove on. Suddenly she saw Gladys' car— the red Corvette with the little blinking lights circling the GLADYS license plate. She felt cold. She pushed herself back into the seat and said to herself, "Listen Gladys Bessinger, let me tell you one thing. It's going to be me sitting at the Las Vegas table with Tom Jones. Me, Ruby McSwain."

"What?" asked Thurston. "Did you say something, Miss Ruby?"

She smiled. "Not a thing, hon. Not a thing." The only thing that mattered to her now was that she was surrounded by all the people she loved, on her way to the big Atlanta Hair Show, hoping she could win, knowing she wouldn't, but being brave enough to carry it off.

It was a hot day to be on a black top highway, especially a highway going across S.C. and 200 miles of central Georgia. It was the kind of day that if you left a can of hairspray in the car it would explode. So Thurston was mixing drinks as fast as he could and Annabella was drinking them as fast as he could mix them.

"Here honey," said Thurston, handing Miss Ruby one of his famous Piña Coladas. Miss Ruby took it, looked at it, smelled it, then sipped it.

"It kind of tastes like ice cream. Make me another one."

"You want another one?" he asked.

"Yeah, but you might as well make two of them. I could drink these all day."

Yvonne sat up front next to Harper, disapproving of Miss Ruby drinking and wishing she were somewhere else rather than seated next to Harper. He was driving the first car and driving her crazy, the way he just kept staring at her as if she were a pizza or something. She couldn't stand him. He gave her the creeps. And he was always talking, and when he wasn't, he was just about to start. And as if that weren't enough, when Thurston said, "Hey, Yvonne, you want something to drink?" and she had answered with, "Can you make me a glass of orange juice?" Harper had pointed his finger at her like a ray gun and went, "Zap! You're a glass of orange juice."

Of course, this cracked everybody else completely up, especially Miss Ruby, who was toasting the Hair Show. "Bottoms up, baby! Tom Jones, here I come."

On this note, Harper belted into "Ninety-Nine Bottles Of Beer On The Wall," and Annabella couldn't get any of the verses straight, which caused Thurston to turn *All My Children* on in the backseat, loud. He put his fingers in his ears and watched Erica do her stuff, only the camera kept zooming in on a man with curly brown hair.

Thurston adjusted the contrast and sat back with his mouth hanging open. "Yum yum, would you look at that guy?" he said to nobody in particular, pointing to the TV. "He's gorgeous. There's got to be a queen behind that camera."

That was how it all began sixteen miles out of town. So nobody could really believe it when a loud whap whap whap whap whap came suddenly from under the hood. Harper screeched over into the emergency lane and Buck just sailed on past in car number two.

"Where does he think he's going?" asked Miss Ruby while Harper got out to see what was going on.

He made a big thing out of getting out of the car and lifting the hood. He was slow, thought Yvonne, oh was he ever slow. It seemed like forever before he was finished, standing by her window with a silly smile on his face, holding up the fan belt like it was a dead snake.

"Isn't it something?" he asked. "There ought to be a law about letting these things get so old."

"Well, can we still move?" asked Miss Ruby.

"Sure we can," said Harper, swinging the old belt back and forth next to Yvonne's window, grinning at her.

"Well, let's go then," said Miss Ruby, touching her famous

updo, patting it down. "Hurry up and put that air conditioning back on. It's hot in here!"

"No can do, Miss Ruby," Harper said as he got back in. "Without the fan belt, we can't run the A.C."

"Well, we'll just have another one of those Grasshoppers then," Annabella said, holding out her glass. "Thurston, whip it up."

Harper started out into the slow lane, and with all the windows rolled down, the wind began whipping Annabella's hair around. It was hair that Thurston had been working on and off all morning, thinking he would never be able to get it right for the cameras in Atlanta, but finally, with the help of extra mousse and gel, and even some of Yvonne's heavy duty hairspray, he had styled it where he wanted it.

Suddenly Thurston was jumping all over the car trying to get the windows back up, screaming, "Annabella's hair! Her hair! Oh my God, her hair!"

"Thurston, are you mad?" asked Yvonne. "We'll sweat to death in here."

"Annabella," he warned, "don't you dare sweat on your hair."

"Don't sweat on my hair? Are you high or something? How am I supposed to not do that?" She lit up a cigarette and began smoking it and Thurston, on remembering Duran's remarks about Annabella's wrinkles, grabbed the cigarette and threw it out the window.

"From now on you are banned from any cigarettes until after the Hair Show."

"Oh brother." Annabella's bangs were wilting down her forehead and her head looked like it was rolling a little.

"And no more drinks until we get there, you understand?" he asked. "You got that?"

"Got it, Herr Hitler," she said, patting her pocketbook beside her for another pack of cigarettes, lighting up again.

"If you smoke," said Yvonne, "I'll have to roll down my window again." Yvonne hated cigarettes and had a little sign back at her station that read: THANK YOU FOR NOT SMOKING.

"Shut up, Yvonne," Thurston said. "Okay, Annabella, one cigarette, but only while I fix your hair."

Thurston took out his little portable butane curling iron and went to work repairing the damage that had been done. He curled her hair back, he fluffed it forward, he curled it forward, he fluffed it back and when he was finished, he began spraying it with Yvonne's hairspray. It was a heavy spray, a tacky spray, misting into the already thick, smoke filled air, making everything sticky to the touch and Harper's hands stick to the steering wheel.

Yvonne was the first to open her window again, and then so did everybody else, except Thurston, who had taken off his labcoat and was holding it around Annabella as if it were a Chinese screen.

"Thurston," said Annabella, "this is insane. I sure hope you don't think I'm planning on driving to Atlanta the whole way like this."

"Can I go to the bathroom?" asked Yvonne.

"I don't know, can you?" asked Harper, cracking himself up with the oldest joke in the world.

Yvonne rolled her eyes to the heavens, and noticed that he was wiping his hands on his neatly folded handkerchief. It was as if he did everything so perfectly right that everything he did came out so perfectly wrong. He assured her that there was a rest area up ahead and began to tell her all about his job selling vacuum cleaners. She wanted to ask him why he was telling her all this, but she was afraid it would only invite him to tell her more. So she sat back and let his words roll over her like the wind coming in through the windows, and thought about all that she had decided since waking up this morning.

It had come clear to her in the night, just like everything came to her, in the form of a dream. Once again, she had been nervous and couldn't sleep, so she had eaten a Slim Jim and some grapes and dropped off soundly after that, only to find herself already at the Hair Show and the hairdressers weren't people but giant Brazilian ants. She opened door after door after door and each door led to a different, even more frightening haircut. At the last door, she opened it and there, cut right into a lady's hair were the words: YVONNE RETIRE.

It had scared her to death.

She had gotten out of bed and eaten another Slim Jim in front of the TV and went through her bankbook and found that she had saved just enough money to carry her through for the rest of her life. Did it really seem so close by, the rest of her life? She didn't know why she hadn't retired already. Hair, the way Yvonne Tisdale had known it, had gone the way of the drive-in movies and it didn't look like it was ever going to change back.

So she decided, right there in front of an Andy Griffith rerun, with half a beef stick in her hand, that she was going to quit the hair business for good and do what she'd always dreamt of doing ever since she could remember. She was going to start taking photography classes down at the adult continuing education center. She already had an idea for a theme, which was why she had brought her camera along. She was going to do a lay-out on the end of the shampoo-and-set era. It would be kind of a farewell gift to herself, and a gift welcoming her into a new world. She wasn't going to tell a soul about it. It was going to be her little secret.

Harper was still talking about rug conditioners when he suddenly pulled into a Rest Area-No Facilities.

"What are you doing?" asked Yvonne. "There aren't any bathrooms here."

He sailed on through without even stopping and said, "Ahh, now I feel rested," and he laughed and winked at Yvonne. Yvonne stared straight ahead gripping her knees. She did not want to encourage any more of that kind of behavior. She couldn't stand him.

The plan was for the caravan of beauticians to stop at the Georgia Welcome Center, just over the state line, where

204

they would picnic and discuss details about the Hair Show. And this is exactly what happened. Only it took a lot longer for it to happen, because while the first limousine sat and waited in the heat for the second limousine, the second limo, the one Buck was driving, was going at a snail's pace.

"Would somebody like to tell me why we're going so slow?" asked Riley, who was sandwiched miserably between Earline and Louise, facing an even more eager Millie, wishing he was back home watching baseball or going through some of his Civil War books.

It was taking them forever to get to Atlanta. It seemed like every time they saw a rest stop, one of the women had to pee. Riley felt like he was going to crawl out of his skin. The perfume Earline was wearing did not blend well with Louise's and they kept trying to get him to join in the conversation which consisted mostly of skin diseases and other illnesses.

Riley shuddered, especially when they talked about treatments and needles. He thought about getting up front with Buck, only that was where all the curling irons and hair dryers were, stacked to the dashboard, rubbing against Buck's arm as he drove.

The only person who was having any fun at all was Ronder, who had taken off her shoes and was reading a pirate romance. "Hon, he can't go any faster," she said, turning the page. "He doesn't have a license."

"What?!" asked Earline, grabbing on to Riley's left thigh.

"What?!" screamed Louise.

"Why doesn't he have a license?" Riley asked.

"D.U.I.," said Ronder, "but it's okay. As long as he keeps under the speed limit he'll be just fine."

Louise and Earline weren't about to let Riley get up in that front seat with all those curling irons. They'd waited too long to get next to him. So they patted his knees and said that Buck was driving just fine as far as they were concerned, and Millie, not to be completely left out, reached across and patted his hand and agreed. Which made him feel even more trapped and hemmed in by their crossing thighs, silky clothes, and smothering perfume.

The two limos finally met up at the Georgia State Line Welcome Center. Harper got out and began cleaning the leaves from the air vents under the windshield. Everyone else was inside looking at pamphlets on Georgia.

"Well, I don't care what you say," said Yvonne. "I'd go to Six Flags before I'd go anywhere."

"I've been there already," said Ruby, trying to impress her. "That's why I want you all to go so bad. They have cloggers there that dance on a stage, and then you can go off on a boat ride. A river boat with a giant wheel."

"Oh my, I can't wait," said Thurston in a dull, flat voice.

"Where's Annabella?" asked Ronder.

Thurston would have died on the spot if he'd known that right at that moment, Annabella was in the bathroom throwing up. She was now convinced that the only people who knew how to drive were Northerners. Harper had driven like he was steering a boat. When Annabella finally staggered out of the car, her hair was ratted up like a bird's nest and her mascara was streaked down her cheeks. It was a good thing that Thurston had gone to the vending machines along with everyone else, and not gone looking for her.

Although Miss Ruby had ordered a gourmet lunch for everyone, everyone was tired of champagne and booze and wanted simple things to drink, like Cokes and Pepsis.

"What are these bars doing here?" asked Yvonne.

"Read the sign, darling," said Thurston. "What does it say?"

"Reach hands through bars for service," read Buck slowly. "What kind of crap is that?"

"You ought to know, baby," said Ronder.

Yvonne put in fifty cents and lost it right away. After banging, through the bars, on the machine buttons, she tried it again. This time she got a bottle of Mountain Dew, even though she had pressed the 7-Up button. As she popped the top off she saw Harper coming out of the men's room. She watched him curiously as he got off the sidewalk and onto the grass, where he began systematically scraping his feet.

"What is he doing?" she asked Ruby.

Miss Ruby explained, "You know, I was wondering that very same thing myself. And I finally figured it out. He does it every time he goes to the bathroom. He's cleaning his shoes. He's a wiper."

It was the worse possible news Yvonne could hear. It ranked right up there with putting kittens to sleep, it was so sad. This was obviously a man who needed somebody to rub his head to sleep at night. Yvonne sipped her drink and thought, But it's not going to be me. Not me, no huh-uh, not me.

"Hon," said Miss Ruby, putting her arm around Yvonne, "can't you see how crazy that man is about you? Couldn't you just go out on a date with him? He wants you to talk to him so bad."

"I'd get my head shaved first," said Yvonne, who was already thinking about something else. She was wondering where she'd packed her camera. Half the trip had already gone by and she hadn't taken one shot.

She found it jammed in among the blowdryers and curling irons in Buck's limousine. She would have been furious, but she was startled by a loud piercing scream biting through the Georgia pines.

It was Thurston. He was staring at Annabella, who had her heels in one hand and was holding her hair up in the other. Tendrils of it were falling down around her shoulders and she looked just like Medusa with no makeup on. He couldn't believe his eyes.

He was holding on to the drinking fountain and Miss Ruby was cupping the water that trickled out.

"Come on honey, drink this," she said. "She doesn't look all that bad. We can fix her up."

"How could she do this to me?" he asked. "What is it about me that she wants to ruin?" He talked about Annabella as if she were a hundred miles away instead of standing right there beside him, smiling and wobbling and trying to reach out to touch him.

"What's wrong, baby?" she asked.

"Get away from me! Don't touch me, you Jezebel!" he yelled.

By the time Yvonne had made her way up from the parking lot, Thurston had held on to that Georgia water fountain and milked the scene for all he was worth. Everybody was patting him, hugging him, holding him up and doing everything they could to keep him neutralized.

Yvonne had no idea what was wrong. She just thought it would make a fine group picture with them all standing around like that, huddled so close together.

She snapped her first Polaroid, and the flashbulb turned Thurston into a wild man.

Yvonne squealed, "What's wrong with you?" when he started after her.

But Buck grabbed Thurston before Thurston got to Yvonne. It was then that Yvonne realized the problem. She went over to Thurston, who was now crying on Buck's shoulder. She said, "Thurston, if all the problem is, is that you want Annabella to look good for the cameras when she gets to Atlanta, well, I see no problem at all. The answer is right here." She swung her camera back and forth like a bell.

Thurston wiped his eyes and Buck pushed him off. Miss Ruby held her breath as Yvonne said, "Let's just take a before picture and then an after picture of Annabella. You know, the kind you took back at the shop? And we'll have one of you sizing her up, fixing her up and then the finished product. Thurston, she'll look great when she gets there. Just think, you'll have a whole photo spread ready for the newspapers. Who could resist?"

Thurston looked at Yvonne then grabbed her, clamping

his arms around her, squeezing her tight. "Oh Yvonne, I do love you so."

So while Ronder laid out the elaborate picnic that Ruby had brought, with white tablecloth, fruit, meats, champagne, the whole nine yards, including caviar, Thurston went to work making Annabella even more "before" looking. He brushed every bit of body he could from her hair. Then, after thinking it over, he poured salad dressing on his brush and brushed it in to make her hair look flat and oily. He was quite pleased with how it was all turning out, but not yet pleased enough.

"Do her face with some of that makeup of yours, Yvonne," he said. "That'll make her look sick."

Yvonne gave him the evil eye and then went to work, putting light powder on Annabella's face where dark blusher should go, and dark blusher where light powder should go. For the finishing touch, she added a lipstick recommended for women with jet black hair, not blonde, applying it to Annabella's top lip only, making it thinner than any top lip should ever be.

Annabella looked horrible. And the best thing was, she looked naturally horrible. She let her natural inclination toward being the actress she always thought she should be, take over. She walked just like she thought white trash would walk, with her hips swinging hard and wide, her hands swinging back and forth, and her head held to one side.

"You look awful!" laughed Ronder.

And that's when Yvonne took her first "before" picture of the beautiful Annabella.

Thurston, of course, was delighted.

Yvonne took a few more shots of Annabella standing with Ronder, and then Annabella standing alone. And while she put more film in the camera, Thurston whisked Annabella away to the ladies room at the Georgia Welcome Center to wash her hair in the sink.

Ladies from all over the state and other states came in

and out, doing lady type things in the ladies room, watching him as if it were normal for him to be in there.

Meanwhile, Yvonne kept snapping shots of Ronder and Miss Ruby: Miss Ruby by a tree, Miss Ruby eating grapes, Miss Ruby sticking out her tongue, Ronder sticking out her tongue at Miss Ruby, and so on and so forth. Then Buck wanted to get in the picture, and Harper begged for someone to take a snapshot of him and Yvonne together. So Yvonne complied, and Miss Ruby took the shot of Harper standing with his arm around Yvonne while Yvonne had her head turned away with one foot out the frame. Ruby even got a shot of Earline and Louise and Millie, posing around Riley at the picnic table. He was eating a chicken wing and they were all smiling at him, offering him another chicken wing, some olives, cake, champagne.

Yvonne was so happy. She didn't even mind Harper asking for another picture.

She had to put in more film again when Thurston came back with Annabella dripping by his side. He had borrowed a big thick orange extension cord from a Georgia ranger, who he swore was gay, and plugged his hair dryer into it. So the next picture was of Annabella sitting on the table having her hair dried by Thurston.

"Hon, I swear he's not gay," said Annabella, looking at the ranger who was watching them.

"He's as gay as I am, darling," said Thurston, switching to a cooler air for Annabella's bangs. "Did you see the way he was looking at me?"

"How could I miss it? He probably wants to arrest you."

"He probably wants to handcuff me to his bed."

"Oh, Thurston, that is so gross," laughed Annabella. "Anyway, I can prove he isn't gay."

"How?" asked Thurston.

"Just you watch." Annabella smiled at the ranger, stroked her chin, and licked her tongue around her lips in a slow, complete, perfect circle.

The ranger hooked his finger at her telling her to come

on over, promising her a Georgia night of wild and passionate love.

Thurston said, "Well, he justs thinks he's straight. He'll be out of the closet before you get back to New York."

"Oh Thurston, you're too much!" she laughed.

Yvonne got the shot of Annabella coming on to the Ranger and decided that it would make a great "after" picture for the papers.

Miss Ruby was laughing at the whole thing, eating caviar, trying to look like she enjoyed it, although to her it tasted the same way seaweed smelled. She'd rather have had a McDonald's hamburger than those little salty eggs spurting around inside her mouth. But it was time for caviar and she wasn't about to miss out on anything.

It was a great time for everyone and Annabella even got to ride the rest of the way in the air conditioned limo, saving her newly coiffed hair for whatever lay ahead for them in Atlanta. Everything would have been perfect if Riley could have only gotten rid of Earline and Louise and Millie. But they were holding fast.

The two limos circled the Peachtree Plaza three times trying to find a parking place. Finally they each found one two blocks away, down a steep hill. Everyone loaded up with suitcases except for Thurston, who was busy complaining about his heels. Halfway up the hill, Annabella began repeating over and over again that there were people at the hotel who parked and unloaded cars for the guests.

But no one listened.

Harper had never been to anything but a motel before and Buck had never been anywhere except to Daytona Beach to stay with some questionable in-laws from a first marriage. It was Harper and Buck who bore the brunt of the load. They carried Thurston's big suitcases and all the curling irons and hair dryers.

There were no cameras waiting for them when they finally walked up to those great front doors, just El Dog, Duran's yellow convertible, parked in a tow-away zone right out front, and a little man with a small reporter's pad and a number two pencil. Thurston limped over to him, trying to separate himself from the rest of the crew, but it was of no use. Yvonne was right behind.

"Well, Thurston," she said, pointing from his heels to her flats as he limped, "so now what are you going to say about my shoes? My ugly, comfortable shoes. Smile." She snapped a photo of him rubbing his ankle, looking mad.

"Darling, scram. This is business," he said, shooing Yvonne away. He waved to the newspaper man. "Hey, sugar, come on over here, would you?"

The little guy waddled over like a duck, eager and sweating to get a good features article.

"Hon," said Thurston, straightening the reporter's tie, "you've got to do something about that walk—and that hair. Darling, I don't know my room number yet, but check the desk. I want you to come on up for a haircut. Listen, by the way, do you think you can get some cameras up there? I'm the one you've all been waiting for."

"Are you one of the European guys?" asked the reporter, all excited.

Thurston shook his head. "No, I am not. I am The Great Thurston."

"I knew you weren't," he said, looking let down. "These Southern accents are enough to give anyone away, aren't they?"

Thurston had hated the little man on the spot, and now he hated him some more. Thurston had taken drama and voice lessons since he was eleven years old, and had been told that he sounded just like Lawrence Olivier. He brushed at his arm where the reporter had touched him.

"Honey," he said, "on second thought, keep your hair just like it is. It really is you, isn't it?"

While Thurston lied to the reporter about all of his bad qualities, making them sound like good ones, and played up on all of his good ones, making them sound like great ones, Miss Ruby found out that Gladys Bessinger was throwing a closed party for the press and the sponsors of the Hair

Show that night. All of a sudden it was too much for Ruby and she began to cry.

"Hon, dry your eyes," said Ronder standing close by holding her makeup case. "There's enough water in here as it is. All these fountains make me want to pee." Ronder squeezed her knees together, tight, shaking them from side to side.

"Okay, okay," said Miss Ruby embarrassed. "Stop that now."

"Okay what?" asked Ronder. "Okay you'll go and change into your new outfit and come back down here fighting like a champ? Is that what you mean by okay?"

On Ronder's advice, Miss Ruby changed into a beautiful cream colored taffeta dress. It looked just like her old wedding gown, the one that Gladys had so envied, only it was newer, brighter, and trailed after her wherever she went, leaving a scent of her favorite perfume. Ronder had sprayed it all over the gown with abandon before they walked out the door.

Miss Ruby had begun sneezing and sounding nasal, "Are you sure that isn't too much?" she had asked Ronder.

"Hon," Ronder had said, "if you want to win this game, you're going to have to play it as if you were Gladys yourself. Believe me, Gladys would wear more than this."

So Miss Ruby told Ronder to spray some more, and informed Ronder while she was doing it that she was going to crash Gladys' party tonight, and Riley was going to be hanging on her arm when she did it.

"What a great idea," Ronder said, spraying a last shot of perfume on Ruby's updo. "You look beautiful, Miss Ruby, just beautiful. Come on, let's go find Yvonne. We need a picture of this."

They found Yvonne downstairs, happily taking pictures, happy to take as many pictures of Miss Ruby as she could. Yvonne was really going to miss Miss Ruby when she retired. She was going to miss everything about the hair business. Mostly the people she had seen walking the lobby were the new generation Hair Designers, but every once in a while she saw a few Beauticians and she saved her film for them.

Earlier, in the bathroom, she had run across five of them, spraying and styling their hair, and she had joined in the most delightful hair conversation she could remember. It was a "Hon do you remember this" and a "Hon do you remember that" conversation and it did Yvonne's old heart the world of good.

"Hon, when it all boils down to it," said a woman with red flame hair done up in a bubble, "everybody wants a little White Minx on their hair."

"Are you entering the Hair Show?" asked Yvonne, all excited.

"No baby, I just came to watch," said the woman as she sprayed and pushed at her hair. She talked into the mirror, never really looking at Yvonne once, but Yvonne didn't mind. She just wanted to listen.

"I've been coming to these Hair Shows for years," said the woman, "and there's no way in hell you're going to see me up on that stage doing the stuff they do now. Hon, I'd just as soon they chop off my head before having some of the things they do to people's hair today, done to mine."

"Ain't it the truth," said a cute little blonde in her sixties. Yvonne would have never been able to guess she was that old except she was talking about her grandchildren, and how one was seven years old and one was fourteen, and how her husband had just had a shoulder operation. And while Yvonne was right up there in age with her, she didn't talk that talk yet.

Yvonne was glad when the woman switched over to talking hair "Do you remember the baloney curls?" she asked. This grew a great round of "Oh yes"s from the rest of the girls, so the blonde continued, "And remember when we used to mix sugar and water and spray our hair with that?"

Everyone groaned.

"That thing would hold a set for a week," said another woman.

"Hard as a rock, baby," said even another woman. She had a blue rinse in her hair. "Not only that, but the bacteria it grew."

"Everyone wore it," said the blonde.

"I bet Jackie Onassis wore that on her hair," said the woman talking into the mirror. "I always thought that if I ever met her, I'd ask her just that."

"She had the cutest little clothes," came a voice from inside one of the bathroom stalls. Yvonne could see the woman pulling up her pantyhose, with a cigarette in between her jeweled fingers.

Yvonne was in heaven.

They told story after story, intimidating anyone who happened to walk in and not know what they were talking about. It was as if they were the only beauticians left in the world. The woman who had been smoking in the stall came out and began to tell her favorite hair story.

"I'll never forget it for as long as I'm alive," she said. "My husband and I were on our way to my father's funeral, when my husband started suffering chest pains on the plane trip down. Well, we had to make an emergency landing, and when we got there, I told them at the hospital that he had an hiatal hernia and they said, 'Well, they may call this an hiatal hernia in Louisville, but down here we call it a heart attack.' Well," said the lady as she lit another cigarette, "you can only imagine what a mess I was. They began to ask me all kinds of questions and I couldn't think to even give them my own name. Finally when they asked my husband's age, I told them he was twenty-seven."

Everyone in the room was quiet and the woman's smoke weaved through their hair. "So anyway," she said, "I got back on the plane and went down to the funeral, then turned right back around, and when I got back to the hospital my husband was much better, thank the Lord, and the nurse at the desk said, 'Hon, I don't mean to be disrespectful or anything, but I'm curious. Your husband's a nice looking man, but there's just no way, with all that gray hair, that he could be as young as you said he was. You said he was twenty-seven.' Well imagine my surprise yall," she said, tracing the tip of her cigarette evenly around the rim of the sink. "Twenty-seven was the number of my hair color. Can you believe that? I couldn't remember anything else but the number of my damned hair color."

Everybody cracked up and Yvonne got a shot of them all standing at the mirror, fixing their hair. And when it was time for them to leave, Yvonne didn't even have to ask for their cards. She'd be able to spot them just by looking at their hair. And when she went to bed that night, she would be a happier woman than she had been in years.

While Yvonne was in the bathroom, Riley and Buck and Annabella had fallen in with a Wrinkle Cream Convention. The group was from somewhere out of New Jersey, from a place nobody had ever heard of before. Everybody had a jar of Wrinkle Cream and everybody had a different gimmick to sell the cream with. One man was rubbing it on his shoes to show whoever was walking by just how good it was. Annabella couldn't get over this. She put her arm around him and said, "Hon, that's alligator skin on those shoes. You'll never get those wrinkles out."

"That's the point," he said. "You'll never remove wrinkles, but you can sure make them look good." He whacked her on the ass and Annabella whacked him right back. It was easy to see that they were going to be great friends.

Miss Ruby showed up with Ronder, and they talked each other into getting a demonstration. Two women in official looking labcoats sat them on high stools and circled the cream around their cheeks with a smooth, professional motion and told them all sorts of lies about their product. But mostly they told them how it would make ninety percent of

their crow's feet disappear within six weeks, which meant
that they would have to buy three miniature bottles before
they would even begin to notice a difference. The $39.95
price tag kept the women talking longer, faster, and Miss
Ruby was just on the edge of ordering a whole supply for
the shop, when Ronder kicked her on the shin and said,
"Hon, you can get the same thing using an egg and may-
onnaise."

"Really?" asked the woman who was doing Ronder's face.

"I swear you can. And you know, if your face is oily, all
you have to do is scrub it with a little oatmeal and avocado,
and whoosh, your problem's gone."

The woman stood there holding the open jar, with cream
on her fingers, holding her mouth open. "Hey, you aren't
one of them Cosmetologists that are supposed to be here
this weekend?"

"Yep. Just got in today."

"We're from Stuckey, South Carolina," said Miss Ruby
proudly.

"Well, I been thinking," said the demonstrator, "what
would you do to my hair if you were me? I just got a perm
two weeks ago and the girl that did it, she left that stuff on
too long or something because whenever I roll it, it just falls
flat on my right side."

Ronder pulled the woman's head real close to her near-
sighted eyes and examined it long and hard. Then she
pulled a strand from out of the back of the woman's scalp.

"Ouch! Why'd you go and do that?" asked the woman,
rubbing her head.

"It's called an elasticity test. See, you take your fingernails
and run it along the hair like it was a Christmas ribbon you
were trying to curl, and then when it's curled, see, you
stretch it out tight and then let go. If it pops back into a
ribbon again, which yours has not, then it means that your
hair is in good shape. Honey, you need a conditioning treatment."

Miss Ruby was so proud of Ronder, she told both of the

demonstrators that Ronder was her daughter, and that if they ever wanted to get her to fix their hair, Stuckey wasn't even a day's drive away. "By the way," she added, "you haven't happened to have run across anybody else from there, have you?"

"Well," said the woman who was doing her face, "come to think of it, there was another lady in here but she wasn't exactly friendly. I must have worked on her for half an hour and she didn't even say thank you or nothing."

"That had to be Gladys," said Miss Ruby, turning to Ronder.

"Another thing," said the woman. "There was this French guy with her, you know?" The woman rubbed her chin with the top of her wrist trying not to get cream on herself. "And you should have seen his clothes. He was wearing this pink outfit that even I would have given my eye teeth for, and those boots. Hon, they were dyed pink lizard skin with lifts."

"That wasn't real skin," said the other woman.

"Well, they were real lifts."

Buck came up and kissed Ronder on the cheek, right on her wrinkle cream, right in front of Ruby and the demonstrators, to demonstrate his love for her.

"Oh go away, you old fool," she said, so happy she couldn't stand it.

"How can I leave you when you look so gorgeous?" he asked, running his finger across her face and then licking it like he was licking icing from a cake. "Ahh, coconut. My favorite."

"Ronder," Miss Ruby asked as she watched Buck head for the bar just one more time, "Its getting late. Where do you think all the hair stylists are? I don't see any."

"Miss Ruby, they're everywhere you look. See that woman over there? The one wearing all black, with the spiked hair? She's a hairdresser."

Miss Ruby looked disgusted. "There is no way the State Board would give that thing a license. She looks like she hasn't had a bath in a week."

"Miss Ruby, the reason I know she's a hairdresser is because she keeps looking at that man's hair. See how it tucks up in the back real funny? Well it's just about to drive her crazy. You can just feel her scissors in her hands right now."

The man Ronder was talking about was Harper, and when he turned around, Miss Ruby was embarrassed for him. He strode over gleefully with a little bounce to his walk, and he was holding a single hors d'oeuvre and a single napkin. Ruby didn't want to get stuck talking to him all night long, because she wanted to find Riley. So she told him that Yvonne was looking for him.

It was all Harper needed to send him off into a tailspin. "Are you sure? Did she say what she wanted? Did she tell you where I could find her? What exactly was it that she said?"

Ronder kicked Miss Ruby and started giggling, and Miss Ruby cracked up too. They weren't really laughing at Harper. They were laughing at Yvonne, who had been taking pictures, but when she spotted Harper, she had ducked behind a statue and was now being accosted by a sleazy sales type.

Ronder said, "She said she would meet you by the water fountain on the second floor by the ladies room."

"Now? Right this minute?"

"Soon, very soon," said Ronder. "And she said that whatever you did, you were not supposed to leave. Just wait for her." Harper darted off, up the escalator, out of sight, and Ronder and Miss Ruby couldn't help cracking up again.

31

The Wrinkle Cream conventioneers were in full swing and the bar was packed. Miss Ruby took some literature from the girls and headed out with Ronder to find Riley, keeping her eyes on the Camelia Room, where a sign was posted outside announcing:

GLADYS BESSINGER'S
PELO BONITO
HAIR SHOW PARTY

Invitation Only

Suddenly it occurred to her where Riley was.

When they had first arrived at the front desk, there had been a letter in Riley's box. Nobody else had gotten anything, just Riley. He had opened it, read it, stuck it in his shirt pocket and hadn't said a word. It had bothered Miss Ruby to no end, and she had kept wanting to reach over and take it from him. But she hadn't. As a matter of fact, she had completely forgotten about it up until now. But now Miss Ruby could picture that envelope, rising up out of his pocket like a tombstone, with an invitation to Gladys Bessinger's Hair Show Party engraved on the granite instead of R.I.P. It might as well have been R.I.P. She had to hold on to Ronder to steady herself.

But Riley wasn't at Gladys' party. He was drunk, drunk, drunk, blending into the walls and the pillars and anything else he decided to lean on. Then he was leaning on Earline and Louise, smelling their perfume and thinking they smelled like Bebe. He began to miss her. And then he looked over and saw Millie, in the hands of yet another Wrinkle Cream salesman, and thought that she looked exactly like someone he used to date.

Thurston, who had taken an afternoon nap, woke up and realized it was late and that he should never have left Annabella alone in her room, where he had sent her earlier to get some beauty sleep, too. He went to her room and, just as he feared, she had vanished. Quickly he dressed and began looking in the bars and scanning the crowds for her. As he entered the main bar he muttered to himself, "Dammit, where is that little bitch?"

Suddenly his heart froze. He was hearing Duran flirting with one of the Wrinkle Cream salesgirls.

"Honey," Duran said, "you don't want to be selling this shit."

Thurston turned around slowly, and there, behind a potted palm, stood Duran. His Duran, but now Lars of Norway was by his side, looking more like a bodyguard than a gay hairdresser. Thurston pulled back so Duran wouldn't see him and the pangs of jealousy went shooting across his chest like a heart attack.

He stood on the other side of the palm and listened as Duran talked the salesgirl into being his model for the Hair

Show. He promised her a bigger and brighter career, and with the new look he was going to give her, he said she would be living in New York or Hollywood before the month was over.

Thurston loved Duran so much. He loved the way he made everybody feel so good about themselves. In all Thurston's life, Duran had been the only one who could pull him out of his dark moods. Now he was no longer there to help him, and all Thurston could do was turn around to face the crowd again and try and pretend it didn't hurt. He felt old and fat next to Duran's new sleek European with that full naturally blond crop of hair. He probably ate raw broccoli and strange Norwegian fish, and he looked much too sane to make a good gay.

Thurston knew now that he should have married Duran and then there wouldn't have been this problem, when suddenly Duran turned around and spoke to him. "Look at her, darling."

Thurston turned and saw Annabella. She was dead drunk.

Duran said, "You'd better get her into bed."

Thurston didn't say a word. All he could think about was that he hadn't brushed his hair in over an hour, and his bald spot felt like it was flaming.

"You know," said Duran, "if you get her into bed right now, and get her to sleep right away, then you might just be able to take second place tomorrow." He was smiling that smile that always told Thurston nothing.

Annabella had been laughing with her eyes closed, sitting on the Wrinkle Cream salesman's lap. She had noticed that his name tag read MR. NORVELLE, and she was spelling out "Mrs. Annabella Norvelle" in her mind. It was something she did automatically with each new man she met. She didn't like the sound of it at all, and when she opened her eyes, she noticed that Duran was pointing at her, talking to Thurston. She noticed, too, that his new boyfriend was in the background. She grabbed the salesman on the head with both of her hands and kissed him right on the top and said,

"Hon, don't go away. Keep everything warm. I'll be right back."

She went waving wildly at Thurston, tripping over everything. "Come on, hon," she said, grabbing his arm, "let's go join the party!"

That's when Thurston remembered what he had said to Ruby about not giving anyone the satisfaction of seeing them lose. He lifted his head up and smiled his most brilliant smile at Duran while offering his arm to Annabella, who gladly took it and tugged him off, leaving Duran just standing there.

"Thurston," said Annabella, "one thing about being rejected. It's just hell on the other guy if he thinks it doesn't bother you. Let's dance."

So Thurston, who really could dance, pushed up his black leather labcoat sleeves, jangled his bracelets out in front of him, and went into a snakey tango move that he knew they didn't teach up in those Swedish mountains.

"Keep dancing, baby!" yelled Annabella over the loud disco music. "He's still standing there watching you. Ohhh, do that little move again with your hips. Yeah, that's the one. Good news. Duran just shrugged his new boyfriend off. I think he wants to stay and watch you. Make it wild, baby. Make it last. Make him weep. But take me with you while you do it."

So Thurston took Annabella everywhere. He took her into his gay world and told her what it felt like to be a man, and what it felt like to be more of a woman than even she knew. He told her where he had been and where he was going to go. And he let her know just how far he had taken Duran, and just how much farther Duran could have gone if he hadn't left. And although Thurston hadn't opened his mouth, she heard every word he said by watching his every move, every twist from his hips, every dip from his waist, and the way he never quit looking her straight in the eye.

When she looked over to see if Duran was still watching,

he was, only now Lars of Norway was pushing the elevator button, trying to pull him away. "Do that grinding thing again!" she yelled to Thurston, and he gave it all he had. When she looked at Duran again, he was smiling to himself and nodding his head, and she knew that Thurston was right where he needed to be.

When the song ended, she wrapped her arms around him and said, "He got every move you made, baby. He didn't miss a beat."

Annabella wanted to dance some more, but Thurston explained to her that it was time for lights out. She whined and cajoled and pleaded and got mad, but to no avail. He was sending her to bed and that was that.

While they stood waiting for the elevator, every man who had had the honor of having Annabella on his lap earlier, and even some who hadn't, came by and gave her their cards, some free samples and a few pats on the behind. And a little part in Thurston, a little leftover part that still made him crawl out of bed in the morning and shave and eye other men's biceps —not because they looked good, but because maybe he wished his were bigger—that little part that made his body jump inside when Annabella had done her little special things out on the dance floor, that little part didn't like those men patting her on the behind at all.

Miss Ruby leaned on Ronder as they passed Thurston, who was half dragging, half pulling Annabella into the elevator, when suddenly Ronder spotted Riley leaning against the statue.

"Miss Ruby, dry your eyes," said Ronder, pointing. "I've found him. There he is. He doesn't look like he's been with Gladys. Probably they've had him trapped all night." She was talking about Earline, who was on one side of him, and Louise, who was on the other.

Miss Ruby looked up from where her tears had stained

her cream colored taffeta gown to where Riley was. At that moment, he looked more like a Greek god to her than the statue he was leaning on. Now they could go show Gladys a thing or two. She was excited now. Her heart was pounding, skipping beats. She couldn't wait to get to him. It seemed like the longest walk she had ever taken.

"Riley, hon," she said when she finally got to him, "I need to borrow you for a few minutes."

"Oh!" cooed Earline, and Louise said, "But we were just having the nicest little talk."

"Sorry, girls," said Ronder, pulling him out of their grip. "He's Miss Ruby's now."

Riley's vision was blurred and his tongue was thick. But none of this mattered because Ruby didn't need him to talk or to make sense. All she needed was for him to take her arm and walk her down the hall and into the Camelia Room.

The first person they saw was Gladys, dancing with one man and whispering something to another whenever she circled by in her silver minidress. On the next circle, when she spun around, she saw Riley nudging Ruby's neck. She stopped dead in her tracks.

But Riley wasn't really nudging Ruby's neck. He was falling on her and telling her that if they didn't leave, he was going to be sick. So Miss Ruby put her arm around him and left smiling, because she knew that Riley, the man whom Gladys had been so in love with for her entire life, was walking out of the Camelia Room on Ruby's arm. It looked like they were heading off to a little love nest.

Miss Ruby soared. She felt great. It was going to be hard to get to sleep, that was for sure; she was so excited. But she had to try. She wanted to make sure she was wide awake for the big event, the thing she had been waiting weeks and weeks for—the Hair Show. Together, she and Ronder got Riley to the glass elevator, and on the way there they spotted Harper up on the next level, still waiting patiently outside the second floor ladies room for Yvonne.

"That is so sad," said Miss Ruby.

"I know," said Ronder. "I'll go back and get him when I go find Yvonne."

Ronder found Yvonne sleeping on one of the lobby couches. "Wake up, Yvonne," she said, shaking her.

"No," Yvonne said groggily.

"Come on, hon. You got a room here. Come on, let's go on up to bed."

"There's no way I'm getting on that elevator," said Yvonne, wide awake now. "I'm not going up in that thing. All that glass. No sirree, not me."

"Hon, it's either that or spend the night talking to Harper. Here he comes now."

Yvonne stood up and saw Harper smiling eagerly down at her from the second floor landing. He was waving and holding up one finger to let her know not to go anywhere because he'd be right down.

Yvonne started pressing the elevator button and tapping her foot. "Please, oh please, hurry," she said.

And it came just in time, just as Harper jumped the last three steps off the escalator, still waving for her to wait.

They all laughed about it before they parted for bed, Miss Ruby, Ronder and Yvonne.

"You'd have thought he thought I was twenty-two the way he was looking at me," said Yvonne, who slept with a stocking on her head to keep the pin curls in place.

"Hon," said Miss Ruby, "the man's obviously in love with you."

"Yeah," said Ronder. "I'm afraid he's got it bad."

"Do you know what he said to me today?" asked Yvonne.

"No, what?" asked Ronder.

"We were downstairs there, near that restaurant," said Yvonne, pulling the stocking away from her ear to rearrange a clip, "and he was just hanging on my every word. So I asked him if he felt like an ice cream cone, and he started feeling his arms all up and down and said, 'Well, no. I think I feel more like an ice cream sundae.' "

Miss Ruby and Ronder cracked up.

"I thought I would scream," said Yvonne, rolling her eyes. "An ice cream sundae."

Miss Ruby and Ronder were grabbing on to each other now, in tears laughing so hard. At first Yvonne didn't think it was so funny, but it didn't take her long to join in, to ham it up.

"Poor old thing," she said with tears streaming down her face, "an ice cream sundae. I can't stand him."

32

The preliminaries for the Hair Show contest consisted of giving a perm, a frosting, a haircut, a style and a fingerwave. It was an all day affair, after which the chosen few were put into the categories that best suited them. Some went into the haircutting competition, and some were placed in the color contest, and some were set up to compete on the permanent wave level.

Cosmetologists were walking around everywhere, entering, watching, cheering others on. Some were holding on to their mannequins, others their models, standing in one line and then another, making small talk to whoever was nearby. They were talking about how this year's Hair Show didn't seem as organized as last year's, but that it looked better; while some said they knew one of the judges, and others said they'd heard the judges were from out of town. Still others said they didn't care, that all they wanted was a cigarette.

Empty faces were staring ahead, looking around, looking scared, afraid they were in the wrong line. Small empty faces from small towns with names like Winnsboro, Pelham,

Gastonia and Lumber Bridge, touching their hair and studying the Atlanta gays, the Atlanta pros, and knowing they stood little, if no chance, next to them. But the small town stylists were to get the biggest surprise because at two'clock sharp the announcement came over the P.A. system that among the finalists for the Best Hairstyle of the Year were two small shops out of one small town in Stuckey, South Carolina: Gladys' Bessinger's Pelo Bonito and Miss Ruby McSwain's Celebrity Styling.

Rumors were spreading everywhere. Rumors that were once innocent had now fish hooked into ugly twisted rumors. Someone was related to one of the judges, or one of their mothers, or somebody had been paid off or something had gone wrong.

But at the afternoon Gala, put on by *Salon Talk* magazine and thrown by the sponsors, everything was made clear.

Gladys Bessinger's shop had won because her shop was the only one with Europeans, and the Europeans had the right look in everything they touched. And Ruby McSwain had come in at a close second, because her shop was the only one that could produce a decent fingerwave, an excellent fingerwave as a matter of fact.

Since nobody else had the European touch, nobody could argue much with Pelo Bonito's victory. It was the fingerwaves that upset everyone. Everyone knew that fingerwaves were out, which is why nobody knew how to do one. So if knowing how to do a fingerwave in the finals didn't matter, why should it matter in the preliminaries? Maybe the rules should change with the times. But the facts stood. They had been forewarned, and the rules hadn't been changed. They should have practiced.

And now, all because Yvonne, who hadn't created anything more elaborate than a simple updo in the last fifteen years, knew how to do a simple S-section, she and Thurston were up in their suites getting ready to go against Gladys and her boys.

But something terrible had happened somewhere between the Gala and getting ready for the finals. Annabella, who was supposed to be beauty resting, had snuck off after stuffing two pillows under her sheets and was nowhere to be found.

Miss Ruby sent Buck and Riley out looking for her and they came back with the bad news. "She's down at the bar with one of those boys from last night," said Buck.

"And she's drunk again. Real drunk," said Riley, who was suffering from a major hangover himself and didn't even want to think about drunk.

"Oh my God! Oh my God!" said Thurston, "I've got to go get her."

Ten minutes later, thirty minutes before he was supposed to go on stage, Thurston was standing in the doorway of Miss Ruby's suite, holding the laughing Annabella up by her armpits. "She stinks," he groaned. "Just look at her. Just look at this beautiful dress. What am I going to do?"

Annabella was in her blue sequined dress, cut to everywhere, slipping out of Thurston's grip onto the floor. "Hon, I'll be fine," she laughed. "I always drink before I go on-stage."

"Just look at her," said Thurston again. "I'm not going on stage with that thing." He stamped over to the bed and dived into the pillows.

"You most certainly are," said Ruby, furious. "You will be up and ready to go on that stage in fifteen minutes or else. Now get cracking. Ronder, put Annabella in a cold tub."

"No, no!" squealed Annabella, laughing, as Ronder and Yvonne dragged her away.

"Now! I said get up from there now, Thurston, and I mean it." Miss Ruby was standing over him like a statue. "I've got a shot at winning this thing. You're not going to ruin it."

Thurston buried his head deeper into the pillow. Maybe it would all go away if he ignored it. It was bad enough going up against Duran, knowing he was going to lose. But he couldn't let Duran see Annabella looking any worse than she already did naturally.

"Thurston," said Miss Ruby, "I'm waiting. One, two, three . . . I'll give you to ten or else I'll give you back to Gladys."

He didn't move.

"Four, five . . ."

"It's no use, Miss Ruby," said Ronder, coming back into the room. "She's out like a light. Yvonne's running the shower over her but she's actually in there snoring. I don't think she's going on any stage tonight."

Nobody said a word for a few minutes. Thurston felt a heavy load lifting off his back, then crashing back down on it again. It must have been the same load that was hitting Miss Ruby, because she suddenly shouted, "SIX! SEVEN! EIGHT! NINE! TEN . . . GET UP DAMN YOU!" She grabbed Thurston by his boots and yanked him off the bed. His knees hit the floor. "I'll be damned if you're going to act like the Queen of Sheba today!" yelled Miss Ruby. "Here. You're going to fix Ronder's hair." She pushed Ronder at him.

Thurston looked shocked, and Ronder grabbed her hair and said, "But I don't want my hair cut, Miss Ruby. I like my hair long."

"I can't do her hair," said Thurston, rubbing his knees, amazed at Ruby's spurt of strength. "Are you kidding? She's got horrible hair."

"Honey," said Ruby, "all I know is I've got a Hair Show to win and you two had better work something out."

The Best Haircut of the Year had already gone to a sleepy looking woman from Tennessee, and the Best Perm, to a gay from Mississippi. And now the crowd was ready. They were sitting on the edge of their seats and standing in the doorway and down the hall just to get a good look at the new Best Hairstyle of the Year. The Hair Show was being held in the Magnolia Room and the Peachtree Plaza was buzzing with the beauticians and gay hair designers, who had competed and lost. They were everywhere, dressed in their different colored labcoats and high heels, and the Shalimar scent was mixing with the chemical fumes in the air.

The judges were all in their places and the stage was set for the grand finale. It was the moment that everyone had been waiting for.

Up onstage there were four hydraulic lift chairs in front of four shiny black shampoo basins, and a model was seated in each chair. Then the backstage curtain moved and the audience quit talking and began to murmur and then there was silence. And then there was Gladys' French hair designer, Raphael, billed to be the biggest winner of the season. He danced and twirled and snapped his fingers until he was by his model's side, and then he danced around her.

Miss Ruby searched the crowd frantically for signs of Gladys Bessinger, but everyone was standing up for the Frenchman. Since the only thing tall about Miss Ruby was her hair, she couldn't see a thing.

Thurston came onstage. He had all the same moves only his were wilder and more exaggerated, and when he got to Ronder, he sat on her lap and spread out his floor length sequined labcoat as if he were still the Sun King. And when he crossed his legs and hooked his toe behind his ankle, the crowd stood back up. They were crazy for him too, and Miss Ruby was thrilled.

Next came Duran, with his black parachute pants and tight black shirt, and zippers that were sewn on to places that zippers had never been sewn before. He moved slow —real slow—and the music he was hearing was not the same music that was coming from the speakers. It was music to do black hair by. And he was humming this music and popping his wrists as he walked. And when he got to Tonya, the former wrinkle cream model, he grabbed her hair and jerked her head back. They had choreographed it beautifully, because she looked up at him exactly the way he had planned for her to look—as if she were his slave and he, the master. The effect was mesmerizing. The look said it all. He was going to make her look like a million bucks.

The audience was going wild when Yvonne Tisdale finally came onstage in her little blue uniform with a butterfly stitched on her collar. They were stomping their feet and clapping their hands and they were ready for the show to begin. She had no moves, just a little portable dryer by her side and a suitcase full of rollers and hairnets. And while Thurston held his position, and the French hair designer, his, and while Duran pulled Tonya's head back just a little farther, Yvonne set her equipment up around Millie Loudermilk, who had decided on the spur of the moment, after being pushed and pushed by Earline and Louise, to be Yvonne's model. Now she looked uncomfortable, as if she had left something cooking in the oven. Yvonne draped a shampoo cape around Millie's shoulders and began brushing her hair and it was the signal for the show to begin.

Thurston and Raphael were the fastest. They were doing things to their models' hair that had never been done before. And it was so exciting that the emcee, who had been asked to sit with the judges earlier, jumped up onstage and started giving his play by play.

His name was Bill Hill, from station WKXO out of Orlando, and he had been doing radio since he was four years old, so his voice just smoothed over the audience, making them feel like part of the show.

"Honey, sugar, honey, sugar," said Bill Hill as he picked two pink carnations out of the flower arrangement from the side of the stage. He put one in Raphael's labcoat buttonhole, and one between Thurston's teeth.

Thurston took one look at Raphael, then one look at Duran, who was winking at Raphael, and he began to do the Mambo and the Rumba, never missing a beat, while he cut Ronder's hair. Ronder squinched her eyes shut tight and whispered, "Not too short, Thurston, okay?"

"Honey, sugar, honey, sugar," continued Bill Hill. "You are not just cutting her hair, you are torturing it." Ronder drew in her breath and the audience went wild.

And Bill Hill picked up on their wildness. He pointed to Thurston and strutted across the stage like a Bantam Rooster, then came back to Raphael, who had managed to braid and twirl his model's hair into the shape of Napoleon's hat.

Bill Hill slid his hand into his jacket and stooped low to look short like Napoleon, and then he walked past Yvonne like this and came up on Duran. "Look at this boy, would you? He's working the model, not the hair. Now wouldn't you ladies out there in the audience like to have one of these for your very own?" he asked with one hand on his hip and the other held out, demonstrating Duran as if he were a new Frigidaire-Freezer on *The Price Is Right*. "But wait," he said. "What is this I see? What are you doing to her hair?"

Duran was shaving Tonya's hair with clippers. He had started at the crown area and was going around and around and around, and Bill Hill was making a big thing out of this, walking around Tonya's chair as if he were the clippers. And he was asking questions the whole time, "What is this thing called black hair? Is there really a difference between black and white hair? Ladies and gentlemen, step right up and ask everything you always wanted to know about black hair but were afraid to ask." He walked over to the edge of the stage and pointed the microphone at a lady in the audience and she giggled and pushed it away. So Bill Hill brought it back to his mouth like he was going to kiss it, and then he spoke real low. "Well, I have a question." He swung around to Duran and asked, "Why oh why do you all wear those plastic bags on your heads all the time?"

Duran pulled away from Tonya and put the still humming clippers against his heart. "It's called love, baby."

"What? But what is this thing called love?" asked Bill Hill, putting Duran's hand back up to Tonya and the microphone to his mouth.

"Honey," said Duran, moving his clippers around again, "blacks don't have oil in their hair. Chances are, if you see a man wearing a plastic cap, he's got a date that night with some foxy looking chick and he wants to look cool, like Michael Jackson. So, he puts on that Afro Sheen or that White Rose Petroleum Gel, and he sticks a cap on over it and hopes that some of that grease will soak in. Now if he's out on the highway and the sun is beating down on that plastic cap, and he's working his ass off, it's got to be at least 120 degrees out there. And baby, that is what I call love."

Meanwhile Thurston and Raphael were neck and neck, coming down the home stretch, and the audience was calling out their names. "Thurston! Raphael! Thurston!

Raphael!" Miss Ruby had long since given up her search for Gladys and was now praying to the gods, praying for Thurston.

The audience was chanting harder than ever now and everything was on the money. The tone of the show, the energy, it was as if it had been rehearsed a hundred times. Bill Hill had never worked an audience so well before. He was tighter, smoother, sleeker. His performance was like a symphony that was being played faster and faster on a turntable. He was making old jokes new and new jokes up. Duran was coming around to the end of his hairstyle, catching up with Thurston and Raphael. The air was full of electricity and nothing, nothing was out of place.

Then Bill Hill turned to Yvonne and it was as if someone had stuck their finger on the needle, scratching it across the record, until it came to the label and went ta-dunk ta-dunk ta-dunk, slowly hitting the label over and over again.

Millie had just gotten out from under the dryer and Yvonne was removing her hairnet. Yvonne's back was to the audience and her shoulders were hunched over. Bill Hill looked at her support hose and her scuffed up nurse's shoes, and sweat began to soak the back of his collar. She had obviously spent many painstaking hours fixing the back of her hair for the Hair Show. The elaborate design of pin curls and pedal curls told him so. She reminded him of his mother. He wanted to run up and hug her and protect her, and at the same time he wanted to throw a plate at the back of her neck. She was slowing things down to a dead halt. She was taking the curlers out of Millie's hair with the same precision a man uses to glue a ship together inside a tiny bottle. Bill Hill couldn't even hear the music anymore, just the audience as their murmuring grew louder and louder, until that was all he could hear. His lower teeth began to tingle—to hurt—like he was chewing on tin foil. And Yvonne was taking one clip, two clips, three out of Millie's hair, slowly, slowly. It felt like the world was coming to an end.

Finally, when all the clips and rollers were out and placed neatly in their assigned little places, Yvonne began to brush out Millie's hair. Bill Hill cracked a small and feeble joke about women brushing their hair with one hundred strokes, and the audience laughed a small and feeble laugh. Nobody knew what to do. So they just waited. And they waited. And then they waited some more.

Miss Ruby covered her eyes with her hands and bent her head down as if in prayer. Louise and Earline were patting her, while Harper and Riley tried to say cute and lively things. Annabella, who was up and dripping from her shower, shook her head and rested it on Buck's shoulder, while he stared back and forth in horror, first at Ronder's new cut, and then at the nightmare Yvonne was in.

Meanwhile, Bill Hill was feeling so bad for Yvonne and her sorry little hairstyle. He watched the judges, watched how they began to shift in their chairs and swing their feet and talk among themselves. Yvonne Tisdale should never have made it to the finals. He was going to have to make his next move count. It was up to him to take everyone's attention away from the disaster that lay before him. So when it looked like she was winding things up, Bill Hill took it as his cue to introduce the other contestants' hairstyles.

"Look!" he said, pointing to Thurston's and Raphael's models.

He picked Ronder up and waltzed her around the stage "Now you can take her anywhere." Her hair, which before had been blond and Farrah Fawcett-like, was black now, with one red streak on the side like an offbeat skunk. It was cut up to zero elevation on the neck so that her ear lobes showed from behind. It wasn't that it was such a new style that brought the audience back to life again. Nothing was really new in the hair business anymore. The styles were the same styles as they always were. They just had different twists now. The Sausage Curl had been transformed into Dominique's Flip. The Bubble was now called Antonio's Punk. Everything old now had a new name and a few spikes and more than one color. And Thurston's style was no different. His was just the same old Dorothy Hammill Wedge Cut, cut just a little higher.

Miss Ruby's heart sank when she finally saw Gladys walking down the aisle, getting ready to pick up her trophy. She looked calm, smooth, everything about her spelled a winner. She was smirking at Thurston's little style, nodding her head at Ruby, acknowledging her, wanting to be acknowledged back. She actually pointed at Raphael at the same time Bill Hill did.

But Raphael's model looked just like last year's winner. Her hat-shaped hair was something that no one would ever wear except in a competition, or be seen anywhere except in a fancy hair book that women looked at but never bought. The judges were disappointed in his performance and so was the audience.

Miss Ruby was ecstatic to see that Raphael hadn't gotten any more applause than Thurston, and she raised her fist in the air in triumph and began pumping it at Gladys, who had stepped back into a shadow. But it was a short lived victory for Ruby, because the audience began to applaud louder than ever now.

When she looked up, she saw that they were applauding Gladys' other boy, Duran. Bill Hill was introducing him and the audience was ready to applaud everything, because watching Yvonne had been so painful.

Duran knew they were applauding him, and he winked at Thurston. It was a wink that said he was sorry, that he'd made a mistake in leaving, and that if Thurston would just take him back, then Duran would never try and pressure him into marriage again.

Thurston turned away because he didn't know how he felt. He just knew that the applause he was hearing was for Duran, not him.

Duran's model, Tonya, had run back to change and she was now standing at the foot of the stage wearing a skin tight black and yellow sequined evening gown. Her iridescent yellow gloves went all the way up to her elbows and her hands were touching her hair.

"Ladies and gentlemen," announced Bill Hill, "the moment we have all been waiting for. I give you the BEEHIVE!"

The crowd went crazy. Yvonne did a slow turn, saw what all the commotion was about and she put down her can of hairspray. She left Millie sitting there, still half finished, and walked over to Tonya to examine her hair.

Duran had shaved a circle and then left a circle of hair. And then he had shaved another circle and left another circle of hair. He had done this all the way around until he had come to the nape of her neck, and there, he had shaved her a little door. And sure enough, her head looked exactly like a real beehive. And she was dressed like a bee.

Yvonne reached up and touched it and circled her fingers around it and the crowd went crazier than ever. They were cheering louder and louder and the judges were getting ready to walk up on the stage and present the trophy to Duran. Gladys was walking with them.

Yvonne looked at Miss Ruby, saw the look of defeat in her eyes, the years of love that the dear woman had invested in the hair business slipping out of her like Annabella had slipped out of Thurston's hands. Then she watched Gladys reach over and pat Ruby on the shoulder and Yvonne just couldn't stand it any longer. She grabbed the microphone out of Bill Hill's hand and said, "That may be a Black Beehive. But that is not a Beehive. I will show you what a real Beehive is."

Yvonne marched her angry little body right back to where Millie was seated and began to spray and tease and spray and tease. Everyone was talking and laughing and Yvonne was crying. The changes that had taken place in her little world of hair were more than she could bear. The gays, the rock and roll, the way nobody cared about hair anymore, or even knew how to do a fingerwave. It all swam around in her head as she teased rat nest after rat nest, up and up and up.

Never in their lives had the crowd seen so much teasing before. Never in her life had Yvonne teased so much before, or sprayed so much before. She sprayed and sprayed and smoothed and sprayed, and thought about Agnes Collins, and how she knew that Agnes had wanted to leave her and couldn't tell her, wouldn't tell her in fact, and how that was the way it was turning out with all her customers. The tears were streaming down Yvonne's face as she sprayed and sprayed some more. Finally Millie's hair began to take on a shape. A tall towering blue-tinted shape. A mass of hair reaching almost a foot high.

At last, Yvonne combed an outer layer over the whole tower of hair and stood back to view her work. Nobody talked. Millie touched the nape of her neck. Miss Ruby smiled. Bill Hill and Thurston didn't blink. Yvonne tapped her comb against the palm of her hand and just stared.

Duran was the first to speak. "That's bad, Mama, bad."

Then Yvonne picked up a can of Happy Hair. "This is not just hairspray," she told the audience. "This is the real thing—lacquer. And for those of you who don't know, and for those of you who forgot, lacquer will do the trick." She sprayed and sprayed again.

Then Yvonne, with the comb still in her hand, reached around and rubbed the small of her back and said, "This, my friends, *this* is a beehive."

The crowd was silent at first. Then they slowly began clapping their hands. And then they were standing and clapping, harder and harder, and when Thurston breezed over to kiss Yvonne, the crowd began screaming, "Yvonne! Yvonne!" louder and louder.

Gladys looked at Ruby and Ruby looked at Gladys. Gladys took a step back and listened to the roaring of the crowd, while Lars of Norway stood by her, supporting her.

And that's when Duran did the only thing left he could do. It was the turning point for Thurston—the thing that made him swear he'd marry Duran the minute they got to Las Vegas. Duran helped pull the judges up onstage and helped them award the trophy that was supposed to go to him, to Yvonne. And it was Duran, Gladys' boy, who personally took the sash—the one that read HAIRSTYLE OF THE YEAR—and draped it over Millie.

That's when Gladys left with Lars of Norway, but not before Ruby had jumped up onstage and grabbed the microphone from Bill Hill. "Gladys! Gladys Bessinger!" she called out.

Gladys stopped in the doorway and turned around. And Ruby, smiling from ear to ear, said the words she had been hearing in the beauty shop all her life, "Well Gladys, that's the way the curl turns."

Thurston was kissing Yvonne on the cheek, over and over again, telling her how proud he was of her. And she knew he meant it. For the first time, she saw that she could never retire from the hair business, and that she could never work without Thurston. She saw that he wasn't the devil after all, just different from her—the kind of difference that brought out the good things in her. She kissed him back and took his hand, and then everyone came up onstage, including Harper, who gave Yvonne a dozen roses and kissed her, too. And Yvonne was so happy she kissed him right back on the lips, surprising everyone, including herself.

The whole audience wanted to touch the Beehive. Louise and Earline were holding on to Riley's arm and Riley was saying, "You remind me of someone, Millie? But I can't quite put my finger on just who?"

"Doris Day?" asked Bill Hill. "You know Doris Day used to wear her hair just like that."

"No, no, that isn't it," he said, pushing him aside and shrugging Earline and Louise off his shoulders. "Hold on. Turn to me a second?"

Millie stood up to face him. Then he reached up and moved one of her spit curls to the right and stood back. "That's it. That is it! Millie, you look just like Jayne Mansfield in Sin City."

"Sin City? I saw that," said Annabella, who was still in

her sequined dress, still wet, still drunk and leaning on Ruby.

"I'll be damned," said Ronder, "I thought she looked familiar." Ronder winked at Yvonne, who stood there holding the gleaming trophy in one arm and the roses in the other. Harper was grinning by her side.

And then Miss Ruby came over with tears in her eyes and said, "You know, Yvonne, I never told you this but I used to wear one of those back in the Sixties. It was great. It used to crunch whenever the boys tried to kiss me and I had to use a pencil to scratch my head."

Yvonne laughed. "And you had to hang your head off the side of the bed to sleep."

Miss Ruby hugged her. "Oh Yvonne, two old bats like us. I bet I still have that satin pillow."